Praise for the novels of *New York Times* bestselling author RaeAnne Thayne

"RaeAnne Thayne gets better with every book."
—Robyn Carr, #1 *New York Times* bestselling author

"As always, Ms. Thayne's writing is emotional, riveting, and keeps you hoping all turns out well."
—*Fresh Fiction* on *The Sea Glass Cottage*

"This issue of the Cape Sanctuary series draws the reader in from the first page to the gratifying conclusion."
—*New York Journal of Books* on *The Sea Glass Cottage*

"[Thayne] engages the reader's heart and emotions, inspiring hope and the belief that miracles *are* possible."
—Debbie Macomber, #1 *New York Times* bestselling author

"Thayne is in peak form in this delightful, multiple-perspective tale of the entwined lives and loves of three women in a Northern California seaside community.... [She] skillfully interweaves these plotlines with just the right amount of glamour, art, and kindness to make for a warmly compelling and satisfying work of women's fiction."
—*Booklist* on *The Cliff House*, starred review

"The heart of this sweet contemporary story is in the women's relationships with each other, and it will suit readers on both sides of the blurry romance/women's fiction divide."
—*Publishers Weekly* on *The Cliff House*

"RaeAnne Thayne is quickly becoming one of my favorite authors.... Once you start reading, you aren't going to be able to stop."
—*Fresh Fiction*

Also available from RaeAnne Thayne

Sleigh Bells Ring
The Path to Sunshine Cove
Christmas at Holiday House
The Sea Glass Cottage
Coming Home for Christmas
The Cliff House
Season of Wonder

Haven Point

Snow Angel Cove
Redemption Bay
Evergreen Springs
Riverbend Road
Snowfall on Haven Point
Serenity Harbor
Sugar Pine Trail
The Cottages on Silver Beach
Summer at Lake Haven

Hope's Crossing

Blackberry Summer
Woodrose Mountain
Sweet Laurel Falls
Currant Creek Valley
Willowleaf Lane
Christmas in Snowflake Canyon
Wild Iris Ridge

For a complete list of books by RaeAnne Thayne,
please visit www.raeannethayne.com.

RaeAnne Thayne

Sweet Laurel Falls

Recycling programs for this product may not exist in your area.

ISBN-13: 978-1-335-44862-0

Sweet Laurel Falls

First published in 2012. This edition published in 2022.

For questions and comments about the quality of this book, please contact us at CustomerService@Harlequin.com.

HQN
22 Adelaide St. West, 41st Floor
Toronto, Ontario M5H 4E3, Canada
www.Harlequin.com

Printed in Lithuania

To the members of the Utah chapter
of Romance Writers of America.
You inspire me with your dedication, talent and sheer grit
and I will forever be grateful for your friendship.

SWEET LAUREL FALLS

CHAPTER ONE

FORGET CHRISTMAS VACATION. This year, Maura McKnight-Parker wanted a vacation *from* Christmas. Wouldn't it be wonderful if she could just crawl into a warm cave somewhere and sleep through the holidays?

With a sigh, Maura took a final look around at the cozy nook where she had arranged several of the plump sofas and chairs normally scattered throughout her bookstore-slash-coffeehouse. Everything appeared ready for the Books and Bites book club Christmas party and gift exchange tonight.

Nibbles? Check. M&M's, spiced nuts and popcorn mix waited in holiday-printed bowls, and she had even dragged out her Christmas china and coffee mugs for said nibbles.

Decorations? Check. Not much to do there, since the halls of Dog-Eared Books & Brew had already been decked the week before Thanksgiving with artificial Christmas trees adorned in elegant blues and whites and silver. Snowflakes and gleaming ornaments in the same color scheme dangled from the ceiling, lightly dancing in the currents of air whenever anybody opened the front door.

Gifts? Yes. She had set up a little tabletop tree with handmade blown-glass ornaments for each of the book club members that she had commissioned from an artist with a gallery in town.

In addition to that pretty bit of swag, she had spent the past few days scouring shelves and boxes in her office and had filled gift bags for all the book club members, brimming with coffee and tea samples and some of the promotional bookmarks, notepads and other tchotchkes authors and their publicists were always sending to the store.

Despite a deep-seated wish that she could just hole up in her house for Christmas like a fox in a cozy den, she had worked tirelessly for days to make this party a success. If she were a scam artist, she would have called this baiting her trap. She had to convince her dearest friends and family members that she was indeed trying to move forward with her life after the hell of the past year. To accomplish that, she needed to put on a convincing show for them.

Maybe then, everybody would back off and give her a little space to find her own way.

"What do you think?" she asked April Herrera, who was taking a load of Books & Brew coffee mugs out of the small dishwasher behind the counter.

The assistant manager for the coffeehouse side of her business gazed at the setup with an enchanted look in her eyes that seemed at odds with her henna-colored hair, pencil-thin eyebrows and various diamond studs. The silk long-underwear shirt she wore underneath her barista shirt and apron hid the various tattoos Maura knew adorned her arms.

Judging only by appearances, April ought to be wild and cynical. Instead, she was just about the sweetest person Maura knew. More important, she was smart and hardworking and intuitive about her customers.

"It looks super in here. Just perfect. You guys are going to have *such* a great time."

Maura tended to have a soft spot for rebellious girls, probably because she'd been one in another lifetime. "Are you sure you can't stay?"

"I really wish I could. Your book club meetings are always a hoot. Your mom cracks me up every time she comes in, and it's hilarious to watch Ruth and Claire together. Do they *ever* agree on a book?"

"Rarely," she answered. Or anything else, for that matter. Ruth Tatum worked in the bookstore, and she and her daughter had what could best be described as a complicated relationship. "You should really stay. You know everyone would love to have you again. Your comments on the last book were really insightful."

"I can't. Sorry. I've really got to take off as soon as Josh gets here. This is my very first time night-skiing with the team."

"How's that going?" she asked.

"Excellent." The young woman's face lit up. "I think they're ready to put me on the schedule on a regular basis."

April was training for the ski patrol and also taking classes in hope of eventually becoming a paramedic. Maura didn't know how she juggled work and class and her two-year-old son, especially on her own. Maybe that was another reason she had taken April under her wing—she could certainly relate to being a young single mother just trying to survive.

"That's terrific. If you need me to make any adjustments to your work schedule here, just say the word. I'm flexible. And I'm happy to babysit Trek whenever you need."

"Thanks, Maur."

"Maybe you can come to the book club meeting in January, if it fits around all the plates you have spinning."

"Definitely!" April started to add something else, but a customer at the coffee counter rang the little bell, and she gave Maura a "later" kind of wave and headed back to take the order.

Personally, Maura couldn't wait for January, to finally

turn that page of her calendar to a new year. Maybe once the holiday craziness was over, she could escape some of the pressure of trying to act as if everything was fine when she was frozen solid inside.

She grabbed one more bowl of spicy nuts and set it on a side table, then moved a bowl of plump, airy peppermints to another spot. Having dear friends and family members surrounding her in Hope's Crossing was both a blessing and a curse. She knew they loved her and worried for her. While she understood their concern and tried to be grateful, mostly she just found it exhausting and overwhelming.

Sometimes that ever-present concern made her feel as if she had been buried alive under an avalanche. It pressed down on her, heavy and suffocating, until all she wanted to do was scramble for an air pocket.

Even her little bungalow on Mountain Laurel Road wouldn't remain a haven for long. In a few days, her daughter Sage would be coming home from college for the holidays, bringing yet another pair of watchful eyes.

She could do it. A few more weeks of pretending, and then she could have the cold nights of January to herself.

After one last look around, she suddenly remembered she'd meant to grab a couple extra copies of this month's book club selection off the shelf, in case anybody forgot theirs and needed it for reference. She had several copies in the display near the front, she remembered, and hurried in that direction.

A light snow drifted past the front display window, the big, fluffy flakes reflecting the colorful Christmas lights on storefronts up and down Main Street. Hope's Crossing was a true winter wonderland and local businesses worked hard to make the town glow with an old-fashioned, enticing charm. Nearly every store had some kind of light display. Hers were LED icicles that appeared to be dripping.

The effort seemed to be working. Her store bustled with customers and, judging by the pedestrian and vehicle traffic on a normally slow Thursday night, the other businesses on Main Street were enjoying the same success.

An SUV snagged the last parking space in front of the café across the street and a few stores down from her. A man in a leather jacket and Levi's climbed out and snowflakes immediately landed on his wavy dark hair and the shoulders of his warm cocoa-colored coat. He looked sharp and put together.

Everyone would be arriving any second now and she should go put the finishing touches on the scene she had created, but for some reason she was drawn to the man she could still barely see.

Some indefinable aspect of him—the angle of his jaw or the way he moved—called to mind the image of her first love. Jackson Lange, sexy and dangerous, young, angry, ferociously smart.

She rarely thought about Jack anymore, except on the rare occasions when his unpleasant father came into the store. Why she would be wasting time wondering about him now when she had so much to do was a mystery.

The man walked around the other side of the vehicle to let someone out of the passenger side, a gesture she didn't see enough these days. She was curious to see his companion, but before she could catch a glimpse of the woman, the front door of the shop opened and Claire and Evie burst through, bringing the scent of snow and Christmas. Their mingled laughter chimed more sweetly than carols.

"I know," Claire said. "That's what I told him. But this is his first Christmas as a stepfather, and I swear, he's more excited than Owen or Macy. I've had to hide the present stash a half-dozen times, and he finds every blasted spot."

"What do you expect, honey?" Evie untwisted her scarf, hand-knitted in a heathery wool that dangled with beads instead of fringe. "He's a trained detective. It's kind of what he does."

The two of them had probably walked over from the bead store Claire owned, just down the street a block. Evie rented an apartment upstairs from Claire. For now, anyway. Evie was dating Brodie Thorne, her friend Katherine's son, and Maura expected their relationship was progressing quickly.

Claire's soft, pretty features lit up when she saw her. "Maura, honey, the store looks fabulous. I keep meaning to tell you every day when I come in for coffee, but you're never standing still long enough."

"Your mom did a lot of the work. It was her idea to hang all the snowflakes and the ornaments. Isn't that brilliant?"

Ruth had been working at the bookstore for months, but Claire still seemed baffled by it. Maura couldn't blame her. No one was more surprised than Maura when Ruth's offer to help out temporarily during those dark days and weeks in the spring had turned into a permanent arrangement that had worked out beautifully for everyone concerned.

"Ruth is a great employee," she assured Claire again. "Hardworking and dependable, with these wonderful, unexpected flashes of ingenuity, like the snowflakes."

"And here she is now," Evie announced.

Sure enough, a moment later Ruth walked in, along with Maura's mother, Mary Ella, and Katherine Thorne. With them was Janie Hamilton, a fairly new addition to town and another lost lamb Katherine had taken under her wing, and right behind them was Charlotte Caine, who owned the candy store in town.

Maura took a deep breath and put on her game face, that forced smile that had become second nature since her world had changed forever eight months earlier. "Welcome, everyone. I'm so happy you can all come."

She stepped forward to hug and brush cheeks with everyone as they all began to shed coats and scarves and hats like penguins molting in the spring. Everyone seemed to have on holiday party clothes: shimmery blouses, festive patterned scarves, dangling earrings and beaded necklaces.

She felt drab in her suede jacket, tailored cream shirt and jeans, though she was wearing one of her favorite chunky wood-bead necklaces she had made at String Fever last year.

"What about Alex?" she asked. "Isn't she coming?"

"Angie's picking her up," her mother assured her. "They texted me a few minutes ago to tell me they're running late. As usual."

"Whew. That's a relief. She's supposed to be bringing dessert, those delicious pumpkin spice cupcakes she makes."

"The ones with the cinnamon buttermilk icing? Oh, yay!" Claire said. "I guess since I'm not trying to fit into a wedding dress anymore, I might be able to let myself have one."

Maura could probably afford to eat five or six, since all her clothes fit her loosely now. Amazing how little appetite she had these days. "Everybody grab coffee or tea or whatever you're drinking from the counter. I've got us set up in the corner."

She ushered everyone over to the coffee counter in time to see April hang her apron on the hook. Josh Kimball had come in to replace her for the evening shift. He waved and grinned his charmer of a grin at her, and she managed to dredge up a small smile for his perpetual raccoon eyes, white in an otherwise bronzed face where his goggles blocked the sun while he was snowboarding.

"I'm off. I'll see you later," April said as she grabbed her coat.

"Thank you for everything. Good luck with the night patrol. See you tomorrow."

"You got it." April swung open the door just as a couple walked in—and suddenly all the air whooshed out of Maura's lungs.

It was the man she had seen a half hour earlier entering the café, the same impractical leather jacket, the same wavy dark hair, the same plaid scarf.

In the hanging track lights of her store, she could clearly see her mistake.

This man didn't simply bear a mild, passing resemblance to Jackson Lange.

He most definitely *was* Jackson Lange.

For one crazy second, her mind became a tangle of half-buried memories, the kind that came from being young and impulsive and passionately in love. The first time he held her hand in a darkened theater, shared confidences on a sun-warmed boulder high up the canyon, tangled bodies and mouths, the peace she found only with him—then the vast heartache and the sharp, gnawing fear after he left.

Someone was talking to her. Evie, she thought vaguely, but the words couldn't register past her dismayed shock.

Jack had vowed never to step foot in Hope's Crossing, with the fierce, unwavering determination only an eighteen-year-old young man could claim.

Yet here he was.

Yeah. Like she needed one more thing to make this Christmas really suck. This was definitely the cherry on top of the fruitcake—for Jackson Lange to come into her store with his undoubtedly lovely wife to have a cappuccino or maybe browse through one of the nonfiction sections. Travel, maybe, or her small but adequate architectural design shelf.

And in the middle of her book club meeting, for crying out loud.

She could just ignore him. If she ducked behind a bookcase, with luck, he wouldn't see her. He probably had no idea she owned Dog-Eared Books & Brew—why would he possibly know that? She could send one of the clerks over to escort him to the farthest corner away from the book club—or better yet, have Josh come with all his delightful snowboarder muscles and throw him out in the cold. She'd never heard of a bookstore having a bouncer, but there was always a first time.

Too late. He turned just at that moment and his blue-eyed gaze met hers. She saw definite recognition there. Oddly, he didn't seem at all surprised to see her, almost as if he had come looking for her. That was impossible, of course. In nearly twenty years, he hadn't made the smallest effort to find her. Not that it would have taken much work on his part. She hadn't gone anywhere.

The years had been unfairly kind to him, she saw, had taken a teenage boy who had been brooding and angry and undeniably gorgeous to all the other teenage girls and turned him into a sexy, potent male, with intense blue eyes, a firm mouth and the resolute jawline that just might be the only thing he shared with his father.

"Are you all right?"

She managed to look away and saw her mother studying her with concern. "What?"

"You've gone pale, darling. And I asked you three times if you made these delicious truffles. What's the matter?"

"I..." She couldn't come up with a way to answer, since every single brain cell had apparently decided to stage a temporary work stoppage.

He was coming this way. She watched him take one step toward her and then another. Her palms went damp and she could feel the blood rush out of her head, which didn't help the small matter of her sudden inability to form a coherent thought.

In a panic, she turned away, as if maybe she could block out the last two minutes and pretend it was just a slice out of her nightmares.

"Why, yes. Yes, I did make the truffles. It wasn't hard at all. The secret is to add the cream slowly and use high-quality flavoring...."

She launched into a whole explanation about the homemade chocolate balls, but eventually the words petered out when she realized nobody was paying attention to her. They were staring at a point above her shoulder.

"You're here!" Mary Ella suddenly exclaimed. "Oh, darling. I'm so happy you made it. I thought you weren't coming until the weekend!"

Her mother brushed past her, arms outstretched. Okay, this *had* to be a nightmare. As far as she knew, Mary Ella would have no reason to even *know* about Jack, as they had kept their relationship a secret that summer, in the tumult that was their respective home lives.

Wondering what alternative universe she had suddenly been thrust into, she finally forced herself to turn around. Mary Ella wasn't hugging Jack, she was hugging someone *behind* him. When her mother shifted, Maura finally caught a glimpse of who it was, and her insides turned to thin, crackly ice.

Her nineteen-year-old daughter, Sage, stood just a half step behind Jackson Lange, hidden from view by the breadth of his shoulders.

Her numb brain *finally* began kicking out messages at a rapid-fire pace, and none of them were good.

Sage. Together with Jackson Lange.

The two of them, in the same room. Not just the same room—the same freaking three-foot radius.

She'd never had a panic attack, despite the past eight months of purgatory, but she could feel one coming on now. Her heart raced and she could feel each pulse throbbing in her chest, her neck, her face. "S-Sage."

Her daughter gave her a long look, but for the first time ever Sage's usually expressive eyes were shuttered.

She knew.

Maura wasn't sure how she was so certain, especially as her daughter's features were closed and set, but somehow she could tell Sage knew the truth. Finally. After nearly two decades.

"Who's your friend, sweetheart?" Mary Ella asked as she stepped away from her oldest grandchild and gave Jack the sort of quizzical look she wore when trying to place someone, as if she thought she recognized him but wasn't quite sure.

"This is Jackson Lange. You've probably heard of him. He's a pretty famous architect."

Maura was aware of the little stir of excitement among her friends. It was fairly common knowledge that Hope's Crossing had spawned the man many considered the next Frank Gehry.

Mary Ella's expression cooled and she took a slight step back. "Of course. Harry's son."

"I haven't heard that particular phrase in a long time." Those were the first words he spoke, and she supposed she shouldn't be surprised that his voice seemed lower, sexier, as it thrummed down her spine.

"Yes. Harry Lange's son." Sage gave her mother that cool look again. "And he's not my friend. Not really. He's my father."

Maura hissed in a breath. Okay. There it was.

This Christmas had just climbed straight to the top of the suck-o-meter.

CHAPTER TWO

OKAY, THIS WAS a huge mistake.

Jack stood beside his daughter—his daughter. Hell. How had *that* happened?—and gazed around at the group of women all staring at him as if he'd just walked in and mooned them all.

When Sage had suggested stopping in at the bookstore to talk to her mother first before he dropped her off at her house and found a hotel for himself for a few days, he'd had no idea Maura would be in the middle of a freaking Christmas party. He noted the cluster of gift bags, the personalized glass decorations on the tree. Somebody had gone to a lot of trouble to prepare for this gathering, and he had just barged in and ruined it.

"Your…father?" an older woman said faintly.

Though twenty years had gone by, he clearly recognized Mary Ella McKnight, with those green eyes all her children had inherited, now peering at him through a pair of trendy little horn-rimmed glasses. She had taught him English in high school, and he remembered with great fondness their discussions on Milton and Wilkie Collins.

She was still very pretty, with a soft, ageless kind of beauty.

"You didn't know either?" Sage raised an eyebrow at her grandmother's obvious shock. "I guess it was a big secret to everyone. I thought I was the last to know."

He had met Sage only days ago, but her sudden barbed tone seemed very unlike the sweet, earnest young woman he had come to know. That she would burst in and spring him on Maura like this without any advance warning seemed either thoughtless or cruel. He should say something to ease the tension of the moment, but for the life of him, he couldn't seem to come up with anything polite and innocuous that didn't start with "How the hell could you keep this from me?"

A woman with chestnut hair who looked vaguely familiar stepped forward and rested a hand on Maura's arm. "Are you all right, my dear?" the woman asked.

Maura gave a jerky shake of her head and swallowed, her features pale. According to what Sage had told him, Maura was still grieving the loss of her *other* daughter, he suddenly remembered, and he felt like an even bigger ass for bursting in here like this.

"Maybe the three of you should go back to your office where you could have a little privacy for this discussion," the other woman gently suggested.

Maura gazed at her blankly for a moment, then seemed to gather her composure from somewhere deep inside. "I'm… I'm sorry. I wasn't… This is a bit of a shock. Yes. We should go back to my office. Thank you, Claire. Do you mind helping your mother lead the book discussion? When Alex gets here, she should have the, uh, refreshments."

He really should have made sure Sage had talked to her mother about all of this before he showed up, but then, he hadn't really been thinking clearly in the three days since the carefully arranged life he thought he had constructed for himself had imploded around him.

Three days ago, he had been living his life, continuing to build Lange & Associates, preparing for an undergraduate lecture at the University of Colorado College of Architecture and Planning. It was the first time he had stepped back in the state since he had escaped twenty years ago, a bitter and angry young man.

His lecture had gone well, especially as he focused on one of his passions, sustainable design. He was fairly certain he hadn't come across as a pompous iconoclast. Among the students who had pressed toward the dais to talk to him afterward had been this young woman with dark wavy hair and green eyes.

She told him she had studied his work, that she had always felt a bond to him because she was also from Hope's Crossing, where she knew he had grown up, and that while she hadn't met him, she saw his father around town often.

He studied her features as she spoke to him about her dreams and their shared passion for architecture, and he had been aware of an odd sense of the familiar but with a twist, as if he were looking at someone he knew through a wavy, distorted mirror.

When she told him her name—Sage McKnight—he had stared at her for a full thirty seconds before he had asked, "Who are your parents?"

"I don't know my father. He took off before I was born. But my mother's name is Maura McKnight. I think she might be around your age or maybe a little younger."

Younger, he remembered thinking as everything inside him froze. She had been a year younger.

"She's thirty-seven now, if that helps you place her," Sage had offered helpfully. "She graduated from high school nineteen years ago. I know, because it was about a month before I was born."

Just like that, he had pieced the dates and the times together, and he had known. He didn't need to bother with

DNA tests. He could do the damn math. Anyone with a brain could clearly see she was his child. They had the same nose, the same dark, wavy hair, the same dimple in their chins.

His daughter. After three days, he still couldn't believe it.

And neither, apparently, could all those gaping women back there. Hadn't she told *anyone* who had fathered her child?

Now he followed Maura through the bookstore, noting almost subconsciously certain architectural details of the historic building, like the walls that had been peeled back to bare brick and the windows with their almost Gothic arches. With jewel-toned hanging fixtures on track lights and plush furniture set around in conversation nooks, Maura had created a cozy, warm space that encouraged people to stop and ponder, sip a coffee, maybe grab a book off a shelf at random and discover something new.

Under ordinary circumstances, he would have found the place appealing, clever and bright and comfortable, but he could only focus on haphazard details as he followed her through a doorway to a long, barren stockroom, and a cluttered office dominated by a wide oak desk and a small window that overlooked Main Street.

Inside her office, Maura turned on both of them. "First of all, Sage, what are you doing here today? What about your biology final tomorrow morning?"

Her daughter—*their* daughter—shrugged. "I talked Professor Johnson into letting me take it this morning. She was fine with that, especially after I explained I had extenuating circumstances."

Maura's gaze darted to him, then quickly away again. "How do you think you did? Did you even have time to study after your chemistry final? You needed a solid A on the final to bring your grade above a C."

"Really, Mom? Is that what you want to talk about right now? My grades?"

A hint of color soaked Maura's cheeks, and she compressed her lips into a thin line as if to clamp back more academic interrogation. Even with the sour expression, she still looked beautiful. Looking at her now, he couldn't fathom that she was old enough to have a daughter who was a college sophomore, but then she must have been barely eighteen when Sage was born. She was seventeen when he'd left, still six months before her eighteenth birthday.

Maura released a heavy breath and finally sat on the edge of her desk, which put her slightly above him and Sage, who had taken the two guest chairs in her office.

"You're right. We can talk about school later. I just… This was all unexpected. I didn't think you would be here until tomorrow, and then I never expected you to bring…"

"My father?"

Maura's hands flexed on her thighs even as she made a scoffing sort of sound. "I don't know where you possibly came up with that crazy idea," she began, but Sage cut her off.

"Please don't lie to me. You've been lying for twenty years. Can we just stop now?" Though the words were angry, the tone was soft and almost gentle. "You've known who he is and where he was all this time, haven't you? Why didn't you ever tell me?"

Maura looked at him quickly and then away again. She hadn't looked at him for longer than a few seconds at a time, as if she were trying to pretend he wasn't really there. "Does it really matter?"

"Yes. Of course it matters! I could have had a father all this time."

"You've had your stepfather from the time you were just a little girl. Chris has always been great to you."

"True. He's still great to me. Even after the divorce, he never treated me any differently than he did L-Layla." Sage's voice wobbled a little at the name. Her sister, who had died earlier this year, he remembered, and felt like an ass again for showing up out of the blue like this, dredging up the past. What would happen if he left town right now and went back to his real life in the Bay Area and pretended none of this had ever happened?

He couldn't do that, as tempting as he suddenly found the idea. To a man who had spent his adult life trying to clear through the clutter in his personal and professional lives, this was all so messy and complicated. But like it or not, Sage was his daughter. He was here now, and had been given the chance after all these years to come to know this young woman who bore half his DNA and who reminded him with almost painful intensity of an innocent part of himself he had left behind a long time ago.

"A child can never have too many people who love her, Mom. You taught me that. Why did you keep my father out of our lives all this time? He didn't have any idea I even existed. If he hadn't come to campus to give a lecture, both of us would still be in the dark."

"A lecture?"

"Right. On sustainable design, one of my own passions. It was wonderful, really inspiring. I went up afterward to talk to him and mentioned I was from Hope's Crossing. It only took us a minute to figure things out."

Maura frowned. "Figure what out? That the two of us dated when I was barely seventeen? How could you both instantly jump from that to thinking he's your…your sperm donor?"

The term annoyed the hell out of him. "Because neither of us is stupid. She told me who her mother was. When I asked how old she was, I could figure out the math. I knew exactly who you were with nine months before her birthday."

And ten months before and eleven months and every spare moment they could get their hands on each other that summer.

"That doesn't prove a thing. You took off. You weren't here, Jack. How do you know I didn't pick up with the whole basketball team after you left?" Defiance and something that looked suspiciously like fear flashed in her eyes.

She had been a virgin their first time together. They both had been, fumbling and awkward and embarrassed but certain they were deeply in love. Even if not for the proof sitting beside him, he wouldn't have believed the smart and loving girl she had been would suddenly turn into the kind of girl who would sleep around with just anybody.

"Look at her," he said, gentling his tone. "She has my mother's nose and my mouth and chin. We can run the DNA, but I don't need to. Sage is my daughter. For three days, I've just been trying to figure out why the hell you didn't tell me."

For the first time, she met his gaze for longer than a few seconds. "Think about it, Jack," she finally said. "What difference would it have made? Would you have come back?"

He couldn't lie, to her or to himself. "No. But you could have come with me."

"And lived in some rat-hole apartment while you dropped out of college and worked three jobs to support us, resenting me the whole time? That would have been the perfect happily-ever-after every young girl dreams about."

"I still had a right to know."

She suddenly looked tired, defeated, and he saw deep shadows in her eyes that he sensed had nothing to do with him.

"Well, I guess you know now. Yes. She's your daughter. There was no one else. There it is. Now you know, and we can be one big, freaking happy family for the holidays."

"Mom." Sage moved forward a little as if to reach for Maura's hand, but then she checked the motion and slid back into her chair.

Pain etched Maura's features briefly, but she contained it. "Okay. I should have told you. Give me a break here. I was just a scared kid who didn't know what to do. You left without a forwarding address, Jack, and didn't contact me one single time after you left, despite all your promises. What else was I supposed to do? I finally tracked down your number at Berkeley about four months after you left and tried to call you. Three times I tried in a week. Once you were at the library, and twice you were on a date, at least according to your roommate. I left my number, but you never called me back, which basically gave me the message loud and clear that you were done with me. What more was I supposed to do?"

He remembered those first few months at school after that last horrible fight with his father, after he had opted to leave everything behind—even the only warm and beautiful thing that had happened to him in Hope's Crossing since his mother's death.

He remembered the message from Maura his roommate had given him and the sloppily scrawled phone number. He had stared at it for hours and had even dialed the number several times, but had always hung up.

She had been a link to a place and a past he had chosen to leave behind, and he'd ultimately decided it was in both their best interests if he tried to move on and gave her the chance to do the same.

That she had been pregnant and alone had never once occurred to him. Lord, he'd been an idiot.

Everything was so damn tangled, he didn't know what to do—which was the whole reason he had agreed to give Sage a ride back to Hope's Crossing to talk to Maura before he flew back to San Francisco.

"Look, we're all a little emotional about this tonight. I didn't realize you were unaware I was bringing Sage back to town."

That little tidbit also appeared to be news to Maura. "You rode here with him?" she asked her daughter. "Is something wrong with the Honda?"

"It hasn't been starting the last week or so. I think it just needs a new battery, but I figured I could drive the pickup while I was home and catch a ride back to school with one of my friends after the break. I can deal with the Honda before school starts next semester."

"You should have called me. I could have driven to Boulder to pick you up."

"Sorry, Mom. My car troubles just didn't seem all that important in light of…everything else."

"I guess that's understandable." Maura forced a smile, but he could clearly see the bone-deep weariness beneath it. What had happened to the vibrant, alive girl who'd always made him laugh, even when they were both dealing with family chaos and pain?

"So what now?" she asked. Though she looked at her

daughter, he picked up the subtext of the question, directed at him. *What else are you planning to do to screw up my life?*

"I think you should get back to your book club Christmas party for now. I'm really sorry we interrupted it."

"Between Ruth and Claire and your grandmother, I'm sure everything will be fine," Maura assured her.

Much to his astonished dismay, tears filled Sage's eyes. "But I know how much you always look forward to the party and the fun you have throwing it for your friends. It's always the highlight of your Christmas. If anything, you needed it more than ever this year, and now I've ruined everything for you."

Maura gave him a harsh look, as if this rapid-fire emotional outburst were *his* fault, then she stepped forward to wrap Sage in her arms.

"It's only a party," she said. "No big deal. They can all carry on just fine without me. And if you want the truth, I almost canceled it this year. I haven't really been in the mood for Christmas."

This information only seemed to make Sage sniffle harder, and he watched helplessly while Maura comforted her. Judging by the mood swings and the emotional outbursts, apparently he had a hell of a lot to learn about having a nineteen-year-old daughter.

"You're exhausted, honey. I'm sure you've been studying hard for finals."

"I haven't been able to sleep much since the lecture," she admitted, resting her darker head on her mother's shoulder. He had a feeling the bond between them would survive the secret Maura had never told her daughter. As he saw the two of them together, something sharp and achy twisted in his gut.

He had an almost-grown daughter he suddenly felt responsible for, and he had no idea what he was supposed to do about it.

"Why don't you take my car home and go back to the house to get some rest," Maura said. "I'll catch a ride with your grandmother or with Claire. We can talk more in the morning when we're both rested and…more calm."

"I'll take her home," Jack offered quietly.

"Thank you, but I wouldn't want to put you to any more trouble. You've done enough by bringing her all this way from Boulder. I'm sure you need to get back to…wherever you came from."

In a rush to send him on his way, was she? "Actually, I'm planning to stay in town a few days."

"Why?" she asked, green eyes wide with surprise. "You hate Hope's Crossing."

"I just found out I have a daughter. I'm not in any particular hurry to walk back out of her life right away."

The surprise shifted to something that looked like horror, as if she had never expected him to genuinely want to be part of their daughter's world on any ongoing basis. Sage, though, lifted her head from her mother's shoulder and gave him a watery smile. "That's great. Really great."

"What do you say we meet for breakfast in the morning? Unless you have to be here at the bookstore first thing."

Maybe a night's rest would give them all a little breathing space and offer him, at least, a chance to regain equilibrium, before any deeper discussion about the decisions made in the past and where they would go from here.

"I own the place. I don't have to punch a clock."

"Which usually means you're here from about eight a.m. to ten p.m." Sage gave her mother a teasing look.

"I can meet for breakfast," Maura said. "Tomorrow I don't have anything pressing at the store until midmorning."

"Perfect. Why don't we meet at the Center of Hope Café at around eight-thirty? We stopped there to grab a bite at the counter before we walked over here, and I'm happy to say their food is just as good as I remembered."

"The café? I don't know if that's the greatest idea. You might not want to…" she started to say, but her words trailed off.

"Want to what?" he asked.

She seemed to reconsider the subject of any objection on his part. "No. On second thought, sure. Eight-thirty at the café should work just fine."

"Okay. I'll see you then. Shall we go, Sage?"

"Yeah." She pressed her cheek to her mother's. "I'm still furious you didn't tell me about my father. I probably will be for a while. But I still love you and I will forever and ever."

"Back at you," Maura said, a catch in her voice that she quickly cleared away.

"Do you think she'll be okay?" Sage asked him after they walked through the bookstore and the lightly falling snow to the SUV, which he had rented what seemed a lifetime ago at the Denver airport before his lecture.

"You would know that better than I do."

"I thought I knew my mother. We're best friends. I still can't believe she would keep this huge secret from me."

He wondered at Maura's reasons for that. Why didn't she tell Sage? Why didn't she tell *him?* Surely in the years since he'd left, she could have found some way to tell him about his child.

The idea of it was still overwhelming as hell.

"You'll have to give me directions to your place," he said after she fastened her seat belt.

"Oh. Right. We live on Mountain Laurel Road. Do you remember where that is?"

"I think so." If he remembered correctly, it was just past Sweet Laurel Falls, one of his favorite places in town. The falls had been one of their secret rendezvous points. Why he should remember that right now, he had no idea. "I know the general direction, anyway. Be sure to tell me if I start to head off course."

Traffic was busier than he expected as he drove through Hope's Crossing with the wipers beating back the falling snow. He hardly recognized the downtown. When he had lived here, many of these storefronts had been empty or had housed businesses that barely survived on the margin. Now trendy restaurants, bustling bars catering to tourists and boutiques with elegant holiday window displays seemed to jostle for space.

Some of the historic buildings were still there, but he could see new buildings as well. Much to his surprise, some faction in town had apparently made an effort to keep the town's historic flavor, even among the new developments. Instead of a modern hodgepodge of architectural styles that would be jarring and unpleasant with the mountain grandeur surrounding the town, it looked as if restrictions had been enacted to require strict adherence to building codes. Even in the few strip-mall-type developments they passed with pizza places, frozen yogurt shops and fast-food places that might appeal to tourists, the buildings had cedar-shake roofs and no flashy signage to jar with the setting.

As he drove up the hill toward Mountain Laurel Road, the surroundings seemed more familiar, even after twenty years. In his day, this area of town had been called Old

Hope, a neighborhood of smaller, wood-framed houses, some of them dating back to the town's past as a rough and rugged mining town. A few of the houses had been torn down and small condominium units or more modern homes built in their place, and many had obviously been rehabbed.

He could easily tell which were vacation homes—they invariably had some sort of kitschy decoration on the exterior, like a crossed pair of old wooden skis or snowshoes, or some other kind of cabin-chic decoration. He saw a couple of carved wooden bears and even a wooden moose head on a garage.

"Turn here," Sage said. "Our house is the small brick-and-tan house on the right, three houses from the corner."

From what he had just seen in town, Maura ran a prosperous business in Hope's Crossing. According to the information he had gleaned from Sage over the past few days, she had been married for five years to Chris Parker, frontman for Pendragon, a band even *Jack* had heard of before.

She must have received a healthy alimony and child support settlement from the guy when their marriage broke up. So why was she living in a small Craftsman bungalow that looked as though it couldn't be more than nine hundred square feet?

Despite its small size, the house appeared cozy and warm nestled here in the mountains. Snow drifted down to settle on the wide, deep porch, and a brightly lit Christmas tree blazed from the double windows in front. The lot was roomy, giving her plenty of space for an attached garage that looked as if it had been added to the main house later.

He glimpsed movement by the side of the house and spied a couple of cold and hungry mule deer trying to browse off the shrubs, which looked as if they had been wrapped to avoid just such an eventuality. The deer looked up when Jack's headlights pulled into the driveway, then it turned and bounded away, jumping over a low cedar fence to her neighbor's property. Its mate followed suit and disappeared in a flash of white hindquarters.

Now, there was an encounter that brought back memories. When he was a kid and lived up Silver Strike Canyon, he and his mother would often take walks to look for deer. She would even sometimes wake him up if a big buck would wander through their yard.

"Thanks for the ride. I guess I'll see you in the morning."

"I can walk you in. Help you with your bag and your laundry."

"You don't have to do that."

He hadn't been given the chance to do anything to help his daughter in nearly twenty years. Carrying in her bags was a small gesture, but at least it was *something*. He didn't bother arguing with her; he only climbed out of the SUV and reached into the backseat for the wicker laundry basket she'd loaded up at her apartment in Boulder, hefted it under one arm and picked her suitcase up with the other.

Sage made a sound of frustration, but followed him up the four steps to the porch and unlocked the house with a set of keys she pulled from her backpack. Warmth washed over them as Sage pushed open the door to let him inside, and the house smelled of cinnamon and clove and evergreen branches from the garlands draped around.

Jack found himself more interested than he probably should have been in Maura's house. He took in the built-in bookshelves, the exposed rafters, the extensive woodwork, all softened by colorful textiles and art-glass light fixtures.

"Looks like Mom went all out with the Christmas decorations. A tree and everything."

He glanced at his daughter. *His daughter*. Would he ever get used to that particular phrase? "You sound surprised."

"I thought this year she wouldn't really be in the mood for Christmas. Usually it's her favorite time of year but, you know. Everything is different now."

He didn't want to feel this sympathy. For the past three days, he had simmered in his anger that she had kept this cataclysmic thing from him all these years. Being here in Hope's Crossing, being confronted with the reality of her life and her pain and the difficult choices she must have faced as a seventeen-year-old girl, everything seemed different.

He felt deflated somehow and didn't quite know what to do with his anger.

Sage fingered an ornament on the tree that looked as if it was glued-together Popsicle sticks. The tree was covered in similar handmade ornaments, and he wondered which Sage had made and which had been crafted by her younger sister.

"I hope Grandma and the aunts helped her and she didn't have to do it by herself," Sage fretted. "That would have been so hard for her, taking out all these old ornaments and everything on her own."

Sage's compassion for her mother, despite everything, touched a chord deep inside him. There was a tight bond between the two of them. Had it always been there, or had their shared loss this year only heightened it?

He spied a cluster of photographs on the wall, dominated by one of Sage and Maura on a mountain trail somewhere, lit by perfect evening light amid the ghostly trunks of an aspen grove. They had their arms around each other, as well as a younger girl with purple highlights in her hair and a triple row of earrings.

"This must be Layla."

Sage moved beside him and reached a hand out to touch the picture. "Yep. She was so pretty, wasn't she?"

"Beautiful," he murmured. All three females were lovely. They looked like a tight unit, and it was obvious even at a quick glance that they had all adored each other.

Maura had been divorced for a decade and had raised both girls on her own. How had she managed it? he wondered, then reminded himself it was none of his business. He was here only to establish a relationship with his newly discovered daughter, not to walk down memory lane with Maura McKnight, the girl who had once meant everything to him.

"Oh, look. Presents." Sage's eyes were as wide as a little kid's as she looked at the prettily dressed packages under the tree. What had she been like as a big-eyed preschooler waiting for Santa to arrive? He would never know that. He'd missed all those Christmas Eves of putting out plates of cookies and tucking his little girl into bed.

"I guess I'd better head out to find a hotel. Are you sure you're okay now?" He couldn't see any evidence of the tears from earlier, but a guy never could tell.

"Yeah. I'm fine. I'm just going to throw in a load of laundry and check my Facebook, then go to bed."

"Okay, then. I guess I'll see you in the morning."

"Okay. Good night."

He turned to head toward the door and had almost reached it when her voice stopped him.

"Wait!"

He paused, then was completely disconcerted when she reached up and kissed him on the cheek. "I'm really glad we found each other, Jack."

On the way here, they had already had the awkward conversation about what she should call him. She didn't feel right calling him Dad at this point in their relationship, so he had suggested Jack.

"I am too," he said gruffly.

He meant the words, he thought, as he walked out into the snowy evening lit by stars and the Christmas lights of Maura's neighbors. Despite everything, the realization that Sage was his daughter astonished and humbled him. And yes, delighted him—even though it meant returning to Hope's Crossing after all these years and facing the past he thought he had left far behind.

CHAPTER THREE

FOR A LONG time after Sage walked out with Jack, Maura sat in her chair with her hands folded together on her desk, staring into space.

Jackson Lange was here in Hope's Crossing.

She'd never thought she would have occasion to use those particular words together in the same sentence. Stupid and shortsighted of her, she supposed. This was his hometown, and despite his avowed hatred of the place, she should have expected that someday he would eventually be drawn back.

One would assume some latent affection for the town where he had lived his first eighteen years must have seeped into his bones. It was only natural. Salmon spent their last breaths returning to their birthplace. Why should she simply have assumed Jackson wouldn't want to come back at least once in twenty years?

In her own defense, she had always assumed his hatred for his father would also serve to keep him away.

In the early years after Sage was born, she used to come up with all these crazy, complicated scenarios in her head for what might happen if he *did* return. She had worked it all out—what she would say to him, how he would respond, the immense self-satisfaction she fully expected to find from throwing back in his face that he had left her yet she had managed to move on and survive.

In her perfect imagination, he would come back on the proverbial hands and knees, telling her what a fool he had been, begging her to forgive him, promising he would never be parted from her again.

Around the time she'd met Christian, she had been more than ready to put those fantasies away as both impossible and undesirable. She had put all her resources into thrusting Jack firmly into her past, and focusing instead on her new relationship and the love she told herself she felt for Chris.

She could never completely assign him to the past, of course, not when her beautiful, smart, clever child bore half his DNA. Sage was always a reminder of Jack. She would turn her head a certain angle, and Maura would remember Jack looking at her the same way. Sage would come up with a particularly persuasive argument for something, twist logic and sense in a way that never would have occurred to Maura, and she would remember how brilliantly Jack could do the same.

In all those early fantasies and all the years to come later, it had never once occurred to her that someday Sage might find him on her own and bring him back to the town he couldn't wait to leave.

Her sigh sounded pathetic in her small office, and she shook her head. Nothing she could do about this now. Against all odds, he and Sage *had* found each other, and now she would have to deal with the consequences of him in their lives. A smart woman would find a way to make the best of it—but right now she didn't, for the life of her, know how she was supposed to do that.

"Having a rough night?"

She turned at the voice and found her mother in the doorway, still lovely at sixty with her ageless skin and Maura's own auburn hair, the color now carefully maintained at To Dye For. Emotions crowded her chest at the sight of the sympathy in her mother's green eyes behind her little glasses, and she suddenly wanted to rest her head on Mary Ella's shoulder, as Sage had done with *her* earlier, and weep and weep.

Her mother and her sisters were her best friends, and she didn't think she would have survived the past eight months without them. Or what she would have done twenty years ago, when she was seventeen and terrified and pregnant in a small town that could still be closed-minded and mean about those sorts of things.

She fought back the tears and mustered a smile. "Rough night? Yeah. You could say that."

"Oh, honey. Why did you keep this to yourself all these years?"

"I didn't think it mattered. He was gone and insisted he wasn't ever coming back. Why did I need to flit around town badmouthing him for knocking me up and then taking off?"

Mary Ella stepped forward and pulled her into a hug, and those blasted tears threatened again. "I have to admit, I suspected. I knew you had become friendly with him. People told me about seeing you together. I also suspected you had a little crush on him. I just hadn't realized things had…progressed. I don't know how I missed it now. Sage looks a little like him, doesn't she?"

"Do you think so?"

"The mouth and her chin."

"She might look a little like him, but she's very much her own person."

"Absolutely." Her mother leaned back a little and smoothed a stray lock of hair away from Maura's forehead. "Everyone will understand if you need to leave. Go home to Sage. We can carry on without you."

She was tremendously tempted to do just that—the going home part, anyway. Right now, she wanted nothing more than to sneak into her house, crawl into her bed and pull the Storm at Sea quilt—the one she and her sisters had made after her divorce—over her head and not crawl out again until the holidays were over.

Nothing new there, she supposed. She couldn't remember a moment in the past eight months when she *hadn't* wanted to climb into bed and block out the world. But she was a McKnight, and the women in her family soldiered on, no matter what.

She had managed to keep herself going all these months. She could make it through this too.

"I'm not about to let Jackson Lange ruin the book club Christmas party for me." She rose on legs that felt a little unsteady. Low blood sugar, she told herself. All she needed was a truffle or something. "Let's go party. I think this evening calls for some of Alex's famous spiked cider. I hope she brought some."

"If I know your baby sister, I have no doubts of that." Mary Ella slipped an arm through hers and walked by her side through the bookstore and back to the gathering.

She might have predicted the reactions of her friends and family exactly. Angie, her oldest sister and the second mother to the six McKnight siblings, looked at her with deep compassion and concern. Alex, younger than her by only a few years, gave her a look that clearly conveyed solidarity against all males of the species. Claire—Alex's best friend, who had always seemed like part of the family and had made it official only a few weeks ago by marrying Maura's younger brother—acted typically solicitous, handing her a mug of something, fragrant steam curling into the air.

It was tea, not Alex's cider, a Ceylon black with cinnamon, clove and orange peels, but Maura figured she could build to the cider.

They were just getting ready to start the annual gift-exchange game, she realized, where everybody picked a wrapped gift and passed it either left or right while someone—in this case, Janie Hamilton—said certain words when she read a passage from a holiday book.

"We saved a spot for you," Claire told her. "Pass left when you hear the word *the* and right when you hear *and*. What are we reading, Janie?"

Janie held up a familiar Dr. Seuss book. "Sorry. My kids have all the Christmas books in their rooms, which are a total mess until I shovel them out. All I could find was *How the Grinch Stole Christmas*."

"My fave," Alex said, stretching her feet out on a cushioned ottoman.

Maura took the empty seat and spent the next few minutes giving an Oscar-worthy performance of someone enjoying herself as, with much laughter, they passed the gifts back and forth, until Janie finished with the Grinch carving the roast beast and everybody ended up with their final gift.

To her delight, her prize was Charlotte Caine's gift, a beautifully presented bag of almond brickle from Charlotte's store down the street, Sugar Rush.

"Thanks, Charley. Just what I needed!" She smiled, thinking how pretty the other woman looked tonight in her white silk blouse and ruby earrings, despite the extra pounds she carried.

The distraction of opening presents gave her a much-needed chance to gather her composure, so she was almost ready when Ruth finally brought up what she knew was on everyone's mind.

"So it's true," she said in her abrupt way. "Harry Lange's son is Sage's father."

She would like to deny it, but what would be the point? Everybody knew now, and she couldn't stopper that particular bottle. Trust Ruth not to shy away from the topic everybody else had been avoiding.

"Yes," she said, with as much calm as she could muster.

"I always knew that boy was a troublemaker," Ruth said promptly.

"He wasn't. Not really." Jack might have been on fire with grief for his mother and with anger and bitterness toward his father, but it had consumed him quietly. To everyone else, he had been hardworking and reliable. An excellent student, a diligent employee at his summer construction job.

"A decent man stays around to take care of his responsibilities," Ruth said stubbornly.

"He didn't know he had responsibilities here, Ruth," she said, wondering if her voice sounded as tired to everyone else as it did to her. "I never told him I was pregnant."

"Well, that was a pretty stupid thing to do, wasn't it?"

A bubble of laughter with a slight hysterical edge welled up inside her. "Yes. Yes, it was. Very stupid," she answered.

"What was stupid?" Angie asked, on Ruth's other side.

"Not telling the Lange boy she was pregnant so he could step up and do the right thing." Ruth said.

Like marry her? Oh, that would have been a complete nightmare. She had believed it then, and nothing had changed her mind in the intervening years. She had loved Jackson Lange with a desperate passion, and he obviously hadn't loved her back nearly as intensely. If he had, he never would have left.

Only after he took off did she realize the twisted way she had subconsciously reenacted her own childhood in their relationship. Her father had walked away from their family in order to pursue his own professional and academic dreams. By falling hard for Jack just months later—an angry young man who already had one foot through the crack in the door on his way out of Hope's Crossing—hadn't she perhaps been trying to replicate and repair her family life by trying to keep him with her, as she couldn't keep her father?

Her love hadn't been enough to keep Jack in Hope's Crossing any more than she had been able to keep her father from walking away from their family.

"Look, you're all my dearest friends," she said now, realizing everyone's eyes were on her, though they made a pretense of carrying on conversation. She supposed it was better to confront the weird turn her life had just taken head-on rather than dance around it. "I don't want to put a damper on the party, but I know everyone is wondering. You're all just too kind to pry."

Except Ruth, anyway, but she didn't need to point out the obvious to anyone there.

"I might as well get this out in the open, then we can go back to enjoying the rest of the party. Jack and I dated in high school. We kept it secret because…well, because of a lot of things going on in our respective families. The timing didn't seem right."

Her mother's lips tightened, and Angie reached out and rubbed a hand on Mary Ella's arm. She wanted to assure her mother that James McKnight's defection of his family and the emotional fallout from that hadn't been the only reason for their secrecy.

After years of mental illness, Jack's mother had committed suicide herself just a few months earlier. Sometimes Maura wondered if Jack had only turned to her out of a desperate effort to push away the pain.

"After Jack left town, I discovered I was pregnant. For a lot of reasons that seemed very good at the time, I decided not to tell him I was pregnant and to raise Sage by myself." She lifted her chin. "Personally, I don't think she's suffered for my decisions. She's bright and beautiful and well-adjusted. Chris has been a great stepfather to her, and she loves him. If our marriage had lasted, I'm sure he would have adopted her."

Okay, she was spilling way too much here. She caught herself and wanted to change the subject, but on the other hand, these were her dearest friends. She would rather be open with them from the outset about Jack and Sage, rather than have them all shake their heads and worry about her behind her back. Hadn't she endured enough of that since Layla's death?

"How did they find each other?" Alex asked.

"As you all must know, Jack is an architect. Apparently Sage attended a lecture he gave a few days ago on campus. She knew he was from Hope's Crossing and they struck up a conversation. In the course of the conversation, they both connected the dots. And here we are."

Silence descended on the group as everyone mulled the information. Claire was the first to break it. "How are you doing with all this?"

"Peachy. Why wouldn't I be? It's all very civil." Except for that moment when she had wanted to smack him and tell him how he had shattered her heart. "It will be interesting to see what happens. My hope is that Jack and Sage can develop a friendship. They have a shared interest in architecture, after all. Perhaps Jack can, I don't know, mentor her. Help her with her studies, maybe."

"That would be great," Angie said. "Does that mean you think he's sticking around Hope's Crossing?"

Oh, she hoped not. The very idea made her stomach cramp. "I doubt it. Jack isn't a big fan of our little neck of the woods. Not to mention that he also hates his father."

"Not a big shocker there," Mary Ella muttered. She had a long-standing feud with Harry Lange, the wealthiest man in town, who seemed to think he owned everyone and everything in town—not just the ski resort he had developed, but everybody in Hope's Crossing who owed a living to the tourists he had brought in to enjoy it.

"Is there anything you need from us?" Claire asked.

A little spiked cider would be a good start. "I'd like to get back to the party. You have all found time in your holiday-crazed lives for this, and I don't want to ruin everything with more drama. Can we just forget about Jackson Lange for now?"

Everybody seemed to agree, to her great relief. Katherine Thorne asked Janie a question about one of her children who had broken an arm sledding off the hill at Miner's Park, and the conversation turned.

She loved these women. Sometimes their idiosyncrasies and their smothering concern drove her crazy, but she didn't know how she would have survived these past months without them. She had a feeling she would be leaning on them more than ever with this new twist on her life's journey.

HER HOUSE WAS quiet when she returned after the party finally wrapped up. She'd become used to it over the past few months since Sage had returned to Boulder and school. After she opened the door and found only the whoosh of the furnace, she finally admitted to herself that some part of her had been looking forward to Sage's return to fill the empty space with sound—her endless chatter about grades and her classes and current events, the television set she always had on, usually to HGTV, her local friends who went to other schools or had stuck around town to work and who always seemed to find excuses to drop in when Sage was in town.

She was destined for another quiet night, she realized.

"Sage? Honey?" she called, but received no answer. Maura knew she was home. Her purse was hanging on the hook by the door, and her cell phone was on the console table. She walked through the house to Sage's bedroom. The door was ajar and she rapped on it a few times softly, then pushed it open.

Sage was curled up in her bed with only her face sticking out of the cocoon of blankets. The lights of one of the little individual Christmas trees Maura had always set up in her girls' bedrooms twinkled and glowed, sending brightly colored reflections over Sage's face.

She rubbed a hand over her chest at the sudden ache there. She loved her daughter fiercely, had from the very first moment she'd realized she was pregnant. Yes, she had been afraid. What seventeen-year-old girl wouldn't have been? But she had also been eager for this unexpected adventure.

Those weeks and months of her pregnancy seemed so fresh and vivid in her mind. In her head she had known that giving up the baby for adoption to a settled, established couple who loved each other deeply would have been the best thing for Sage, but she had been selfish, she supposed.

She couldn't even bear the idea of losing this part of Jack that she already loved so much.

She could also admit to herself now that, at the time, she had been so angry at her father for leaving and at Jack for repeating the pattern that she had managed to convince herself her baby didn't need a father in her life, except to donate half the DNA. She could certainly raise this baby by herself without help from anyone.

Yeah, it had been immature and shortsighted—but then she had only been seventeen. Younger than her daughter was now.

Sage had always been a restless sleeper, even as a baby, but her exhaustion over finals must have tired her out. She didn't move when Maura stepped forward to click off the lights on the little tree or when Maura smoothed the blankets and tucked them more securely, then walked quietly from the room.

She paused outside the next bedroom and almost didn't go inside but finally forced herself to move. She switched on the little tree beside the empty bed and watched the colors reflected on the pale lavender walls, cheerful yellows and blues and reds and greens.

Angie, Mary Ella and Alex had insisted on coming over Thanksgiving weekend to help her put up the rest of the decorations, but she had placed this little tree here herself, as well as the little solar-powered tree on the gravesite. She had decorated it with all Layla's favorite ornaments—little beaded snowflakes Layla had made at String Fever, a glass snowman she had received from one of her good friends, a few small, pearlescent balls that seemed to shimmer in the glow from the lights.

She hadn't changed anything in here yet. It still looked like a fifteen-year-old girl's room, with a couple of lava lamps, a big, plump purple beanbag where Layla had loved to study, and huge posters of bands on the wall—most notably, Pendragon, her father's acoustic rock band. Though he was twice her age, Layla had had a bit of a crush on Chris's drummer.

Some day she would do something with the room. Maybe turn it into a home office, since most of the bookstore paperwork she brought home ended up spread out on a desk in her bedroom.

Not yet, though. She couldn't bring herself to change anything yet, so she left it untouched and only came in occasionally to dust.

After a few minutes of watching the lights, Maura cleared her throat and turned off the lights before she walked back into the quiet hallway.

As much as she ached with pain for Layla and the life that had been cut short by a whole chain of stupid decisions by a bunch of teenagers, Maura couldn't stop living. She had another daughter who needed her, now more than ever.

CHAPTER FOUR

DESPITE THE RADICAL changes to the rest of the town, the Center of Hope Café had changed very little in the twenty years since Jack had been here.

That might be new wallpaper on the wall, something brighter to replace the old wood paneling he remembered, but the booths were covered in the same red vinyl and the ceiling was still the old-fashioned tin-stamped sort favored around the turn of the century.

Even the owner, Dermot Caine, still stood behind the U-shaped bar. He had to be in his mid-sixties, but he had the familiar shock of white hair he'd worn as long as Jack could remember and the same piercing blue eyes that seemed capable of ferreting out any secret.

Despite the calorie-heavy comfort food the café was famous for, Dermot had stayed in shape and looked as if he could beat any comers in an arm-wrestling contest, probably from years of working the grill.

Just now he was busy talking to a couple of guys in Stetsons. Jack looked around for Maura and Sage but couldn't spot them. He didn't see anyone else he recognized either. It looked as if the Center of Hope was popular with both locals and tourists, at least judging by the odd mix of high-dollar ski gear and ranch coats.

He stood waiting to be seated for just a moment before Dermot walked over, no trace of recognition in his gaze.

No surprise there. Jack had been gone twenty years. He probably looked markedly different than that kid who used to come into the café to study after the library had closed for the night.

It sure as hell had beat going home.

"Hello there and welcome to the Center of Hope Café." Dermot had a trace of Ireland in his voice. Jack could easily have pictured him running a corner pub in a little town in County Galway somewhere, surrounded by mossy-green fields and stone fences. "You've got a couple of choices this lovely morning. You can find yourself a vacant spot at the counter, or I can fix you up with a booth or a table. Your preference."

"I'm actually waiting for two more. A booth would be fine."

"I've got a prime spot right here by the window. Will that suit you?"

"Perfectly. Thank you." He shrugged out of his jacket and hung it on a convenient hook made from a portion of an elk antler on the wall beside the booth. As he slid into the booth, Dermot set out a trio of menus and opened one for him.

"Here. You can have a little sneak peek at the menu before the rest of your party comes. We also have made-to-order omelets, if that suits your fancy. The breakfast special this morning is our eggs Benedict, famous in three counties. Can I get you some coffee or juice while you're waiting?"

Ordinarily, he would have liked to extend the courtesy of at least ordering beverages for Sage and Maura. Since he had no idea what they would like, he opted to play it safe and order only for himself. "I'll have both. Regular coffee and a small grapefruit juice. Thank you."

Dermot nodded. "Coming right up." He paused for just

a moment, his blue eyes narrowed. "Have you been in before? I usually have a good eye for my customers. I keep thinking I should know you, but I'm afraid my memory's not what it once was and I can't quite place you. Sorry, I am, for that."

"Don't apologize. I would have been surprised if you *had* recognized me. It's been twenty years. You used to serve me chocolate malts from the fountain with extra whipped cream while I did my homework in the corner." It was a surprisingly pleasant memory, especially considering he didn't think he had many of this town. That hadn't involved Maura, anyway.

"Jackson Lange," Dermot exclaimed. "Lordy, it's been an age, it has. How have you been, son?"

How did a man encapsulate his journey over the past two decades? Hard work, ambition, amazing good fortune in his chosen field and not such good fortune in his painfully short-lived marriage. "I can't complain. How about you? How's Mrs. Caine?"

His cheerful smile slipped a little. "I lost her some fifteen years back. The cancer."

"I'm sorry."

"Aye. So am I. I miss her every single day. But we had seven beautiful children together, and her memory lives on in them and our eight grandchildren."

He gestured to the other two menus. "And what about you? Are you meeting your family here, then?"

He thought of Sage, the daughter he hadn't known existed a handful of days ago. "Something like that."

"I'll treat you right. Don't you worry. Our French toast is still legendary around these parts. We still cover it in toasted almonds and dust it with powdered sugar."

He usually was a coffee-and-toast kind of guy, but he

had fond memories of that French toast. An indulgence once in a while probably wouldn't kill him. "Thanks. I'll keep that in mind."

Dermot smiled at him and headed to the kitchen, probably for his juice. Through the window, Jack watched Main Street bustle to life. The woman who was trying to change the marquee on the little two-theater cinema up the road had to stop about five times to return the wave of someone driving past, and a couple of women in winter workout gear who had dogs on leashes paused at just about every storefront to talk to somebody.

The scene reminded him of a small village outside Milan where he had rented an apartment for two months during the construction of a hotel and regional conference center a few miles from town. He used to love to grab a cappuccino and sit on the square with a sketchbook and pencil, watching the town wake up to greet the day.

In his career, Jack had worked on projects across the world, from Riyadh to Rio de Janeiro. He loved the excitement and vitality of a large city. The streets outside his loft in San Francisco bustled with life, and he enjoyed sitting out on the terrace and watching it from time to time, but he had to admit, he always found something appealing about the slower pace of a small town, where neighbors took time to stop their own lives to chat and care about each other.

Dermot walked out with his juice and a coffeepot. "Still waiting?" he asked as he flipped a cup over and expertly poured.

"I'm sure they'll be here soon."

"I'll keep an eye out, unless you would like me to take your order now."

"No. I'll wait."

A few moments later, while he was watching the dog

walkers grab a shovel out of an elderly man's hands in front of a jewelry store and start clearing snow off his store entrance, Maura and Sage came in. Their faces were both flushed from the cold, but he was struck for the first time how alike they looked. Sage was an interesting mix of the both of them, but in the morning light and with her darker, curlier hair covered by a beanie, she looked very much like her mother.

The women spotted him instantly and hurried over to the booth.

"Sorry we're late," Maura said without explanation, but Sage gave a heavy sigh.

"It's my fault," Sage said. "I was *so* tired and had a hard time getting moving this morning."

"You're here now. That's the important thing." He rose and helped them out of their coats. Sage wore a bulky red sweater under hers, while Maura wore a pale blue turtleneck and a long spill of silver-and-blue beads that reminded him of a waterfall.

He was struck by how thin she appeared. The shirt bagged at her wrists, and he wondered if she had lost weight in the months since her daughter died.

"I've been enjoying the café," he said after they slid into the other side of the booth together, with Sage on the inside. "It hasn't changed much in twenty years."

"The food's still just as good," Maura said. "Unfortunately, the tourists have figured that out too."

"I noticed that. It's been hopping since I got here."

The conversation lagged, and to cover the awkwardness, he picked up their menus from the table and opened them, then handed them to the women. He hadn't worked his way through college tending bar at a little dive near the Gourmet Ghetto for nothing.

"So Mr. Caine recommended the French toast."

"That's what I always get when we come here for breakfast," Sage told him. "It's *sooo* good. Like having dessert for breakfast. Mom usually has a poached egg and whole wheat toast. That's like driving all the way to Disneyland and not riding Space Mountain!"

"Maybe I'll try the French toast this morning too," Maura said, a hint of rebellion in her tone.

She seemed to be in a prickly mood, probably unhappy at the prospect of sharing a booth and a meal with him.

"Sorry I didn't order coffee for either of you. I wasn't sure of your preferences."

"I usually like coffee in the morning," Sage told him, "but I'm not sure my stomach can handle it today. I'd better go for tea."

As if on cue, Dermot Caine headed toward their booth and did an almost comical double take when he saw Maura and Sage sitting with him. Jack wondered at it, until he remembered his comment about waiting for his family, in a manner of speaking.

Well, if the word wasn't out around town that he was Sage's father after the scene at the bookstore the night before, he imagined it wouldn't take long for the Hope's Crossing grapevine to start humming.

"Sage, my darlin'. Home for the holidays, are you?"

"That's the plan, Mr. C." She beamed at the older man, who plainly adored her.

"And how is school going for you?"

Sage made a face. "Meh. I had a chemistry *and* biology class in the same semester. I don't know what I was thinking."

"Well, you're such a smarty, I'm sure you'll do fine." He turned to face Maura. Somehow Jack wasn't surprised when he reached out and covered her hand with his. "And how are you, my dear?"

"I'm fine, Dermot. Thanks." She gave him a smile, but Jack didn't miss the way she moved her hand back to her lap as soon as Dermot lifted his away, as if she couldn't bear to hold even a trace of sympathy.

"I'm guessing you'll be wanting water for tea."

"Yes. Thank you."

"Make that two," Sage said.

"Sure thing. And what else can I bring you? Have you had time to decide?"

They all settled on French toast, which seemed to delight Dermot Caine to no end. "I'll add an extra dollop of fresh cream on the side for you. No charge," he promised.

After he left, awkwardness returned to the booth. What strange dynamics between the three of them, he thought. Twenty years ago, Maura had been his best friend. They could never seem to stop talking—about politics, about religion, about their hopes and dreams for the future.

Over the past few days, he had seen Sage several times, and their conversation had been easy and wide-changing. He had years of her life to catch up on, and she seemed fascinated with his career, asking him questions nonstop about his life since he'd left Hope's Crossing and about some of the projects he had designed.

Maura and Sage seemed very close as mother and daughter, and he would have expected them to have plenty to talk about.

So why did these jerky silences seem to strangle the conversation when the three of them were together?

"I guess you found a hotel room," Sage finally said after Dermot returned with cups of hot water and the two women busied themselves selecting their tea bags.

"It wasn't easy," he admitted. "I ended up stopping at a couple different places and finally found a room at the Blue Columbine."

"That's a really nice place," Sage said. "My mom's friend Lucy owns it."

Good to know. He would have to take a careful look at the basket of muffins that had been left outside his door that morning to make sure nobody had slipped rat poison into it. "The bed was comfortable. That's usually what matters most to me."

"You didn't want to stay up at the Silver Strike?" Maura asked with a sharp smile that seemed at odds with her lovely features. "I've never seen the rooms there, but I've heard they're spectacular. Fodor's gives the place a glowing review."

His mouth tightened. She really thought she had the right to taunt him about that damn ski resort, after everything? Did she not understand she was on shaky ground here? He wasn't sure he would ever be able to forgive her for keeping Sage from him all these years. He certainly wasn't in the mood to deal with her prickly mood or veiled taunts about his father's ski resort.

"I'll pass. A B and B in town is fine with me for now."

"For now? How long are you planning to stay in Hope's Crossing?" she asked bluntly.

Sage sat forward, eyes focused on him with bright intensity as she awaited his answer. He chose his words carefully. "I'm not sure yet. I was thinking about sticking around for a week or two, until after the holidays."

For all their surface resemblance, the two women had completely disparate reactions. Sage grinned at him with delight, while Maura looked as if Dermot had just fed her a teaspoon full of alum with her tea.

"That's great. Really great!" Sage enthused. "I was afraid you were leaving today."

"How can you spare the time?" Maura asked woodenly. "You're a big-shot architect, just as you always dreamed."

"It's a slow time of year for me, which is why I was able to accept the lecture invitation. After the holidays, things will heat up. I've got a couple of projects in the region, actually, one in Denver and one in Montana, and a big one overseas in Singapore coming up, but my schedule is a little looser than normal this month."

Maura stirred her tea, then took a cautious sip before speaking in a polite tone that belied the shadow of dismay he could see in her eyes. "Do you really want to spend that much time in Hope's Crossing?"

He shrugged. No doubt she was thinking his presence would ruin her whole holiday. He didn't care. He wasn't really in the mood to play nice, not after she had kept his daughter from him for nineteen Christmases. "I was thinking maybe Sage and I could take off for a few days to Denver to study some of the architectural styles."

"Really?" Sage's eyes lit up as if he had just handed her keys to a brand-new car. "That would be fantastic! I would *love* it."

Maura avoided his gaze to look out the window, and he could almost taste her resentment, as thick and bitter as bad coffee. When she finally looked back at the pair of them, she offered up a small, tense smile.

"That would provide a good chance for the two of you to spend some time together. If you do stick around, there are plenty of things to do around here as well. Art galleries, restaurants, hundreds of miles of cross-country ski trails. I'm sure you remember how lovely the canyon can be when it has fresh powder. Of course, that's what all the skiers love too, and what brings them here in droves."

It was another caustic dig, another reminder of what had finally forced him to turn his back on Hope's Crossing—his father's final, vicious betrayal and the gross misuse of land his mother had intended to leave to him.

Eventually he would probably have to drive up to the ski resort to see for himself how greed had destroyed his mother's legacy. But not today.

"We should go up for the Christmas Eve candlelight ski," Sage exclaimed. "We haven't done that in a few years, have we, Mom? It's so beautiful to watch all the little flames dancing down the mountainside."

"That sounds great," Maura said.

Not to Jack. The last place he wanted to be on Christmas Eve was up at the ski resort. He started to give some polite answer when his attention was caught by someone else coming into the café. He couldn't see the man's features from here when he turned away to speak to Dermot, but something inside Jack froze.

He didn't need to see him clearly to know who was currently trying to push around the restaurant owner, despite the futility of anyone thinking they could intimidate Dermot Caine.

His father.

The biggest son of a bitch who had ever lived.

Dermot cast a quick look in their direction and grabbed Harry's arm, obviously intent on steering him the opposite way.

"Hold your horses. Let me at least take my coat off, you daft Irish fool."

Those were the first words he had heard his father speak in nearly two decades. He was taken completely by surprise at the twisted, complex mix of emotions that washed over him like flood waters through a rain-parched arroyo.

At the overloud voice, Maura turned around to follow the sound of the commotion. When she turned around, he didn't detect any hint of surprise in her expression.

Was his father a regular at the cafe? He must be. He suddenly remembered Maura's reaction the night before when he had suggested they meet here for breakfast, her initial hesitation and then the too-quick agreement. She must have expected Harry to show up eventually.

This was a damn setup. He should have known.

What happened to her? When they were wild teenagers in love, Maura had been his anchor, the only bright spot in a world that had never been all that great but had completely fallen apart after his mother's suicide. It was obvious that sweet and loving girl had disappeared twenty years ago.

"Low," he murmured.

She sipped at her tea again and gave him an innocent look that didn't fool him for a second. "I don't know what you're talking about."

"You're a liar now too?"

Sage looked back and forth between the two of them, trying to interpret the simmer of tension, but Maura quickly distracted her. "The Christmas Eve ski is always fun. What else would you like to do this year?"

"I always love the wagon rides they have through Snowflake Canyon to look at the lights."

"We can add that to the schedule," Maura assured her.

They talked about other traditions, leaving Jack to simmer in his frustration. He had known he would eventually have to see his father. He just hadn't expected it to be twelve hours after he arrived in town.

Dermot must have remembered the vast rift between

him and his father. To Jack's relief, he had seated Harry in an area of the restaurant that angled away from them, out of sight of their booth. At least he wouldn't have to come face-to-face with the man. Even so, any culinary anticipation for the cafe's much-vaunted French toast had turned to ashes in his gut.

A bleached-blond college-age kid with the slouchy dress and manner of a ski bum brought their food over a few moments later, three plates brimming with golden French toast with little crackly pieces of sugar-coated fried dough and sliced almonds on top.

"Hey, Sage, Maura. Stranger Dude. Dermot's tied up in the kitchen for a while," he explained. "He asked me to take care of you. So if you need anything else, give me a shout-out."

"Thanks, Logan."

"How's school?" Sage asked.

"Good. I think I made the dean's list. I had a killer final in statistics, but I think I aced it. You?"

"Pretty good. Not dean's-list good, but I was happy with it. Did you have Professor Lee for stats? I've got him next semester."

"He's brutal, man."

"Hey, I might need a ride back to Boulder after the break. When are you taking off?"

"Haven't thought that far in advance. My first class isn't until ten-thirty the Monday school starts, so I might get in a few runs as soon as the lifts open before I head back."

"I'll text you after New Year's to figure things out."

"Okay. Like I said, if you need anything, let me know."

The conversation between the young people gave Jack a chance to regain his perspective. It wasn't Maura's fault Harry ate breakfast at the café. He had sensed something off in her reaction when he'd made the suggestion to eat here the night before and should have pursued it.

Besides, he was an adult. He could certainly spend a few minutes in the same restaurant with the man he despised. Yes, it had been petty of her to set him up like that, but if he were going to hold a grudge, he had bigger grievances against her. As far as he could see, there was no reason to let Harry ruin a perfectly delicious breakfast.

"So we talked about cross-country skiing and sleigh rides and Christmas Eve candlelight skis. What else do I need to see in Hope's Crossing while I'm here?" he asked Sage.

She launched into a long list of her favorite things to do in town. By the time she finished, even *he* was thinking maybe Hope's Crossing wasn't the purgatory he remembered.

"Sounds like you two have plenty to keep you busy until school starts up again," Maura said. She had only eaten about four or five bites of her French toast and one nibble of the crispy bacon that accompanied it.

Sage suddenly looked stricken, as if she had only just remembered that her mother might have expected to spend some of the holiday break with her. "We could do a lot of this together, the three of us."

There was no "three of us." Just two people who had once loved each other and the child they had created together.

"No, this will be good," Maura assured her with a smile that only looked slightly forced. "You know how busy I'm going to be up until Christmas Eve and then the week after with all the holiday returns. This way I won't have to worry about you being bored while I'm stuck at the store."

She checked her watch and set down her napkin. "Speaking of busy, I probably need to run. Mornings are hectic in December. It seems like everyone in town decides to take a coffee break at the same time and fit in a little shopping too."

The purpose of suggesting they meet for breakfast had been to come to some sort of agreement on how their tangled relationship would proceed from here. He wasn't sure they had accomplished that particular goal, but they seemed to have reached an accord of some sort, Harry's unexpected presence notwithstanding.

"Do you need some extra help with the rush?" Sage asked.

"You don't need to come in," Maura assured her. "You should spend the day with your, er…with Jack while you have a chance."

"Well, yeah, I want to. But to tell you the truth, I haven't had a chance to do any Christmas shopping yet, and I could use a little extra money. I hate to dip into my college fund for presents if I don't have to."

"Don't worry about me," Jack assured her. "I've got plenty of work to catch up on. Maybe we could always meet this evening."

"Are you sure you don't mind?" Sage asked.

"Not at all." The two of them didn't need to spend twenty-four hours a day together. It was probably better to take their interactions in small doses while he was still adjusting to the idea of even *having* a daughter.

Besides, he didn't want Maura to think he planned to monopolize every moment with Sage while he was in Hope's Crossing.

"In that case," Maura said, her features a little more relaxed, "I would love to have you work at the store today.

We've been slammed the last few days, and I'm sure Ruth could use help restocking."

With that settled, they returned to their breakfast. He was happy to see Maura eat a few more bites and finish off the citrus slices that came with it. When breakfast was over, they wrangled for a moment over the bill, but he solved the issue by taking his credit card and the ticket to the cash register, leaving her to glower after him.

"I'll walk you over to the store," he said to the two of them after signing the credit card receipt handed him by the snowboarding academic. "The only place I could find to park was in that alley behind your store."

"Parking is our big problem downtown, as you have probably figured out. The Downtown Merchants' Alliance is talking about building a big parking structure a block to the west, if we can do it in an aesthetically pleasing way that fits in with the rest of the town."

After leaving the café, they walked up half a block to the light so they could cross the street. As he looked up the length of Main Street, he was struck again by the charm of the town, with electrified reproductions of historic gas lamps lining the street and brick-paved sidewalks instead of concrete. The town leaders seemed to have gone to a great deal of trouble to manage the growth in that pleasing way Maura was talking about that stayed true to its character, with none of the jumble of styles so many communities adopted by default.

Beneath the wooden sign reading Dog-Eared Books & Brew, he held the door open for the two women and stepped inside the welcoming warmth to say goodbye to Sage.

"What time do you think you'll be free for dinner?"

"I don't know. Can you give me a second, though, before we figure out details? I've had to pee since before Logan brought our breakfast, and I'm not sure I can wait even five more minutes."

"Uh, sure."

She gave him a grateful smile and hurried to the back of the store, leaving him to watch with bemusement at her abrupt exit.

Maura gave a short laugh. "That's Sage for you. Sorry about that. When she was a little girl, I always had to remind her to take a minute and visit the bathroom. She tended to hold it until the very last second, because she didn't want to bother wasting time with such inconsequential things when she could be creating a masterpiece skyscraper out of blocks or redesigning her Barbie house to make better use of the available space."

He could almost picture her, dark curls flying, green eyes earnest, that chin they shared set with determination. A hard kernel of regret seemed to be lodged somewhere in his chest. He had missed so much. *Everything.* Ballet recitals and bedtime stories and soccer games.

This whole thing was so surreal. He had always told himself he didn't want or need a family. His own childhood had been so tumultuous, marked by his mother's mental chaos and Harry's increasing impatience and frustration and his subsequent cold distance. In his mind, family was turmoil and pain.

Jack had always just figured that since he didn't have the desire—or the necessary skills—to be a father, he was better off just avoiding that eventuality altogether. That had been one of the things that had drawn him to Kari, her insistence that her career mattered too much for her to derail it with a side trip on the Mommy Track.

Mere months into their marriage, she'd done a rapid about-face and started buying baby magazines and comparing crib specifications. Even before that, he'd known their marriage had been a mistake. She hated his travel and his long hours, she couldn't stand his friends, she started drinking more than she ever had when they were dating.

Bringing a child into the middle of something that was already so shaky would have been a disaster. They started counseling, but when he found out she had stopped taking her birth control pills despite his entreaties that they at least give the counseling a chance to work, he had started sleeping on the sofa in his office.

She filed for divorce two weeks later and ended up married to another attorney in her office a month after the decree came down.

Yeah, he had always figured he and kids wouldn't be a good mix. But these little glimpses into Sage's childhood filled him with poignant regret.

Nothing he could do about that now. He realized that Maura was watching him warily and he forced himself to smile. "I like your place."

She tilted her head, studying him as if to gauge his sincerity, and he was struck again by her fragile beauty. With that sadness that never quite left her eyes, she made a man want to wrap his arms around her, tuck her up against his side and promise to take care of her forever.

Not him, of course. He was long past his knight-in-shining-armor phase.

"Thanks," she finally said. "I like it too. It's been a work in progress the last five or six years, but I think I've finally arranged things the way I like."

She untwisted her striped purple scarf and shrugged out of her coat before he had a chance to help her, then hung both on a rack nestled between ceiling-high shelves.

"A bookstore and coffeehouse. That seems a far cry from your dreams of writing the great American novel."

She seemed surprised that he would remember those dreams. "Not that far. I still like to write, but I mostly dabble for my own enjoyment. I discovered I'm very happy surrounded by books written by other people—and the readers who love them."

"It's a bit of a dying business, isn't it?"

She frowned and stopped to align an untidy shelf of paperback mysteries. "I don't believe a passion for actual books you can hold in your hands will ever go away. We have an enormous children's section, which is growing in popularity as parents come to realize that children need to turn real pages once in a while instead of merely flipping a finger across a screen. Our travel section is also very popular, as is the young adult fiction."

She shrugged. "Anyway, I've made sure people come to the store for more than just books, though it's still the best place in town to find elusive titles. We've become a gathering spot for anyone who loves the written word. We have book groups and author signings, writer nights, even an evening set aside a couple times a month for singles."

"You've really built something impressive here."

She paused and looked embarrassed. "Sorry. You hit a hot button."

"I don't mind. I admire passion in a woman."

In a *person.* That's what he meant to say. In a *person.* Anyone. But it was too late to take the word back. Maura sent him a charged look and suddenly the bookstore felt over-warm. He had a random, completely unwelcome memory of the two of them wrapped together on a blanket up near Silver Lake, with the aspens whispering around them and the wind sighing in the pine trees.

She cleared her throat and he thought he saw a slight flush on her cheeks, but he figured he must have been mistaken when she went on the offensive. “What is this whole business about sticking around town for a few weeks, Jack? You don’t want to be here. You hate Hope’s Crossing.”

He didn’t want to take her on right now. He ought to just smile politely, offer some benign answer and head over to browse the bestseller shelf, but somehow he couldn’t do that.

“If I want to see my daughter—the daughter you didn’t tell me about, remember?—I’m stuck here, aren’t I?” he said quietly.

“Not necessarily. Why can’t you just wait and visit Sage in Boulder when she returns to school? Or have her come visit you in San Francisco. You don’t have to be *here*.”

“I’m not leaving. Not until after Christmas, anyway.”

“You’re just doing this to ruin my holidays, aren’t you?”

He could feel his temper fray, despite his efforts to hang on to the tattered edges. “What else? I stayed up all night trying to come up with ways to make you pay for keeping my daughter from me. Ruining your holidays seemed the perfect revenge for twenty years of glaring silence. That’s the kind of vindictive bastard I am, right?”

“I have no idea,” she shot back. “How am I supposed to know what kind of bastard you are now?”

“Insinuating I was a bastard twenty years ago to knock you up and leave town.”

“I didn’t say that.”

“You must have thought it, though, a million times over the years.”

That was the core of the anger that had simmered through him since that life-changing moment after his lecture. What she must have thought of him, how she must have hated him to keep this from him.

For twenty years their time together had been a cherished memory, something he used to take out and relive when life seemed particularly discouraging.

He had wondered about her many times over the years. His first love, something good and bright and beautiful to a young man who had needed that desperately.

To know that she must have been cursing his name all that time for leaving her alone with unimaginable responsibility was a bitter pill.

"You didn't *tell* me, Maura. What the hell was I supposed to do?"

"Not forget me, as if you couldn't wait to walk away from everything we shared. As if I meant nothing to you!"

As soon as she blurted out the words, she pressed a hand to her mouth as if horrified by them.

"I loved you," he murmured. "Believe whatever else you want about me, but I loved you, Maura."

"Yet you hated your father and Hope's Crossing more."

"Maura," he began, knowing he had no defense other than youth and idiocy and his own single-minded resolve to make something out of his life away from this place. Before he could figure out how to finish the sentence, chimes rang softly on her front door and a new customer came in.

He saw the man out of his peripheral vision for only a fleeting instant, but something made him shift his head for a better look. Instantly, he wished he hadn't. Did his father have a freaking tracker on him?

CHAPTER FIVE

"IS THAT BOOK on spelunking here yet?" Harry Lange growled before he had even walked all the way through the doorway, as if every employee had been lined up inside merely waiting for him to make an entrance. "I could have had it a week ago if I had ordered the damn thing online."

His words were directed at Maura, Jack realized. Harry must have seen her when he walked inside. It took another beat for his father to recognize *him,* but Jack knew the instant he did. Harry's jaw sagged and ruddy color leached from his aging features as if somebody had just slugged him in the gut.

Maura looked from Harry to him and quickly stepped forward. "I'm not sure, Mr. Lange. I'll have to ask Ruth. She's the one who handles the special orders. If you can wait a few moments, I'll see if I can find her."

Harry didn't seem to have heard her. He continued to stare at Jack, mouth slack and his eyes awash with a hundred tangled emotions Jack didn't want to see.

So much for slipping into town and back out again without seeing his father. Twice in the space of an hour must be some kind of cosmic joke.

The familiar raw fury for his father welled up, but now that he was confronted with the actual man instead of only memories, it seemed muted, somehow—as if the color and heat had bled from it as well.

"J-Jackson?" Harry's voice sounded strangled, as if he were choking on one of the little mints from the checkout at Dermot Caine's café.

"Harry." The single word came out clipped, cold.

"I…hadn't heard you were in town."

"It was a spur-of-the-moment thing." One he was quickly coming to regret.

"I see. How long will you…" His voice trailed off, and Jack began to think maybe the pale cast to his features was from more than just surprise.

"I'm still working that out."

For politeness' sake, he should probably move closer to his father so they didn't have to raise their voices to be heard a dozen feet apart, but he couldn't seem to generate the necessary forward momentum. Lord knew, Harry wouldn't be the one to budge. That much apparently hadn't changed.

Maura was finally the one to move first. She took a step forward. "Mr. Lange, are you all right?" she asked suddenly, taking another few steps.

"I… No. Not really. Damn it."

His father lurched as if someone had struck him from behind. He knocked a hip against a display table of new releases and swept a hand out to steady himself, scattering books to the floor. Even so, he was unable to keep his balance. Jack could see him start to head to the floor, but he was too far away to reach him in time. Maura was closer, but even she couldn't prevent Harry from toppling. A hard crack sounded above the bustle from the coffee bar as the side of his head made contact with the edge of the table before he slumped to the ground.

"Mr. Lange!" Maura exclaimed, kneeling next to the prone figure.

"Is he okay?"

"I don't know. He was standing there one minute, then hit the ground the next. Mr. Lange!"

She turned his father onto his back, and his aging features were ashen and still. Was he dead? Had Jack managed to knock him off just by showing up in town? He froze for a moment, aware of his own strange mix of emotions—shock and dismay and most surprising, a completely unexpected regret.

"He's unconscious!" Maura said. "Come on, Mr. Lange. Wake up."

"He hit the edge of the table pretty hard."

"Give me your coat."

"Why?"

"Just give it to me, Jack!"

He reluctantly handed over the custom-sewn leather jacket he had picked up during his time in Italy. She bunched it up and tucked it under Harry's head. Even that bit of commotion didn't make his father snap out of it.

"Come on, Harry, this is stupid. Wake up." His father's eyelids fluttered a little at his voice, but his eyes didn't open.

If he had ever imagined a reunion with his father—which he absolutely *hadn't*—he was pretty sure this wasn't what he would have predicted, with his father sprawled out on the ground looking lifeless and ashen.

"Harry!" he barked.

That seemed to do the trick. Harry's eyelids jerked a few times, and seconds later he finally opened his eyes fully. They were dazed and blank for a moment before they sharpened, his gaze fixed on Jack with shades of that same stunned disbelief. "What…happened?"

Jack couldn't seem to say anything, frozen in place by

the years of bitterness and hatred he had fed and nurtured for this man.

"You fell," Maura finally answered.

She tugged and pulled the jacket to a better position under the old man's head and seemed unfazed when he batted away her hands.

"Get away from me," he snapped. "I just need to catch my breath."

She eased away, picking a cell phone out of her pocket. "Fine. You should know we charge extra for napping in the middle of the store."

"Smarty."

She gave him a tart look even as she started hitting buttons on her phone.

"What are you doing? Put that away! I hope you don't think I'm going to let you take a picture of me for all your girlfriends to cackle about."

Jack noted with concern that, despite his protests, his father's voice still sounded feeble and his features hadn't lost that pallid cast.

"I hadn't planned to take a picture, no. But that's a great idea."

"What are you doing, then?"

"Calling nine-one-one. You need to go to the emergency room to be checked out."

If anything, that made Harry look even more horrified. "Forget it. I'm fine. I just lost my balance, that's all." He tried to scramble up, and Jack finally had to move forward to help Maura keep him in place.

Harry gave a sharp intake of breath when Jack grabbed his arm and gazed at him with an expression he couldn't decipher.

"You passed out in my store," Maura said sternly. "I'm

not about to leave myself open to some future lawsuit where you claim negligence. I'm calling the paramedics. You can fight it out with them."

Harry jerked his gaze away from Jack to summon a half-hearted glower, but he subsided back against the cushion of his jacket. Really? He was going to give in without a fight? For the first time, Jack began to wonder if something was seriously wrong with Harry's health.

"This is just want you wanted, isn't it?" Harry said bitterly. It took a moment for Jack to realize the words were directed at him. "It probably gives you no end of pleasure to come back after all these years and see some weak, pathetic old man on the floor at your feet."

Any concern and sympathy he might have briefly entertained for Harry dried up like the Mojave in August. "You're not that old."

Harry frowned at him and gave Maura a nasty look in turn. "At least help me up. I'm fine. I don't need to be lying on the damn floor. Help me to one of those chairs over there."

She looked undecided, then gazed around the crowd of curious customers that had begun to gather around.

"If we do, will you promise to stay put instead of trying to juke around us and run out to avoid the EMTs?"

"Very funny. I'm not running anywhere. Now help me up."

She sighed and reached for one of Harry's arms, gesturing for Jack to take the other. He would have liked to ignore her. Hell, he would have liked to yank his eight-hundred-dollar Milano leather jacket out from under Harry's head and make his own escape from Dog-Eared Books & Brew, but common decency—as well as a completely ridiculous desire not to look like a bigger ass to her than he already did—compelled him to step forward and grab Harry's other arm.

His father was still not quite seventy. Jack imagined without the pallor he would still be fairly hale and hearty. Still, the old man felt almost frail as he and Maura supported him toward a plump armchair in the nearby travel section.

"What's going on?"

At the new voice, he looked over and found Sage gazing at the three of them in puzzled consternation.

"Mr. Lange is feeling a little under the weather," Maura replied. "He passed out."

"I didn't pass out," Harry snapped. "I just lost my balance. If you left a person with half a foot of aisle room in this place, I would have been fine."

"See, that definitely sounds like you're blaming me. Should I be calling my lawyer?" Maura returned.

"I'm not going to sue anybody."

Don't believe him, he wanted to tell Maura. If Harry saw any advantage to himself in a given situation, he wouldn't hesitate to lie, steal and betray to get his way.

"O. M. G.!"

Maura blinked at Sage's sudden exclamation. "What?"

"If Jack is my father, that means Mr. Lange is my grandfather!"

He bit back a four-letter word. Of all the moments for Sage to blurt out that little bit of information!

Harry's eyes widened and he looked back and forth between the two of them. Maura was the one who had turned pale now. She looked as if she wanted to disappear behind a bookshelf, and Jack wanted to join her.

Harry did *not* need this information, something else he could figure out how to manipulate for his own purposes.

"What did she say?" Harry asked.

"Nothing," Maura muttered. "Now would be a really good time for you to go back to sleep."

"Who are you?" Harry asked Sage, his thick eyebrows arched like bristly caterpillars.

"My daughter," Maura said quickly.

He narrowed his gaze. "Your daughter died in that car accident up Silver Strike Reservoir this spring. I was there, wasn't I? I saw the whole thing."

That was news to Jack. What had been his father's involvement in the accident that killed Layla Parker?

"This is my older daughter, Sage."

He should just keep his mouth zipped here. He knew damn well telling him about Sage was a mistake—but he also knew Harry well enough to be certain he would just keep pushing and pushing until somebody told him.

"And mine, apparently," Jack finally said.

Maura sent him a quick, surprised look, as if she expected him to deny the whole thing. Harry, on the other hand, just stared.

"Have you taken a DNA test?" he asked.

None of your damn business, he wanted to say. He didn't want his father mixed up in this complicated mess, but he was coming to realize he didn't have much control over things. Harry just might have more contact with Sage than he would. He lived in Hope's Crossing, after all. While Jack would be back in San Francisco, Harry would be free to pick up the phone whenever Sage was in town and meet her for lunch at the café or the resort or any blasted place he wanted.

"She's my daughter. I'm convinced of it, and that's all that matters."

Harry opened his mouth to argue, but before he could,

the door to the bookstore burst open, and a pair of burly paramedics hurried inside with emergency kits and dedicated focus.

"Back here," Maura called and waved. They shifted directions and headed toward them.

"I don't need the damn paramedics," Harry grumbled.

"Well, you've got them," Maura retorted. "Hey, Dougie."

One of the paramedics, a guy who looked like he could probably bench-press half the bookstore, grinned at her. "Hey, Maur. What have we got?"

"Maybe nothing. I don't know. I just thought it would be better to call you to check things out."

"That's what we're here for. What happened?"

"Mr. Lange isn't feeling well. He had some kind of incident. We were talking one moment and he fell over the next. I think he was unconscious for about thirty seconds to a minute."

"I didn't pass out," Harry asserted. "I just lost my balance."

"And then went to the Bahamas for the next little while," Jack answered.

"Either way, it's a good idea to check things out," the other paramedic said.

"That's what I figured," Maura answered. "He hit his head on a table pretty hard when he fell."

She stepped away from Harry and let the paramedics do their thing.

"Is he going to be okay?" Sage asked him, her voice low.

He figured his father would be harassing the paramedics all the way to the hospital, haranguing them on everything from their driving to the accommodations. "It's just a precaution. I'm sure he'll be fine."

For the first time, he noticed Sage looked a little pale

too. This had to be weird for her, to find herself suddenly related to the old bastard.

"I don't need a stupid gurney."

"Sorry, Mr. Lange. We have to follow the rules."

"This is ridiculous."

"You can always refuse treatment," Dougie, Maura's friend, said to Harry.

Jack fully expected his father would do just that, but after a pause, Harry shrugged. "No. I'll come. I don't want to see the idiots in the E.R., though. Call Dr. Osaka and tell him to meet us there."

"Whatever you say, sir."

A moment later, the paramedics finally succeeded in loading Harry onto the gurney and rolled him out of the bookstore.

"Are you going to follow the ambulance to the hospital?" Maura asked.

"He doesn't need me. He's made that more than clear." He turned to Sage. "So we're meeting for dinner. What time works for you?"

She still looked a little green around the gills, and he had a feeling food was the last thing on her mind. "Well, I was thinking I could work until four or so. Any time after that?"

"Let's say six-thirty. I'll pick you up at your house."

"Great. I'll see you then."

He picked up his jacket, shook it off from being on the ground, then shrugged into it. With a stiff nod to Maura, he headed out into the snow-crusted streets of Hope's Crossing.

The encounter with Harry served as a stark reminder of everything he'd been thinking. What the hell did he know about being a father? When he was a kid, his own example had been distant, preoccupied with work, then increasingly sharp—bordering on cruel—as Jack had reached adolescence.

By the time his mother eventually took her own life out of despair and loneliness and mental illness, Harry had given up any effort at establishing a relationship and had shown nothing but disdain for him.

Maybe Jack ought to just cut Sage a break now and slip back out of her life as quickly as he had come. She hadn't had a chance yet to establish any real feelings for him. She had her mother, her grandmother, a strong support network here in Hope's Crossing. Why on earth did she need *him?*

He stopped himself before he could go further down that road. The idea of leaving now, after he had only just found her, was unbearable. He wanted to be a father to her, in whatever limited capacity he could manage.

If that meant achieving some sort of peaceful accord with Maura, he was willing to do that too. He had to think that somewhere inside the prickly, sad-eyed woman she had become were some traces of the smart, funny, tender girl she had once been.

He was willing to do whatever might be necessary to find her again.

COMPARED TO THE excitement of an ambulance and paramedics and a wobbly Harry Lange, the rest of Maura's day seemed depressingly uneventful.

Even with the hectic holiday season and the various challenges it presented to a business owner—the crowds and the chaos and even a couple of teenage shoplifters she had to turn over to Riley—she found that every day seemed very much like the one before. Tomorrow would probably be more of the same.

Every once in a while she had a wild urge to do something crazy. To leave the store and take off cross-country skiing for the day, or drive into Denver for some retail therapy, or just walk away from everything and catch a flight to some secluded beach in Mexico.

She was grateful for her job and her business, for the comfort of routine. But she still sometimes wanted to chuck everything and escape, even in the middle of the holidays.

She looked around the store. It was nearly six-thirty, and the crowd had thinned a great deal as people headed home or to one of the many restaurants for dinner in Hope's Crossing. They would probably see a bit of a spike again in about an hour, but nothing to compare to the afternoon crowds.

"Sierra, do you think you and Joe can handle the registers by yourselves?"

"Absolutely, Maur," her employee assured her, flipping stick-straight blond hair out of her eyes. "We're totally dead now. Go home and grab some dinner and put your feet up and watch something brainless on TV!"

That idea sounded really lovely, if only she didn't have about four hours of paperwork to do. But one of her favorite things about being a small-business owner was that she could do said paperwork at home with her feet up on the coffee table if she wanted—or even if she didn't want to.

"I think that's just what I'll do. Thanks for everything today."

"No prob. See you tomorrow."

Maura headed back to her office to pick up her laptop. On impulse, she sat down and grabbed the phone and quickly dialed the number to the Hope's Crossing hospital, a small forty-bed unit that served the town and the smaller surrounding communities.

"Yes, I'm checking on a patient. Harry Lange," she told the operator.

"Are you a family member of Mr. Lange's?"

Does being the recently discovered baby mama of his estranged son count? She sincerely doubted it. "No," she had to confess.

"In that case, I'm afraid I can't release any information on Mr. Lange's condition. I'm sorry."

"I understand. Can you transfer me to his room?" That would at least let her know if he had been admitted.

"Yes. Hold on a moment, please."

So he was still there. She wasn't sure why she cared about the man's condition, as demanding and arrogant and downright unpleasant as she found him. Much to her chagrin, some stupid part of Maura actually felt a little sorry for Harry Lange. Despite having everything most people thought necessary for a life to be deemed a success, Harry's unhappiness was palpable. His own choices had left him sour and bombastic and bitterly alone.

Apparently one of those choices was to ignore the phone in his hospital room. The phone rang eight times in the room before she was bounced back to the chirpy operator. "I'm afraid there's no answer in that room."

"I'll call back. Thank you."

She hung up the phone. Maybe she ought to swing by to check on him. She frowned at the thought. Why would she even consider it, except for the fact that he had been standing in her store when he'd had his little incident?

Harry Lange was none of her business. She should despise everything about the man—because of him, Jack had turned his back on all they might have had together.

"Trouble with a vendor?"

She turned at her mother's voice and found Mary Ella in

the doorway. She looked bright and pretty in a turtleneck with her little reading glasses hanging by a new beaded chain Maura hadn't seen before. If she could look half as smart and put-together as her mother when she had six decades under her belt she would consider herself blessed.

"Not a vendor. I was just calling the hospital to check on Harry Lange."

Mary Ella's finely arched eyebrows shot way up. "Okay, that statement is just wrong on so many levels. What happened to that old son of a—er, monkey? And why on earth would you be calling to find out about it?"

"You hadn't heard? I figured the gossip would have spread all over town by now."

"I've been at home working on that quilt I'm making for Rose's oldest and cleaning the house before they get here next week. I haven't talked to a soul. What happened?"

"How's the quilt coming?"

"Fine. Now, what happened to Harry?"

Her mother's urgency made her blink. Mary Ella *despised* Harry. They had a long-standing feud and could barely tolerate being in the same room with each other on the few community occasions where that might be necessary.

"This morning he stopped into the bookstore to pick up a special order. Wouldn't you know it, he walked in just as Jack was about to leave. Seeing his long-lost son must have been too much for him. I don't know if it was shock or disgust or something else, but he stumbled a little, hitting his head on one of the display tables. Considering he passed out for a moment, I insisted on calling the paramedics."

Mary Ella sank into one of her visitor chairs. "Is he all right?"

"Privacy laws, remember? They can't tell me anything. He seemed fine when the paramedics came. He was sitting up and snapping at everyone before the paramedics made him go to the hospital."

"Why am I not surprised?"

"Because Harry is a bastard. You're the first one standing in line to call him that."

"I am, aren't I?" Mary Ella murmured.

"I'm sure he'll be fine. He'll be stomping around town bossing people around before we know it." Maura decided to change the subject. She had spent enough time worrying about Harry Lange—and his progeny—today. "So what brings you here? Isn't it the Beadapalooza over at String Fever?"

Claire's annual event attracted beaders from around the county, drawn to slashed prices and the great offers on bead kits. It was usually the perfect way to de-stress from the holidays, with the bonus of allowing people the opportunity to make a few last-minute gifts.

"Exactly. That's why I'm here. Claire sent me over to see if you are coming."

She refused to feel guilty for skipping this year. The book club the night before had been more than enough socializing for her. She thought about trying to come up with an excuse to appease her mother, but finally opted for the truth.

"Mom, this whole thing with Jack… I'm just not ready to face everyone again. It's been bad enough this year since Layla… Well, it's been bad enough. And now this. I can't bear to have everybody talking about me and Jack and our history together now. I'm going to pass. Please give my love to Claire. Next year will be better." She hoped.

"Oh, honey." Mary Ella's mouth trembled and Maura really hoped her mother wouldn't start crying, because then *she* would start crying.

They were both saved by a bustling outside the door, then a strange, squeaky sound. A moment later, Sage appeared in the doorway. "Oh, good. You *are* still here. Are you leaving soon? I was hoping I could catch a ride home with you."

She frowned. Sage had on her red peacoat, but it looked bulky and unnatural. Maybe she was hiding a Christmas present under there. Maura ordered herself not to ask, though she really hated secrets. "I thought you were having dinner with your, er, with Jack tonight."

"We changed our plans. He called just after I left the store this afternoon and said his assistant scheduled a couple of conference calls and he couldn't get out of them. I think he felt really bad, but I'm cool with it. He's picking me up for breakfast tomorrow. Right after I hung up with him, Josie texted me. She's back from UCLA for the holidays, so we've been hanging out at her house."

"Oh, how is Josie? Is she liking Stanford?"

"She's good. I guess she likes it okay, but all she wanted to talk about was her new boyfriend. James. Not Jamie or Jim or Jimmy. *James*. He's a senior in pre-med and sounds boring as hell."

Maura saw her mother bite her lip to fight back a smile. She wanted to chide Sage for swearing, especially in front of her grandmother, but since she did the same all too often, she didn't feel that she had much standing.

"Don't you have any boring boyfriends to talk about?" Mary Ella asked.

Sage's expression suddenly grew closed, as it did whenever Maura asked the same thing. "Oh, you know how it is. I don't have time for much of a social life. I've got to ace my generals, or I won't be able to get into the undergraduate environmental planning program."

That mysterious squeak sounded again. It was definitely coming from Sage's direction. Was it a burp? Maura looked closer, but her daughter adjusted her arms a little and gave the two of them a casual smile. "Can you believe Josie is thinking about changing her major again? This will be like her fourth time."

"You should be fortunate you've always known you wanted to be an architect," Mary Ella said.

Sage's torso suddenly wiggled oddly, and she moved as if someone had just tickled her ribs.

"All right. What's going on, Sage?"

Her daughter put on the same innocent face she used to wear when Maura would walk into her room and find crayon marks on the wall. "What makes you think something is going on?"

"I don't know. Either you've got an alien inside your coat or a serious case of indigestion."

Sage sighed and unzipped her peacoat. A furry little tan face peeked out cheerfully. "Josie brought a shih tzu puppy home from college. I guess she got in trouble at school for having it in the dorm and thought she could convince her parents to keep it here, but they already have three dogs and don't want another one."

"No," Maura said without hesitation. "Absolutely not."

"Come on, Mom. Look how adorable this face is. How can you say no?" Sage lifted the tiny puppy about four inches away from Maura. The animal looked like an Ewok, cuddly and cute. As she looked into those little black eyes, the puppy titled its head and stretched its mouth out in what looked suspiciously like a grin.

Something cold and hard seemed to dislodge inside her. It scared the hell out of her.

"His name is Puck. Isn't he precious?"

"Sage. I can't take on a puppy right now. I don't have time! I'm working twelve hours a day here at the store."

"I'll do everything while I'm here. There's really not much, anyway. He's almost potty trained."

She and Mary Ella groaned simultaneously. *Almost potty trained* was often worse than not trained at all.

"I thought maybe he could come to the store with you. I mean, it's called Dog-Eared Books & Brew, isn't it? Don't you think you should have *some* kind of canine around the place to live up to the name?"

"No. Not really."

"Why not? Claire takes Chester to the bead store with her, and Evie even uses Jacques for therapy."

Neither of those dogs was a puppy—or a yippy, hyper little breed. "No, Sage. This is not a good time to get a dog. You're going back to school in a few weeks, and I'm just not ready to take on a pet."

Her daughter pouted a little, her cheek pressed against the dog's. But she had never been one to dwell long on disappointments. "Well, can we at least keep him until the holidays are over? Josie said she has a friend back in California who might be able to take him. She thought she could take him back with her, but I guess her family's having tons of company over for the holidays—her dad's whole family is coming to ski—and her mom said she can't handle a puppy in the midst of everything else."

Maura didn't know what to say. She hated to disappoint Sage, but didn't they have enough strain in their lives right now, with Jack suddenly bursting back into the picture after all these years?

"I thought, you know, having a cute little dog to keep us company might be a good distraction for both of us, Mom. Help us not to miss Layla so much over Christmas."

She gave a mental groan. Trust Sage to come up with the one thing Maura couldn't refuse. It broke her heart to think of Sage trying to devise a way to ease her mother's pain and her own at the loss of her sister.

"Finding your father isn't enough of a diversion?"

"For me. Not so much for you."

Oh, having Jackson Lange back in Hope's Crossing definitely qualified as a distraction. She had been so scatterbrained today, she had barely been able to function.

She scrutinized the little dog. Okay, he *was* cute. What would be the harm in babysitting him for a few weeks? They hadn't had a dog around the house since their much-beloved ancient golden retriever had gone to the big fire hydrant in the sky the summer before Sage started high school.

"Only until Josie goes back to school. And you have to promise to do all the work, even if you're putting in hours here at the store. Feed him, water him, clean up any messes. Everything. I mean it."

"I will, I swear. Thanks, Mom." Sage stepped forward and kissed her cheek. The little sneak of a dog reached in and gave her cheek a lick too.

Two days ago her life had seemed so simple. Raw and empty and filled with pain, but not all these complications. Now she had Jack to deal with, and Sage and her grief and her secrets, and now a fuzz-faced dog.

"Keep in mind the most important thing. You're cleaning up all the messes," she repeated, just to be clear.

"I know. I know. I won't forget. I'm going to go out and show Sierra and Joe. Just come grab me when you're ready to go home."

She gave her grandmother a kiss—and held the dog up

to do the same—before she blew out of the room as quickly as she'd entered.

"You're a sucker, my dear," Mary Ella drawled.

"You don't have to tell me that. I always have been. I learned it from you, the woman whose children talked her into three dogs, four cats, a couple of gerbils, a tank full of fish and a fainting goat."

"I miss that goat. My yard has never been as well groomed as when we had him around to eat the grass. Maybe I should get another one."

"I know a little shih tzu who could use a new house. Can't promise he'll eat the grass, though."

Mary Ella smiled and rose. "I'd better run, though after quilting all day, I'm not sure these old fingers will be able to do much beading."

"Does that matter? You go to String Fever for the fun and gossip as much as anything."

"True enough." Mary Ella paused and placed a hand on Maura's cheek. "I pray for the day when you will want the same thing again."

"I will. Someday." Absurdly, she wanted to lean into her mother's soft fingers and weep, but she forced herself to straighten her shoulders. "If you find anything out about Harry, let me know. I should probably be ready in case he decides to sue me for every penny, since my store is about the only thing in town he *doesn't* own."

Mary Ella smiled again, but Maura was almost certain she saw anxiousness in her green eyes.

CHAPTER SIX

A GRANDDAUGHTER.

All this time he had a granddaughter, living right under his nose.

Harry Lange fidgeted in the damn hospital bed, trying to find a more comfortable position. He abhorred the Hope's Crossing hospital, even if he had given the place enough cash over the years they should have named a wing after him. The fawning doctors, the busybody nurses, the obsequious administrators who had already been in to check that he was receiving top-quality care.

This was the third time in a year he'd had the misfortune to require treatment at this blasted place. Every visit left him more determined than ever not to return unless it was to the basement morgue.

Most people in town considered him a bastard who plowed his way through life, taking what he wanted without fear or second doubts. That wasn't precisely true. If he dared, he would grab these IVs and yank them out of his arm, unpeel the cardiac leads and head for the door.

He might be strong-minded but he wasn't stupid. He had a bad heart. That was the cold, stark truth. Oh, the doctors gave it all kinds of five-dollar words, but it boiled down to a bum ticker, so he was forced to lie here helpless and let the idiots fuss over him while his son was here in Hope's Crossing for the first time in twenty years.

Jackson.

That moment when he had walked into the bookstore, turned his head and seen his son standing there, strong and handsome and hearty, was one he would remember for a long time. Oh, Harry had seen Jack over the years—not that his son had any idea of those surreptitious trips, which Harry had made in disguise when his sources let him know of some building dedication or architectural award.

Jack never would have seen him at any of those places. Harry had made sure of that. Those few glimpses of his son had been both incredibly rewarding and bitterly painful, and had left him aching for more.

He reached for the water bottle beside his bed, cursing the stupid lines tethering him to the equipment. Wouldn't you know? The simpleton nurse had left it just out of his reach. He was straining with one arm to reach it without falling out of the bed, when he heard the door open.

"Help me here, will you, you idiot?" he barked, without taking his gaze off the unattainable water bottle.

A long silence greeted him, and finally a voice answered, "Still as charming as ever, I see."

Off balance and extending his arm beyond a safe reach, Harry would have fallen sideways out of bed if he hadn't caught himself at the last minute.

His heart fluttered, and he thought with horror that maybe he was having another attack of angina from the damned atrial fibrillation he'd been dealing with for a year, but then he realized it was just completely understandable shock at the sight of his son in the doorway.

"Son."

Jack's mouth tightened at the word, but he moved closer to the bed and picked up the water bottle Harry had been scrambling after like a pig snuffling for apples.

"This what you were trying for?" Jack asked.

He grabbed at it, feeling ridiculous. "Yeah. Stupid nurses always leave it just out of reach. What's the point of making sure my water bottle is full when I can't grab it?"

Jack didn't make a comment, only raised an eyebrow. Harry had wondered himself if the nurses didn't do it out of some kind of passive-aggressive spite. He sipped at his water, wishing they could be meeting under different circumstances, not when he was lying here in a damned hospital gown.

"I didn't expect you to show up."

Jack shrugged. "Call it a crazy impulse. Maybe I just wanted to see how close you were to kicking the bucket."

He refused to show any reaction to that. He had reaped what he'd sown with his son, hadn't he? "I've still got a few miles left in me. The idiot doctors say I've got atrial fibrillation. A-fib. I've been on medicine for it, but I guess it's not working as well as we thought."

Jack seemed to digest that information. "Are they keeping you long?"

"Just overnight while they run some more tests." If they couldn't figure out the right medication, he was going to have to go to Denver for a procedure to reshock his heart, but he decided not to tell Jack that. He quickly changed the subject.

"What's this about you having a daughter? You were a smart kid. Didn't you have the brains to use protection?"

Jack sighed. "It was a shock to me too. I haven't spoken with Maura in twenty years now. She never said a word to me about a pregnancy. I'd like to think I would have taken responsibility if I had known. Every child deserves a father willing to stand up and be a man and take part in raising him."

The implication being that *Harry* had done nothing of the sort. Which was true enough, but not the whole story, something Jack wouldn't have been able to see twenty years ago.

"She's a smart girl, that one. I understand she was valedictorian and earned an architectural scholarship at UC–Boulder. I guess she's a chip off the old block, right?"

Jack frowned. "How do you know anything about Sage? A few hours ago, you had no idea who she even was."

Harry had his sources, who had been busy all afternoon and evening finding out everything they could about this new relation of his. Right now, he figured he probably knew more about Sage McKnight than her own mother, and he was pleased beyond measure that his granddaughter showed such promise, despite her upbringing with that flighty woman.

"The mother, Maura. She's a piece of work. Hooked up with a musician a few years after you left. From what I hear, their marriage only lasted about five years—long enough to make another kid. The girl who died."

Annoyance tightened his son's mouth, so much like his mother's. The girl shared the same mouth. Harry had ordered his people to send any pictures they could find of her, and he was amazed now that he'd never picked up on the resemblance when he had seen her around town over the years. Amazing what a person could miss when he wasn't expecting to see it.

"A real tragedy, that accident," he went on. "All of Hope's Crossing has been in a tizzy since April, pointing fingers, trying to figure out what went wrong. I'll tell you what went wrong. Nothing new here. A bunch of headstrong kids take a couple of drinks, smoke some weed, and think it all gives them immortality and nothing can touch them."

This *wasn't* what he wanted to talk about with Jack. Harry had waited twenty years for his son to return, and this wasn't at all the way he'd pictured their reunion.

He fidgeted and smoothed the blankets. "You didn't come here to talk about something that happened eight months ago to strangers in a town you hate."

Jack met his gaze head-on. "To tell you the truth, I'm not sure why I came here. It was a mistake. I should go. Sorry to have bothered you."

No. Not yet!

Jackson turned as if to go, and Harry racked his brain for some way to keep him here. He finally blurted out the first thing that came to his mind.

"I thought maybe you were angling to be hired to design the town's new recreation center."

His son gave a short laugh that didn't sound amused in the slightest. "Despite what you may think, I don't need to come to Hope's Crossing trolling for business. My firm does fine."

Better than fine, Harry thought with pride. They were one of the most respected design companies on the West Coast, and his son had built the whole thing out of nothing. Of course, he couldn't mention he knew that very well, that he had followed his son's career intensely from the moment he'd finished his graduate work at UC–Berkeley.

"Given your connection to me, I figured you might think you have some kind of in. Well, you don't."

Jack looked if he didn't know whether to be amused or offended. "I would never assume such a thing, even if I knew what the hell you were talking about."

"It's still in the initial planning stages, but I can tell you it's going to be a huge project and one of the most innova-tive facilities in the nation, with indoor and outdoor recreation opportunities. You can get a project prospectus like everybody else, so don't think you can worm the information out of me when I'm on my deathbed."

"Now you're on your deathbed."

Harry shrugged. With his heart problems of the past year, he felt closer than he ever had in his life. Regret was a miserable companion to a man in the twilight of his life, especially since he had always considered himself invincible.

And the man standing reluctantly by his bedside was his biggest regret. The Grand Poobah of his failures.

"You can call my assistant if you want more information about the recreation center. I'm sure it's a project of larger magnitude than you're used to. Probably out of your league."

"No doubt," Jack murmured.

Before Harry could come up with something else to say, the door opened without warning and his nurse backed in carrying a dinner tray.

"Time for your dinner and evening meds." She turned around and blinked a little when she saw Jack. "Oh. I'm sorry. I didn't realize you had company."

She gave his son a quick look and then a longer, more assessing one. Yeah, Jack had always been a good-looking cuss. Much like Harry when he'd been younger.

"This is my son, come to visit me on my deathbed," Harry said.

"Your...son? Oh."

The nurse looked as surprised as she would if Harry had just introduced him as his pet monkey. She was so young she probably didn't even know he had a son. She would have been just a kid when Jack left.

Harry had been alone for two decades in that big house in the canyon. Twenty years. Too damn long.

For a time, he'd thought he wanted things that way. He had been convinced Jack was a stubborn, self-righteous little prick who didn't understand the way the world worked. Jack didn't want him in his life, and Harry had been perfectly content to give him his way. Amazing how a little heart attack could change a man's perspective.

"How lovely to have your family with you." She smiled. "Sorry I'm so late with your dinner, but your food was held up in the kitchen. Better late than never, isn't it?"

"Is it? It's lousy either way. I still don't understand why the fool doctors won't let me have my chef bring me something decent."

"We had this argument the last time you stayed with us. You know your nutritional content has to be screened carefully for sodium, potassium and magnesium. What would happen if we just let you have any old thing?"

"I might actually eat it," Harry muttered.

"Oh, you." She fussed around his IV tree for a moment, then started switching out bags.

"I'll go and let you have your dinner," Jack said.

Harry wanted to call him back, assure him he wanted him to stay, but he didn't want to sound weak in front of either his son or the nurse.

"Call my office if you want to see the prospectus," he said gruffly.

Jack gave him an "are you kidding" sort of look before he left.

Harry watched him go, furious with himself. What the hell was wrong with him? Twenty years of silence, and when he finally saw his son again, he could only come up with inane conversation about *nothing*.

Would he ever see him again? Or was this the only moment he would have to remember until he died?

He lay in the hospital bed under the watchful eye of the nurse, wishing he could rub away the sudden ache in his chest that had nothing whatsoever to do with his heart problems.

"DOES EVERYTHING LOOK OKAY?"

Maura pasted on a smile for her daughter. "Relax, honey. The pork loin looks beautiful and smells even better. It will be delicious."

"I shouldn't be so nervous. It's only dinner. It's just… It's my dad, you know?"

Yes, she did remember that little fact. Maura forced a smile. "I know. Everything will be perfect."

Three days after Christmas, her dining room still looked festive. A garland was draped around the chandelier, and the mantelpiece of the old fireplace was covered in more garlands, gleaming ribbons and chunky candles.

The table was set with her best china, white plates with delicate blue borders. It was old and delicate, exquisite, really, a wedding present from Chris's parents. The set had once belonged to Chris's maternal great-grandmother, who had been one of the original silver queens in Colorado.

After the divorce, she had tried to give it back to Jennie Parker, but her ex-mother-in-law had insisted she keep it in order to hand it down someday to Layla….

Her heart gave a sharp kick at the memory, and she bit her lip, refusing to give in to the sudden burn of emotions. She knew this emptiness would never fully go away, but the past week, the pain had seemed fresh and new. Layla had loved the holidays. She was always the one who'd insisted on decorating the tree the day after Thanksgiving, who would drag them out to go caroling with the church choir through the neighborhood, who would wake up before the sunrise on Christmas morning so she could rush in to see the pile of presents.

Without her, the season seemed not a time of hope and renewal but of bitter loss.

Christmas morning, three days earlier, had been particularly poignant. She and Sage had both put on cheerful faces as they'd opened their gifts to each other, but she could tell her daughter was feeling the same ache.

Christmas night they had gone to the noisy, crowded McKnight party at Mary Ella's, where all her siblings gathered with their families. Claire and Riley had been there with Owen and Macy, Angie and Jim, of course, with their children, and Alex. Even her sister Rose had driven out with her family from Utah in the middle of a snowstorm in order to make it back to Hope's Crossing to spend Christmas in Mary Ella's small house.

She suspected Rose and Michael had come for her sake, to lend emotional support on her first Christmas without Layla. While she had been touched at the gesture and happy to see her just-older sister, she had thought a few times that the avalanche of concern just kept piling on.

She touched the edge of a place setting and straightened the silverware a little, remembering how when she and Sage had returned home from the noise and craziness of the family gathering, they had sat here in the living room by the fire, watching the lights twinkle on the tree, snowflakes gently falling and the little shih tzu puppy wrestling with a leftover ribbon. She had been able to hold it together, until she'd looked over and seen tears trickling down Sage's cheeks.

"I miss her," Sage had said softly. "Sometimes I miss her so much I don't think I can bear it."

"Oh, honey. I know," she had said. What else could she

say? She knew from experience no words were adequate to soothe this pain, so she had held Sage and the two of them had cried that they would share no more Christmases with Layla.

Today Sage hadn't had time to grieve for her sister, too busy shopping and cleaning and cooking. Maura was glad for that, even if Sage was doing all this work for her father. Jack was due to arrive in half an hour for one last evening with his daughter before he left in the morning to return to the coast.

One more day and he would be gone. She had hardly seen him since that first morning after he'd arrived in town, just brief moments when he'd picked up or dropped off Sage on their way to some outing. This would be the longest time she had spent in his company since their ill-fated breakfast at the Center of Hope Café.

If she had her choice, she would have tried to get out of this dinner and let Sage have a quiet evening with her father. What could she do, though? Sage had asked her to stay, and she couldn't find a decent excuse to refuse.

Maybe after he left, she would be able to breathe again.

She looked around the beautifully presented dining table again, but couldn't see anything out of place.

"So put me to work. What can I help you do?" she asked.

Sage shook her head. "Nothing! Absolutely nothing. You've been working at the store all day. Jack won't be here for forty-five minutes. You can go take a nap or read a book or play with Puck—whatever you want, as long as it's something relaxing, not working here in the kitchen with me. This is my gift to the both of you. My parents."

Okay, she probably shouldn't feel so squeamish about being lumped into that category with him. It was the truth, after all, but considering herself a co-parent with Jack still felt so strange after all these years on her own.

"Are you sure? I don't mind helping."

"Positive. Everything's under control. Why don't you go take a soak in the hot tub?" Sage suggested.

The idea had instant appeal. The hot tub on the edge of her patio overlooking Woodrose Mountain was her one indulgence, especially on winter nights with the snow falling gently on her face. "I wouldn't feel right leaving you in here to do all the work."

"Mom, go!" Sage ordered. "I'm serious. You'll only be in the way. I've got this."

She wanted to argue but saw the futility of it. A soak actually *would* be perfect and might soothe her psyche a bit, give her a little inner peace to handle the ordeal of the next few hours.

"Okay. I won't be long."

"Take your time," Sage said.

Maura finally surrendered and hurried into her bedroom to change into her swimming suit, and grab a towel and the book she was currently reading for the January book club meeting.

She hadn't shoveled the path to the hot tub since the last storm, and the two inches of new snow froze her toes in her flip-flops. But she danced quickly through it and worked the lid off, then slid into the always-hot water with a sigh of pure bliss.

Oh, she had needed this, she admitted. The stress of the holidays had just about done her in. She should make time to come out here every night, instead of saving it for a once-or twice-weekly treat.

When Chris lived here with them, he had put the hot tub in the backyard to soak sore muscles after a day on the slopes. After the divorce, it had become her escape from dealing all day with two girls by herself. Once they were in bed, she used to love coming out here to gaze up at the stars and read a book and feel like herself again, a woman with dreams and regrets, instead of only someone's mother.

Tonight she decided not to bother with her book after all and left it on the edge of the hot tub. She turned the jets on High, leaned her head back and lifted her face to the cold night air.

She just might have dozed off from weeks of jagged sleep. She dreamed of Jack, of their first time together, on a blanket high up Silver Strike Canyon. Of tangled limbs and mouths, of two painfully awkward adolescents trying to work their way through the emotions and the heat and intensity that had built up over their weeks together, while the river bubbled beside them and a red-tailed hawk cried somewhere overhead.

After about twenty minutes, the sound of a barking dog in the distance yanked her back to the reality of a winter's evening. She hadn't been asleep long. Maybe even not fully asleep at all. Her fingers and toes were shriveled, but the rest of her was a big, loose ball of relaxation. She probably should go back into the house, even though she didn't want to let go of the sweetness of that dream.

She rose, turned off the hot tub jets and reached for her towel—just in time to see the very grown-up version of that boy standing at the window inside, looking out at her through the frost-etched glass.

Heedless of the plumes of steam that curled and caressed around her, she froze while a heat that had nothing to do with the water temperature seeped through her. She remembered that dream, remembered the heat and wonder of being with him.

After a long, charged moment, she managed to shake off the clinging tendrils of the past and turned away. She wrapped the towel quickly around her, hit the button to close the hot tub's automatic cover, then slipped her feet into her cold flip-flops for the trip through the snow back to the house. Her face was more hot than the rest of her now, but at least she had private access to her bedroom from here, and wouldn't have to drip her way through the rest of the house and risk encountering him in her swimming suit.

More than she already had through the window, anyway.

Drat the man for coming early.

After a quick shower to rinse off the hot-tub chemicals and the rest of her embarrassment, Maura threw on a pair of soft gray slacks and her favorite wine-colored tailored shirt, along with a necklace set Claire had made her out of turquoise-and-burgundy glass beads artfully strung on coiled silver wire.

She wasn't dressing up, she told herself as she touched up her makeup and quickly took a flatiron to her hair—she was only trying to look nice. Okay, and maybe stalling as long as she could here in the safety of her room. Finally she forced herself to give one last look in the mirror, took a deep breath and walked into the kitchen.

She found Jack standing at her kitchen island wearing an apron that read Hope's Crossing Chili Cookoff: We're Smokin' Hot. His long, artistic architect's hands were shredding lettuce into a bowl, while Puck curled up at his feet.

Sage was on the other side of the island, smashing potatoes in her grandmother's old mustard-colored earthenware bowl. She raised an eyebrow with a sweeping gesture toward the entirely too appealing man across the island. "Okay, explain to me why you basically barred me from the kitchen earlier but here Jack is, looking quite at home in my favorite apron?"

Sage shrugged. "He insisted on helping."

"So did I," Maura complained. "You wouldn't let me do a thing."

"I guess you're not as persuasive as I can be," Jack said.

Oh, she was quite sure of that. "I could have done the salad," she muttered, embarrassed all over again that he had caught her dozing in the hot tub while Sage was in here working by herself.

"It's done now," Jack said. "Shall I set this out?"

"Yes. Everything else is ready, I think. Mom, do you want to put Puck in my room?"

"Sure. I would hate to think I didn't do my part," she said drily. "Come here, dude. Time to be banished."

The little dog cocked his furry face and gave her the canine equivalent of a pout as she scooped him up. The two of them had reached an accord of sorts. He mostly stayed out of her way, maybe sensing that her heart wasn't open to him right now. She didn't mind his temporary presence in the house, especially as Sage enjoyed him so much and had stayed true to her promise to take care of him.

Maura carried him down the hall, refusing to acknowledge the comfort she found in the small, warm weight in her arms. Puck whined a little when she set him down on the brightly colored area rug in Sage's room, unhappy with being excluded from the evening's festivities.

"Cry me a river, kid. You're the lucky one. I'd much rather stay in here with you," she muttered.

"Everything's ready, Mom," Sage called out.

Yeah. She would definitely prefer to hide out here with the little dog. "Sorry. It's only for a while. I'll let you out again after dinner," she promised.

Puck must have sensed she meant business and accepted his fate with equanimity. As she closed the door, he was circling the floor a few times, preparing to settle in.

Back in the kitchen, she found Jack had taken off the apron. He looked impossibly gorgeous in a tawny fisherman's sweater and jeans, and her stomach did a long, slow churn, an unwelcome warmth seeping into places that had been cold and empty for a long time.

She didn't want this. Drat the man, anyway. She wasn't ready for heat and hunger and *life* again.

"What's the matter? Did I forget to set something out?" Sage asked anxiously.

Maura realized she was frowning and quickly smoothed out her features. It wasn't *Sage's* fault she was having this blasted reaction to the presence of an entirely too sexy man. No matter her unease around Jack, she refused to ruin all her daughter's culinary efforts.

"Nothing's wrong, honey. I was just thinking this is bigger than the spread your grandmother put on for Christmas dinner."

"Not quite."

"It looks great from here," Jack assured her. Sage beamed at him, though Maura couldn't help but notice the lingering shadows under her daughter's eyes, which didn't seem to disappear no matter how much Sage slept.

They sat down and began to dish up the bounteous feast. At first, the conversation seemed to sputter and fizzle like an improperly laid-out fire, but Sage did her best to add tinder and kindling.

"Jack designed an office tower in Singapore. He's going there in a few months when they start building it. Isn't that awesome!" she exclaimed.

"Awesome," Maura murmured.

He raised an eyebrow but didn't comment.

"Where's the coolest place you've designed a building?" Sage pressed.

"Cool? That's relative. I designed a high-rise apartment building in Seoul last year. That was interesting. But I don't take on any project unless I think it's cool in some way. I would be bored otherwise."

Maura studied him, trying to reconcile this confident man with the passionate boy she remembered. "You've accomplished everything you talked about doing."

She raised her glass of ginger ale, and he lifted his own to clink it against hers and then Sage's.

"Funny thing about this business, though. There's always another mountain."

"What's your next summit?" She genuinely wanted to know, she realized. When was the last time she had been curious about *anything?*

He hesitated for a moment, twisting the stem of his wineglass between his fingers. "You're going to wonder if I'm crazy. No, scratch that. No wondering about it. I *am* crazy. I don't know why I'm even considering it."

"What?"

"The town is considering bonding for a new all-season recreation center up above the reservoir."

Sage's eyes widened. "This town? Hope's Crossing?"

He nodded. "My, uh, Harry told me about it when I went to visit him in the hospital after he fell in the store."

He went to visit his father? Maura stared, caught off guard. If he'd just told them he had swum across the icy waters of Silver Strike Reservoir that morning, she wouldn't have been more surprised.

"What is Harry's involvement?" Maura asked.

"It's his land, if you can believe that. He's considering donating it to the city for the facility."

Okay, that was even more shocking than the idea of Jack going to visit his father in the hospital. Harry didn't do anything out of the goodness of his heart, simply because he didn't *have* a heart and whatever he had that might resemble one wasn't at all good. He was a man who didn't make a move unless he could find some way to squeeze a dollar out of it, and he was famously antiphilanthropic.

She studied Jack. "You're actually considering this? Doing something for the benefit of a town you despise?"

"I don't hate the whole town. I never did."

"No. Just all the people who live in it."

"That's a bit of an exaggeration, don't you think?"

Was it? He had seen cruelty and inequality all around him, especially in the way some people treated his mother's mental illness.

"Anyway, I can't say I've been miserable during the time I've spent in Hope's Crossing these last few weeks. For the most part, people have been very welcoming. The B and B even left me a present with my muffins on Christmas morning."

She smiled. "Let me guess. A scarf. Lucy's mother is a prodigious knitter."

"It's a very nice scarf and will definitely be just the ticket during our chilly Bay Area summer mornings when the fog rolls in."

She tried to imagine him in his natural milieu of San Francisco. Where did he live in the city? she wondered. Riley had lived in Oakland for years and had only returned to be the Hope's Crossing police chief the year before.

Maura had gone to visit him with her girls several years ago and done all the tourist things—the cable cars, walking across the Golden Gate Bridge, visiting the sea lions on the wharf. They might have even passed by Jack's office.

"Hope's Crossing is a nice town," she said after a moment. "I think if you spent a little more time here, you might see that. We even have our own Angel of Hope."

"Angel of Hope?"

"It's actually pretty cool," Sage said. "Somebody goes around secretly doing good works for people. And not little things either. Major stuff. Taryn Thorne, one of the other kids injured in Layla's car accident, got a video game system from the Angel, the kind where you don't need a remote. They're not cheap. And my friend Brooke's mom had all her utilities secretly paid while she was going through a divorce."

He looked intrigued. "And you don't know who's doing all the good works?"

"There are a million theories buzzing around town," Maura said. "Some completely unbelievable. Personally, I think not knowing is a big part of the excitement."

"We had a visit from the Angel," Sage said. "After Layla died, somebody left an envelope with money in it on the doorstep with a note that we could use it for funeral expenses or find some other way to honor her life. Mom and I agreed to donate it to Habitat for Humanity. They've got a housing development going up west of town."

"Really? In Hope's Crossing, along with the million-dollar ski lodges up the canyon?"

"A community can't survive with only vacation homes. We need year-round residents and they need to be able to afford housing," Maura said. It was one of her pet issues and hit very close to home. Too many of the old-timers had been forced out of their homes because they could no longer afford property tax once valuations started going sky-high after the ski resort was built.

"We volunteer to help build whenever we can," Sage said. Her daughter was barely picking at the delicious meal, Maura noticed. She had eaten only a little of the pork and a few of the potatoes she had spent so much time mashing.

Maybe she was too excited at having her father there, or maybe she hadn't quite beaten the flu she seemed to have picked up since she had been home.

"If you take the project in Hope's Crossing, would that mean you would have to commute from California?" Sage asked.

"I don't know whether I'm even going to submit a proposal," he said. "Even if I do, there's no guarantee I would be awarded the project."

"Oh, sure. That makes sense." Sage poked at her food, dragging her fork into little ski trails through her mashed potatoes. She gazed down at her plate and spoke in a deceptively casual voice. "Since you're leaving tomorrow, I was, uh, just wondering when I would see you again."

"We'll work something out," Jack said quietly. "You're not getting rid of me now."

Maura set her own fork down, not hungry anymore. Good thing Jack had a healthy appetite, or all of Sage's hard work would have been for nothing.

CHAPTER SEVEN

DURING THE REST of the meal, they talked about Sage's studies and Jack's projects. It wasn't as awkward as Maura had feared, but she couldn't ignore the little twang of tension between her and Jack, and the small sizzle of awareness.

She didn't want to be attracted to him, but she didn't seem to have any more control over her hormones than she'd had as a teenager.

Finally, everyone seemed to be finished either eating or pushing food around the plate, and the ordeal was over.

Maura smiled and took the napkin off her lap. "Sage, you've been working so hard all day. Why don't you and Jack go in by the fire and relax? I'm happy to take care of the cleanup in here and in the kitchen."

"I can't let you do that, Mom. I left a big mess."

"Between the three of us, we can have the job done in a flash." Jack said.

There is no "three of us," she wanted to say. They weren't a unit and never had been. For Sage's early years, she and Maura had been alone against the world. Okay, they hadn't exactly been alone, since her mother and sisters—and even Riley—had rallied around her. But Jack certainly hadn't been in the picture to stay up late with a sick child or work on potty training or read her to sleep.

Now he had burst into their lives with his stories about his high-powered career and the excitement of traveling around the world, and she could see Sage lapping it up like Puck at his water dish after a long game of fetch, and she *hated* it.

She caught herself, appalled at the thoughts. She was jealous, she realized. Plain and simple. She didn't want to see Sage establishing this bond with Jack. She wanted to turn the calendar back several weeks, to when she didn't have to share her daughter with anyone.

She had lost one child with devastating suddenness. Now it felt as if the other one was slipping away, inch by inch.

She would only push her away further by acting petulant and bad tempered. She forced a smile. "Sure. All three of us can clean up. I really don't mind doing it myself, but we can all make the work go faster together."

After they carried the dishes in from the dining room and loaded the dishwasher together, Maura filled the sink with sudsy water that smelled of green apples and began washing the dishes.

"Towel?" Jack asked, and Sage pointed him to the drawer beneath the work island where the dish towels were stored. As he reached for them, his hip brushed Maura's and she froze as the masculine scent of his aftershave teased her but the moment passed quickly.

For the next few minutes, she washed the dishes and he dried them before handing them to Sage to put away. This was entirely too domestic, she thought. Like a regular nuclear family working together at the end of a long day.

When the final dish was washed and the last bit of water gurgled down the drain, she dried her hands on another towel she pulled from the door, wishing she could clean up the mess of her life as efficiently as they had cleaned up the kitchen. "I imagine Puck is tired of his bedroom confinement. I'd better go let him out."

"I can do that," Sage said.

"No. It's okay. Stay and talk to your, uh, Jack."

The little shih tzu greeted her as if he hadn't seen her in months, jumping around and doing cute little dancing circles in the air. He wasn't much of a barker, something she very much appreciated.

She scooped him up with a quick look down the hall to make sure Sage wasn't watching. It wouldn't do to let her daughter think she was softening about keeping the dog.

"You did okay in here by yourself, didn't you? I don't see any accidents. Good job," she murmured, pressing her cheek to his furry face and receiving a gleeful lick in return.

Through the windows in Sage's darkened bedroom, she could see snowflakes softly falling, kissing the window. Her favorite sort of winter night, soft and quiet. Peaceful. She wanted to be out there, she thought, in the quiet solitude, rather than here with all these awkward currents and the solid proof of all her mistakes.

She could hear the voices recede behind her as Sage and Jack moved into the family room near the fireplace. Suddenly she wasn't at all sure she could sit in there with them and make after-dinner conversation for another hour or so.

"How would you like to go for a walk?" she asked the dog, seizing on any excuse to escape. Puck wagged his tail so hard it was a blur, and Maura was surprised at her own rusty chuckle. "All right. Don't hurt yourself. Let me find your leash and my coat."

In only a few moments, she slipped into her favorite black knee-high UGG boots and her parka, then clipped the leash on the dog and headed into the family room with him dancing around her feet with eagerness.

"Puck needs a walk. I think I'll just take him around the block. We should be back in a few minutes."

"Alone? In the dark?" Jack asked, eyebrows raised.

"This is Hope's Crossing, not San Francisco. But if it makes you feel better, I've got a flashlight *and* pepper spray on my key chain."

He rose. "You know, now that you mention it, a walk actually sounds nice after such a great and filling dinner. What do you say, Sage?"

Sage made a face. "Normally, I'd love that. Mom and I like to take walks together in the evening, but I've been on my feet all day. Right now I don't want to move a muscle from the fire."

Jack looked from Sage to Maura and back again, obviously torn about whether to go with her or stay here and talk to his daughter on his last night in town.

Sage made the choice easier for him, unfortunately for Maura. "You two go ahead and take a walk. I'm great here, I promise. I told my roommate I would Skype for a few minutes to help her with an essay she has to finish for an online course."

"Are you sure?"

"Positive. I'll be fine. It's too cold out there for you to be gone long, anyway."

She was stuck with him now. Maura didn't see a reaction on Jack's handsome features. No doubt he wasn't any more eager than she was to be forced into closer contact, without the buffer Sage had provided so far.

"Let me grab my coat," he said.

While Jack shrugged into his very sexy leather jacket, Puck tugged anxiously on his leash, no doubt the only one excited about this walk now.

Christmas lights still blinked around them from her neighbor's houses as they headed out into the quiet night. This was always a bit of a melancholic time for her, the week between Christmas and New Year's, when people kept their decorations up as if clinging to the last moment of celebration.

They walked in silence past a few houses to the corner, then turned onto the next street.

Jack was the first to break it. "Sage seems like a really terrific kid," he said.

Their daughter seemed to be the one topic they could agree about. "She's amazing. She's always been very grounded. Layla… Layla was fire and passion and all these swinging emotions, from the time she was little. It was like she was hormonal from the time she was a toddler, but Sage has never been that way."

"You've done a good job with her." He paused and seemed to be weighing his words. "It couldn't have been easy on your own."

She glanced at him to see if his words held hidden barbs, but he seemed sincere. She gripped Puck's leash a little more tightly while a steady warmth seeped through her.

"No. It hasn't always been easy. But always worth it."

He didn't answer for a long moment, and the only sounds besides the crunch of their steps in the snow were the occasional passing car on another street farther down and Puck's snuffles. The lights of Hope's Crossing were a bright glitter below them.

Again, he was first to break the silence. "I'm still furious, you know. That you never told me you were pregnant."

She exhaled heavily, her breath coming out in long puffs. "Well, I'm still furious that you walked away without once looking back. So I guess that makes us even."

After a long moment, he startled her by chuckling softly. "How about we both agree we've got a right to be angry with each other and try to figure out where we go from here?"

"You're leaving tomorrow, Jack. Why do we have to go anywhere, except back to my house?"

"My job is fairly flexible. I can work anywhere. I'm thinking about temporarily relocating to Colorado, especially if I decide to pursue the recreation center project."

"Really? You would do that for Sage?"

"I missed twenty years of her life. I'm not sure I want to miss out on the rest of it."

"She's an adult. Trust me, the last thing she's going to want is her father hovering over her."

"I wouldn't hover. Just…be closer. If she needed me."

Her chest ached at the wistfulness in his voice. Should she have tried harder to reach him while she had been pregnant? She had been so certain of her decision to exclude him from Sage's life, but for the first time she began to wonder how much of that had been based on rational thought, and how much had been an immature girl's reaction to her own pain, that he hadn't loved her as she had loved him.

"I suppose you're an adult too," she said. "If you want to uproot your life in some effort to make up for…for lost time or whatever, I'm really in no position to say otherwise. Sage might not want you underfoot all the time, but I'm sure she would enjoy having you closer."

He nodded, hands in his pockets. "Thank you. I appreciate you saying that. I'm still trying to figure everything out."

He released a breath. "I always loved this spot. When I've thought of Colorado over the years, I've pictured this place on a summer evening, with the trees sweeping low in the water, and the water flowing over the moss with the mountains all around. I'd forgotten how beautiful it was in winter."

To her surprise, their steps had led them to Sweet Laurel Falls, one of her favorite places on earth. A small parkway ran parallel to Sweet Laurel Creek, and benches had been set where there was a view of the falls, really just a series of cascading levels where the creek rippled down the mountainside. They stood on the snow-covered pedestrian bridge over one of the lower levels, and from here the water still looked an impossible green from the moss growing on the rocks beneath the surface, in vivid contrast to the ice that had formed along the edges and the snow piled along the banks.

"In another few weeks, that waterfall will be completely iced over, with only a little trickle of water underneath." Right now she felt like that icy waterfall, with only a tiny trickle of life buried deep inside her.

"It must be beautiful."

They stood together without speaking for a long moment, elbows on the bridge railing as they watched the moonlight drift through the snow clouds and create pale shadows on the spill of water. His scent teased her, of cedar and leather. Some part of her wanted to lean against him and just inhale, to soak up some of that warmth. If she turned her head just so, their mouths would be on the same level. Would he taste the same as she remembered?

The thoughts sidled through her head and she caught herself, horrified.

No. Absolutely not. She wasn't ready for that ice to thaw.

She eased away from him, feeling the cold where their bodies had nearly touched. "Um, we should probably head back. Puck's little paws are likely frozen. I should have put his booties on before we left."

For a moment, he watched her with an inscrutable expression, and she had to dearly hope none of those crazy stray thoughts showed on her face.

"Leave the guy a *little* dignity," Jack finally said. "Here."

Before she knew what he intended, he reached for the leash, then scooped up Puck with one arm while he unzipped his jacket with the other, and tucked the dog inside. She watched, amused and touched despite herself, while he zipped the jacket back up with Puck's little furry face sticking out the top. The dog looked inordinately pleased with himself, as if he had orchestrated the whole thing.

"What were you saying about a guy and his dignity?" she asked.

He made a face as they headed back through the lightly fluttering snow to her house, in what turned out to be an oddly companionable silence.

"Would you like some cocoa before you head back to the B and B?" she asked as they approached her front door. The invitation was mostly polite, but he *had* been kind enough to carry Puck all the way.

"Sure. That sounds great. Thanks. We may complain about our chilly summers in the Bay Area, but they don't compare to late December in the high Rockies."

The moment they opened the door, Jack pulled Puck out from his coat and unhooked the dog's leash before setting him down. The scrabble of his nails sounded on the hardwood floor as he headed into the kitchen to his water bowl. Maura shrugged out of her coat and hung it in the closet, then went in search of her daughter. She found Sage stretched out on the couch in the family room, sound asleep with the television playing softly in the background.

Rats. If only she had waited a few moments to extend the cocoa invitation to Jack, she could have used the excuse of Sage sleeping to send him on his way for the evening. She was stuck with him a little bit longer.

"Zonked out," he murmured beside her, and she realized he must have followed her. She glanced over and found him watching their daughter with a wary sort of tenderness that made her chest ache all over again.

Maybe having him in Sage's life wasn't such a terrible thing.

Sage had reminded her of something she used to say, that a child could never have too many people to love her. Maybe there was truth in that. Jack obviously cared for Sage. How could she possibly resent that?

Before she could say anything, she heard that click of nails on hardwood again. Finished with his water, Puck was apparently ready for more fun. He scampered into the room, past them both. Before she could grab him or call out to stop him, he headed straight for the couch and jumped up, straight onto Sage's legs.

"Puck!" she grumbled sleepily, and pushed the dog off her legs.

"Sorry. He moves faster than I do," Maura said.

Sage turned her attention to the doorway, blinking a little to clear away her sleepiness.

"Oh. You're back."

"Sorry we woke you."

"It's okay. I couldn't reach Michelle, my roommate that wanted to Skype. I guess I dozed off while I was waiting for her. I don't think I was asleep very long. How was your walk?"

Maura thought of those tantalizing moments back at the falls when his heat had tugged at something deep inside. "Um, good. I'm making cocoa. Do you want some?"

"Sure. That would be great. Thanks."

She sat up and stretched, her shirt pooching out a little. Maura frowned. Sage had gained weight since she'd left for school in August. She really hoped she wasn't stress eating in the dorm to ease her pain over losing Layla.

Though her mother always insisted on hot cocoa the old-fashioned way, Maura didn't have the time and patience for that, not when she bought high-quality gourmet mixes that tasted just as good, mixed up with water heated in the microwave.

After preparing a mug for each of them, she carried a tray back into the family room. Jack smiled his thanks when she handed him a mug, and she tried to ignore the little tingle as their hands brushed.

Sage took only a small sip of hers before setting it down on the coffee table. She took a deep breath and faced them both. "Okay, I have to talk to both of you. I wanted to do this at dinner. That's actually the reason I wanted Jack to come over, but then when it came down to it, I just… I couldn't ruin the meal."

Apprehension congealed in Maura's stomach. This, whatever Sage wanted to say, must have been the reason she was so distracted throughout dinner.

She set her own mug down and reached for Sage's hand. "What is it, honey?"

Her daughter gripped her fingers for a moment, then released them and folded her hands together in her lap. "I'm not going back to school when it starts next week."

The vague apprehension turned to a full-fledged groan. They had fought about this all summer. After Layla's death, Sage had come home to be with her and had wanted to take a semester off to help at the store.

"You are," she said now, sounding like an old, scratchy

record of the conversation they'd had throughout July and early August. "You have a scholarship."

"I know, Mom. Don't you think I know? That's exactly why I need to take a semester off. My grades last semester sucked! I mean, seriously sucked. I'm barely going to be able to hold on to the scholarship as it is, and if I don't get my act together, I won't have the credits to get into grad school."

"I can't believe you want to run away, just because things are tough right now."

"I'm not running away! I've got everything figured out. I talked to my counselor before I left, and she said we can work things out with the scholarship for me to take one semester off. I can take some online courses that will help bring my GPA up again, even finish the last of my generals online so I can be ready next fall to start taking classes for my major."

"No. Absolutely not." Oh, she did *not* want to have this fight while Jack was sitting there watching them, but she also wasn't about to let Sage walk away from her dreams.

"Mom, listen to me."

"Why should I, when you're not being reasonable? You've been given a chance of a lifetime. I won't let you throw it away."

"I'm not going to throw anything away. Would you just trust me, for once? I know what I'm doing. I came up with a viable plan to take online classes and you won't even listen to it! You're *completely* unreasonable when it comes to school."

She dug her nails into her palms and curbed her sharp retort. Sage was probably right about that. Maura had missed out on her chance to go to college. She'd been too busy working as a checker at the grocery store and nursing her newborn. Maybe that's why she had been so insistent that Sage had to seize every opportunity that had been offered to her.

"What are you going to do here? Work as a barista at the store?"

"You say that like it's a terrible thing. I like working behind the counter, Mom."

"Not for the rest of your life. You have bigger dreams."

"Yes. And that's all they will remain—dreams—until I can bring my grades up again. I'm just not sure my head is in the game right now."

Well, get it in the game! she wanted to yell, but she knew that wouldn't accomplish anything other than to ramp up the tension.

"Okay, let's calm down here," Jack interjected into the conversation.

She had to fight the urge to smack him, to tell him he didn't get the right to come in and change everything. He hadn't been there all along the way, to sit at the kitchen table doing math homework or helping with book reports or editing scholarship applications.

Not by any choice of his own, she reminded herself, which took most of that particular wind out of her sails.

"Honey, I think this is a mistake," she said, fighting for a calm, even tone. "Once you stop to take a break from school, returning will only become harder."

"I know that's your big concern. Just like I know there's no way you'll let me turn into some kind of slacker, living in your basement and hanging out with my friends all the time. You'll push me to go back until my eyeballs bleed."

"We don't have a basement," Maura muttered.

"Metaphor, Mom." Sage rose from the couch and crossed

to her. When her daughter held her arms out, Maura could only hug her in return.

"We want the same thing for me. I want to be an architect. Nothing's changed. If anything, I want it more now than ever. I'm going to go back and finish up. It's just… so much has happened this year. I was still reeling from Layla and now, finding Jack and everything… I just need time to absorb, you know?"

Did she have to sound so damn reasonable? How could Maura argue?

"I have a possible solution," Jack said.

Sage turned to him, her cheek still pressed to Maura's. "Oh?"

"What if you come to work for me while you take a brief break from school? At Lange & Associates, you could gain practical experience working in a real architectural firm, which might help you determine whether this is really what you want to do with your life before you invest more time and energy in school. And also in the plus column, this would offer me the chance to come to know my daughter a little better."

Beside her, Sage's jaw sagged and she pulled away a little for a closer look at her father. "Are you serious? That would be *incredible!*"

She looked as if she'd just won the lottery, the Publishers Clearing House and a round-the-world cruise in one fell swoop.

Maura, on the other hand, felt sick. The room seemed to spin a little and a hard ball of nausea lodged in her gut. Sage, living in the Bay Area? How would she bear it? Riley had gone away to live there and had come back a completely different person, hard and angry and *damaged* somehow.

Granted, he had been an undercover police officer in one

of the most violent areas of the country, and that probably had more than a little something to do with the change in him. Sage would be working in an office somewhere with Jack to watch over her, nothing like Riley's experience.

Somehow that didn't make Maura feel any better.

She forced herself to sip at her cocoa and gripped the handle so hard her knuckles turned white.

"Don't you think that's the *perfect* idea?" Sage asked her when she didn't immediately answer.

What was she supposed to say to that? "It's…an idea. California seems like a long way right now."

She felt the weight of Jack's gaze on her and tried to compose her features into a blank slate, giving away nothing of her inner turmoil. Somehow she didn't think she succeeded very well.

"I didn't mean the San Francisco office," he said. "We're fully and efficiently staffed there. But if I were to open a temporary office in Colorado, I'll definitely need help."

"Really? You want to open a temporary office here?"

"I'm thinking about it," he told Sage. "With the project in Denver I was telling you about and the possibility that I might submit a proposal for the recreation center, having a more regionally based office isn't a bad option."

Some of the tension coiled inside her seemed to ease, but she still couldn't shake the feeling she was losing her daughter. She felt as if she stood belaying for Sage at the bottom of a rocky cliff. Once Sage reached the top, she would slip free of her ropes and disappear forever.

"Denver wouldn't be so bad, Mom," she said. "Just a little farther than Boulder. I could easily come home for the weekends."

"Sure. Of course."

"Actually, I was thinking I could probably find empty

office space for a short-term lease in Hope's Crossing. I wouldn't need much."

What sort of strange dimension had she just entered, where Jackson Lange would seriously consider setting up an office in Hope's Crossing, even temporarily?

"Here? That would be fantastic!" Sage exclaimed. "Brilliant! This way I could still help you in the store on evenings and weekends."

Maura was suddenly aware of her deep exhaustion. From the moment she had climbed out of the hot tub and found him watching her, she had felt as if her emotions had been on some insane amusement-park ride, jostled this way and that, zinging around corkscrews and loop-the-loops, plunging here, climbing here. She couldn't take any more and suddenly wanted nothing more than to be hiding out in her bedroom.

Sage wouldn't be leaving her, apparently. For a little longer, anyway, she could still stand at the bottom of the cliff and hold the rope while her daughter climbed higher. On the flip side, if Jack opened an office in Hope's Crossing, that would mean she was stuck with him. Instead of going back to San Francisco, he would be here, just a few miles away.

"That's a very generous offer, Jack," she managed.

"Not generous at all. I'm gaining more than anyone out of the deal."

"This could be a wonderful opportunity," she said to Sage. "You will still need to remember that your online classes take priority. An internship, even with the best architectural firm around, won't benefit you if you don't return to school and finish your degree."

"I know." Sage jumped up, much more ebullient than she had been when she had broached the topic of school. "This is fantastic. I can't believe it. This went so much better than

I had hoped. I was dreading talking to you about school, but you've been totally cool about it. Thank you. Thank you both so much for being awesome parents."

Maura wasn't *cool* about anything. Not the decision to leave school, not the self-motivation required for online classes and especially not Jack sweeping in to save the day. He was supposed to be leaving town today. She figured any further interaction between them would channel through Sage. Suddenly he was not only invading her family but the town she loved.

She saw this as a huge mistake on Sage's part—and on Jack's. What was he thinking to imagine for a moment that he wanted to live and work in Hope's Crossing again, even for their daughter's sake? He wouldn't be able to stand it for long, she suspected. Temporarily relocating to town in order to help Sage through this rough patch sounded lofty and helpful, but Jack couldn't be seeing the bigger picture of actually having to stay here longer than a few weeks. He couldn't just change his zip code and expect his life to go on as usual. Soon enough, he would tire of the slower pace, the sometimes intrusive neighbors.

She had no control over any of it. Not Sage, not Jack. Good grief, she barely had control over herself, judging by that moment at the falls when she had wanted to lean into his heat and soak it through her skin.

She could only cross her fingers and hope Sage didn't end up with a broken heart—and that she wouldn't either.

WHAT JUST HAPPENED in there?

After saying good-night to Sage and Maura, Jack walked out into the cold Colorado night, where he was surrounded by the familiar scents of snow and pine and *home*.

Something about this place must be messing with his

head. What else would explain an otherwise sane man suddenly committing to a plan that would compel him to stay in Hope's Crossing? He still couldn't quite believe he was even considering throwing his name into the hat for the community recreation center. Now he was about to open up a damned branch office here.

And why? One reason. Because he hadn't been able to bear the shadow of pain in Maura McKnight's eyes when she thought her daughter would be leaving her to move with him to San Francisco.

Man, he was a sucker. Why should it matter if she suffered a little at the loss of face time with her kid? Wasn't this what they called karmic justice? She had robbed him of nearly twenty years with his child. While he might be gradually coming to accept her reasons and finding a little more compassion for a scared teenage girl, that didn't ameliorate his own loss.

A cold wind slid under his jacket as he retraced the steps he had taken earlier on his way back to his B and B. He supposed he could have driven the few blocks to Maura's house in his rented SUV, but living in a city where parking was both exorbitant and elusive had given him a healthy appreciation for the convenience of walking. Old habits, and all that.

Of course, he hadn't expected to find himself bisecting the evening with another walk, when he and Maura had taken Puck on this very same route.

That moment when they had been standing so close together near the falls, when she had leaned against him almost imperceptibly, caught his breath all over again. He was weak when it came to Maura McKnight. He always had been.

He had thought about her over the years with softness,

the same kind of fond recollection he had for his first car and the first building he had ever designed. Over the years, he had even thought about looking her up a time or two, but had decided he would rather cherish those memories than be confronted with a reality that might have turned out far differently than he imagined.

She was his first love, but in his head, he had always compared what they shared to a bonfire of paper and plywood. The flames burned hot and fierce, certainly, but they also burned out quickly, leaving nothing but smoke and ash. How could it have turned out any other way, as young and heedless as they had both been?

Like it or not, their worlds were entwined now through Sage. He wasn't about to walk out of his daughter's life, which meant he would by necessity be in Maura's as well. At least for the next few months, he was bound to see her around town.

He didn't know exactly how he felt about that. Earlier, by the falls, something seemed to shiver between them, something soft and tender and enticing. He shook his head. Crazy. This town definitely took away all reason and good sense. Must be something in the water.

He was just about to turn onto Blue Sage Road, just one block east of the B and B, when a deep-throated dog began to bark wildly a few houses down. Hoping it was on a leash or behind a fence, he crossed to the sidewalk on the other side of the street. He wasn't in the mood to lose any bite-shaped chunks out of his hide right now.

On alert, he scanned the road for any big, angry guard dog coming at him. Out of the corner of his gaze, he spotted movement several houses from him, on the same side of the street. Human. Definitely human, at least judging by the long black coat that flared as the guy sidled behind a tree.

So the loud dog wasn't barking at him, probably. That was a bit of a relief, he supposed. Maybe that was why the other guy was commando-sneaking behind another tree.

Okay, weird. The black clothes, the sneaking around, darting in and out of the trees. Not a particularly good combination. Was this a thief, targeting holiday-emptied houses in town? Wouldn't it be just his luck to witness a crime on his last night in town?

The guy was definitely up to something as he moved one house closer to Jack's position. So far he didn't seem to have seen Jack, not even when he had crossed the street, probably because he was just out of range of the only streetlight on the corner.

Somebody in San Francisco might consider this none of his business, but Jack didn't work that way. He reached for his cell phone and began to dial nine-one-one, and had his finger just above the send button when he realized the mystery man wasn't heading into one of the darkened houses on the street, with their lodge-chic decorations.

Instead, he appeared to be heading up to the doorstep of the smallest house on the street, a clapboard single-story house with green shutters. Several children's bikes were parked on the front porch, and all the lights were blazing from the windows.

The guy probably wasn't a thief, then, but why all the skullduggery? He watched as the figure crept up to the porch and dropped something on the mat, rang the doorbell, then raced back down the sidewalk to hide behind a huge pine tree on the edge of the property. In his dark clothing, he blended into the night, shadow and shape becoming one.

From his vantage point, Jack could see a tired-looking woman wearing a housedress with her hair slipping from a ponytail open the door and peer out.

"Who's there?" the woman called, and Jack slid further behind his own camouflage, not wanting to take the blame or the credit for something to which he was merely an innocent bystander.

"Come on, you kids. Knock it off. It's cold. You shouldn't be out messing around, bothering regular people. Go home."

From inside the house, Jack could hear a child crying and another one yelling. The woman started to close the door, and then she must have caught sight of whatever the mysterious visitor had left on the mat. She bent down and picked up something that looked from here like a business-size envelope. Jack couldn't see it clearly, but as he watched, the woman frowned at the envelope and opened it. He saw a flash of green and the woman's mouth dropped open. She looked at what was obviously a wad of money, then walked to the edge of her porch.

"Hello? Who's there?" she called.

The only answer was the barking of the neighbor's dog and her own children bickering from inside.

"Thank you. Thank you. God bless you. Whoever you are, thank you!"

The last words rang out with a near sob that sent shivers down his cynical spine.

When was the last time he had done something purely altruistic for someone? Oh, he contributed to various charities and always tried to carry a little extra spare change for the homeless who often stayed out of the wind and damp in the doorways he passed on his way to work, but this seemed different, somehow. Much more personal and *real.*

The conversation earlier with Sage and Maura about the town's Angel of Hope rang through his memory. He must have just witnessed the guy in action. What else could it be?

The door closed as the woman finally went inside to

share her news with the rest of her family. Jack should have moved on. He was cold and damp and uncomfortable, but he wasn't about to move until the Angel, if that's who it was, moved first.

The guy waited a few more moments, probably to make sure the coast was clear, then he hurried down the street, moving stealthily from tree to bush, as if he expected a light to blare down from a search helicopter at any moment.

When he was almost at the end of the street, the Angel stopped for just a moment and lifted a hand as if to rub his chest, then he dropped his fingers and hurried down the street.

Jack narrowed his gaze in the darkness, a completely crazy thought clanging through his head. Impossible. Even though the height and the general weight might match up, he would never believe it.

Not knowing the son of a bitch as he did.

CHAPTER EIGHT

A HALF HOUR into her book group, gathered with her closest friends—and a relative or two or three thrown in for good measure—Maura came to a particularly grim conclusion.

"You are all a bunch of dirty rotten liars, aren't you?" she finally exclaimed. "All this talk about character development and imagery is a bunch of bull. Not a single one of you has read this month's book."

Mary Ella and Ruth exchanged guilty looks, and Claire's cheeks turned pink. Her sisters Angie and Alex nudged each other and became inordinately fascinated with the cozy display of mystery novels on the shelf beside them.

"I wanted to read it, my dear. Honestly, I did," Katherine Thorne said with a rueful smile. "I had the best intentions. I loaded it onto my e-reader to take on my cruise to the Caribbean over the holidays, but I ended up reading mysteries and romance novels the whole time. And I won't feel guilty about it either, so don't try to make me."

"I read a review online," Mary Ella confessed. "The reviewer said it was rich in symbolism and layered with existential angst. To be honest, I just didn't have the energy for it. You know how Januaries are."

Maura glared at them all. "Why didn't any of you tell me you didn't want to read the book when I offered suggestions for the month? Jeez, I gave you like five choices. We could have picked something different."

"Make a note," Alex said, lounging on the sofa. She looked pretty and bright as always, with her curly blond hair and the green eyes they shared. "Next January, pick something easy and uncomplicated for our tired little seasonally affected brains."

"Claire, help me out here."

"I'm sorry. I meant to read it, honestly I did. It's been sitting on my bedside table for a month. But with the wedding and the holidays and how busy the store was—and then Macy and Owen both having the flu right after school started again—I just haven't had a *minute*."

"You don't need an excuse, Claire." Evie Blanchard gave her a mischievous grin that would have seemed out of character a few months earlier, before she'd started dating Brodie Thorne and the shadows lurking in her eyes had begun to fade. "You're still a newlywed. I think all of us can agree you probably have better things to do with your free time."

"Evie!" Claire exclaimed, her pink color turning a fiery red even as a sudden glint appeared in her eyes.

"Ewww." Alex made a face. "Anybody have any brain scrub?"

"If you do, pass some my way," Mary Ella muttered, though she smiled with customary good nature at her new daughter-in-law. Despite the teasing, her mother and sister—really, the whole McKnight family—was thrilled at Riley's brilliant choice in Claire. She was the perfect woman for him. She was calm and patient and loving, everything Riley needed after returning hard and angry from his time as an undercover police officer.

"What about Evie?" Claire said. "She's barely left Brodie's side since September."

"I'm here, aren't I?" Evie replied, though she wore that same kind of knowing, well-satisfied smile.

A completely unexpected envy pinched at her as she studied her two dear friends. Except for a few dates here and there, Maura had been alone since she and Chris had called it quits years ago. She had tried to convince herself she needed to focus on raising her daughters, not bringing in man after man to complicate their lives and dilute her attentions. But that was small comfort on cold winter nights when she really missed having someone to snuggle on the sofa with and watch the flames dance in the fireplace while the snow piled up outside and storm winds howled under the eaves.

"I'm hearing rumors," Mary Ella said. "Any truth to them?"

"Katherine," Evie exclaimed to Brodie's mother.

"I didn't say a word, I swear," Katherine protested.

"It wasn't Kat," Mary Ella said. "I just happened to be in Reverend Wilson's office this week, working on organizing the choir music, when a certain handsome young restaurant owner who shall remain nameless came in asking about Saturdays in March when the church might be available."

Evie was the one blushing now, and Maura mentally threw up her hands, though she smiled at the same time. Any chance of having an intelligent discussion about books was hopeless now that another wedding was apparently in the air.

"Oh, no. Not you too!" Alex exclaimed.

"I didn't mean to spoil your surprise, my dear." Mary Ella sent her an apologetic look.

"It's all right," Evie assured her. "I was going to tell everyone tonight anyway."

She held up her left hand, where a beautiful emerald glistened. "It's true. We're looking at March. I hope you can all be there. I'm going to be sending out invitations in the next week or so. I know it's short notice, but Taryn is doing so well, we just wanted to celebrate and start moving on with our lives together."

"Oh, congratulations, honey," Maura said. She hugged her friend, and for the next half hour, Evie made the rounds of the book group, showing off her ring and accepting congratulations and talking wedding plans.

Maura listened to the discussion with her heart a little lighter than when she had started the evening. She loved weddings and was genuinely happy for Evie and Brodie. After all these years, Taryn would have a loving stepmother, Katherine would gain a dear friend for a daughter-in-law, and Brodie couldn't find a better woman than Evie.

After the pain of the last year, they all deserved to be happy. Taryn had survived the accident that killed Layla, her best friend, but had been seriously wounded. Despite her own misgivings, Evie, a former physical therapist, had agreed to help with Taryn's recovery. In the process of helping the girl heal from both her physical and emotional wounds, Evie and Brodie had fallen in love.

Maura sat back now and listened to the conversation flow around her, about flowers and decorations and picking out dresses.

"Too bad nobody brought champagne," Angie said. "We need to toast to the happy couple."

"I can grab some ginger ale from the refrigerator in the back," Maura said. "And don't forget we still have Alex's yummies. What did you bring this week?"

"A new cheesecake recipe I'm trying out. White chocolate."

Everybody moaned with appreciation, except Ruth, who wasn't crazy about chocolate—white, milk or semisweet—

and Charlotte Caine, whom they all knew was trying hard to lose weight.

Alex, who could be surprisingly thoughtful at times, especially when it came to food, produced an angel food cake for the two of them. "No chocolate. And only one-hundred-fifty calories," she told Charlotte.

For the next few minutes, Maura was busy finding glasses and ginger ale for everyone while her sister served up dessert.

"So what else is new with everyone else?" Claire asked when they all seemed settled with refreshments.

"I'm already planning another cruise," Katherine said. "I'm thinking the Panama Canal this time. I'm going to see if I can drag Ruth along to this one."

"We'll see," Ruth said with a grunt.

"I think you need to go on one of those Sexy Senior Singles cruises," Alex said. "Mom, you should go with them too."

Mary Ella rolled her eyes. "I'm not looking for romance—any more than you seem to be."

"Neither am I," Ruth said. "Now, sex, on the other hand…"

Everybody laughed hard at that, even Maura, until Alex turned to her. "Speaking of sex. Or at least *sexy.* I see we've got a new business opening up in the old insurance company office."

Maura could feel heat seep into her cheeks and she sipped at her ginger ale, hoping nobody noticed. She still wasn't quite sure how Jack had taken his fledgling idea over the holidays of opening an office of Lange & Associates in Hope's Crossing and turned it into firm reality in only three weeks. "It's a temporary situation. Jack has some projects in the area and he needed a local base."

"Has Sage started working for him yet?" Angie asked.

"Last week. So far she loves it."

"I was so hoping she would be here tonight so I could ask her what it's like to work so closely with a world-renowned architect," Mary Ella said.

"She's only been working for him a week, so I'm not sure she's really qualified to answer that yet. I do know the work must be tiring. I think she's been in bed by eight-thirty every night. I'm hoping she didn't catch a touch of Owen and Macy's bug."

Maura did her best to conceal her worry for Sage from her mother and the other women. Something was wrong with her daughter. She knew it in her gut. Since Sage had returned from several days spent in Boulder to fix her car and clean out her dorm room ten days earlier, she had been withdrawn and quiet.

During her first year of college, whenever Sage would return home on breaks, the two of them would stay up talking for hours. She couldn't manage to turn off her daughter's chatter and she hadn't wanted to, even when she was exhausted from working all day.

This time around, Sage seemed to want to do nothing but read, watch television and sleep.

If this didn't improve in a week or two, especially now that Sage had the added stimulation and challenge of working with her father, Maura planned to insist she make a visit to their family doctor.

"So how is it having Jackson Lange back in town?" Evie asked.

Maura concentrated on the bite of very delicious cheesecake melting in her mouth. "Fine, as far as I know," she finally said. "I haven't seen the man since the holidays."

That was one good thing about Sage working for him.

She spent all day with him at the small office up the street, and they hadn't socialized much together, which meant Maura's interactions with Jack had become nonexistent.

"I heard he's renting a place up in the Aspen Ridge development," Angie said. "Gina Coletti has a place there and said he's in the same unit with her."

Sage hadn't mentioned that, but then Maura had tried very hard not to ask about her daughter's father. Aspen Ridge was only a few streets away from her house. She wasn't sure how she felt about Jack living so close to her.

"It's only temporary," she said again, wondering just who she was trying to convince. She quickly and deliberately changed the subject by turning to Evie. "How's Taryn these days? I haven't seen her since before Christmas."

"She amazes me every day. You heard she was back in school, right? She started after the holidays. With the tutors she had in the fall, she's not even very far behind. Can you believe that? And she's catching up quickly. We'll have to drop by the bookstore after school one day to say hi. I think Taryn would like that."

"I'm so happy she's improving. Please tell her I would love to see her."

"I will." Evie paused, then lowered her voice while the conversation flowed around them. "I should probably tell you that she and Charlie still email when they can. He happened to mention in an email that you sent a Christmas package to him at the juvenile detention center."

Maura avoided her friend's gaze, embarrassed to have that small gesture become common knowledge. "He has plenty of time on his hands. I thought he might enjoy exploring some good books while he's there."

Evie squeezed her fingers. "Just for the record, you're one of the very best people I know, Maura."

What a joke that was. Inside she felt bitter and shriveled and angry at the world. "It was no big deal. I run a bookstore, Evie. Books are kind of easy for me to lay my hands on." She paused, compelled to ask, though she didn't really want to know the answer. "How much longer does he have?"

"Nine months."

"What's in nine months?" Alex asked, overhearing. "Don't tell me you've got another announcement, Evie!"

"No!" the other woman exclaimed. "Nothing so exciting, I'm afraid. Or pleasant, for that matter. I was telling Maura that Charlie Beaumont has nine more months in his sentence before he's released from juvenile detention."

Alex's teasing smile slid away, replaced by the sharp, hard lines of anger. "Not nearly long enough for the little bastard. He killed our Layla and almost killed Taryn. For that, he gets less than a year in youth corrections? It's heinous."

Evie opened her mouth, but closed it again. Maura knew Evie was somewhat sympathetic to the boy, who had been driving impaired when he'd slid into a tree. Charlie Beaumont had been a huge part of Taryn's recovery. Maura knew that. Facts had emerged at Charlie's sentencing hearing that cast a new light on the details leading up to the accident, but she wasn't nearly as forgiving.

If not for Charlie's decision to drink and drive and then to try outrunning a police officer—her brother Riley—Layla might be waiting home for her right now to giggle and gossip and talk about school.

"I heard Mayor Beaumont is trying to get him out early on good behavior so he can go to Genevieve's wedding," Ruth interjected.

"I think Gen would prefer he stay locked up," Claire

said. "She doesn't want anything to ruin her perfect day, especially not her juvenile delinquent of a brother. Her extremely gorgeous fiancé and his snobby family might not like it."

Maura didn't want to talk about Charlie Beaumont—or for that matter, Genevieve and her grand society wedding in only a few month's time—so she again deftly maneuvered the conversation back to safer waters by asking Claire about the second annual Giving Hope Day, which was in the planning stages.

As Claire launched excitedly into her spiel about how this one would be bigger and better, Maura sat back, marveling at how adroit she had become at social manipulation when the need arose. Yet another unwanted skill she had developed over the past year.

THE BOOK CLUB—if it could legitimately still call itself anything remotely literary after tonight—wrapped up around the time the store closed. She ushered the last of her friends out, then spent another twenty minutes cleaning up while the clerks went through their closing procedures.

"Need me to vacuum in here?" April Herrera asked.

"No. I've got it. Thanks. Good night."

She had a cleaning crew, but over the past year she had reduced their work to twice a week for deep cleaning, while she and her employees took care of the superficial cleaning the rest of the time.

By the time she finished vacuuming the store, her arms ached and she had a slight headache from the noise of her heavy old unit, but the carpets didn't have so much as a stray piece of lint. She returned the vacuum to the stockroom, then gave the store one last cursory look before she locked the door.

In the dim lights, the books gleamed on the shelves and it smelled rich and familiar, of coffee grounds and leather and the delicious mix of ink on new paper. She always had to stop and inhale when she walked into her store, absorbing the smell of new books—of humor and obscure facts and adventures waiting to be discovered.

She loved this place. Pride and contentment were familiar companions as she looked around at what she had built on her own. Yes, Chris had insisted on very generous child support payments and alimony after the divorce. His career by then had exploded, and he had erroneously given her much of the credit for pushing him and believing in his vision of his music.

She couldn't deny his seed money had been a huge help in the beginning, but her own elbow grease and ingenuity had certainly played a part in the success of Dog-Eared Books & Brew. With luck and hard work, she really hoped she could keep the store thriving.

But not tonight. Tonight she wanted to collapse into her bed and block out the world. Tired and more than ready for the long day to be over, she unlocked the door and let herself out, then locked it again.

The storm that had dropped a couple of inches of new snow on the ski slopes earlier seemed to have passed over, leaving the night icy but clear and beautiful.

She tightened her scarf and headed for her vehicle, parked off Main Street in one of the rare side lots. Parking was such a pain. As an old silver-mining town founded before the turn of the twentieth century, Hope's Crossing hadn't been designed to accommodate modern traffic, forget about the hordes of tourists who could descend on any given winter weekend to ski and shop and eat. She didn't mind the walk, though, especially with the bright sprawl of stars overhead.

With the new snow, everything looked fresh and clean in the moonlight.

She would have a better view of the stars if she took her snowshoes up the Woodrose Mountain trail on a midnight hike above the ambient light of the city, but she rarely had the energy for much anymore except soaking in the hot tub after a long day of work.

Her path to her vehicle led her past the former insurance agency, now with a tasteful sign in sans serif script that read Lange & Associates, Architectural and Design Services. Just as she reached the edge of the storefront, the door opened and out of the corner of her gaze she saw Jack walk out. She might have thought he had been lying in wait just for her to pass by, if he hadn't immediately turned around to lock the door behind him without even acknowledging her presence.

He wore that same tailored leather jacket and a gray scarf. On some men she might have considered the scarf an affectation, but on Jack, it looked masculine and sexy.

Something in her stomach tugged, sweet and pliable as taffy, and she frowned, greatly tempted to slide into the shadows and keep walking. She sighed and slowed her steps. She was many things, but she generally tried hard not to be rude.

"Hi."

She was a little gratified when he jerked in surprise at her greeting and looked up with a distracted manner.

"Oh. Hi. Sorry. I didn't see you there."

"It's the dark coat. It can be good camouflage when I need it. Lets me sneak around town ninja-style without attracting attention."

"Hmm. Seems to be an epidemic of that around here," he said.

"What do you mean?"

"Nothing. It's not important." He shouldered his leather messenger bag and walked toward her, and that taffy ache stretched tighter. "You keep late hours."

"That's funny. I was about to say the same about you. I didn't realize brilliant architects had to burn the midnight oil too."

He laughed roughly and the sound seemed to slide down her nerve endings like the barbs of a feather. "I can't answer for the brilliant architects. I know the rest of us do, if we want to be able to afford that oil to keep the lights on."

She smiled, amused at his attempt at humility. She had heard enough about his career to know which category most of his peers would fit Jackson Lange into. And if they happened to give out prizes for the sexiest among them, he was certain to win that too, especially right now with his wavy hair rumpled and that appealing evening shadow just begging for a woman to slide her fingers across…

Not *this* woman, of course.

"What are you doing out so late?"

"Book club meeting. And I use the term loosely."

"Which term? *Book club* or *meeting?*"

"Either. Both. Tonight it was mostly a gossipfest."

"Sounds ominous. I'm glad I was safely tucked away here working."

"My friend Evie is getting married. That's an exciting bit of news. She's marrying Brodie Thorne. Did you know him?"

"He was a few years behind me in school, I think. Didn't he ski jump or something?"

"That's the one. They're getting married in March." She

paused. "His daughter was Layla's best friend. She was injured in the same car accident, and Evie has been helping her heal."

He didn't seem to know what to say to that, and she wondered why she was blabbering on about people he didn't know and likely didn't give a damn about. Probably because she couldn't seem to fight this little hitch in her breathing, the hard pulse of her heartbeat.

"Well, have a good night," she said, and turned to continue on her way.

"Wait. Where are you parked? I'll walk you to your car."

"You don't have to do that. I'm not far, in the little lot behind the bike shop." She *really* didn't think spending more time with Jack Lange was a great idea right now, with her defenses sagging from exhaustion—especially when he looked so dangerously irresistible.

"Well, there you go. I'm in the same lot."

Naturally. She should have expected that, since many of the downtown business owners parked there and instructed their employees to do the same, to leave room for customers in the closer parking spaces. What else could she do but shrug and walk beside him as he headed toward the lot?

They walked in silence for a few moments, and she tried not to notice the heat of him, which drew her on the wintry night as a fire in a fifty-gallon drum attracted hobos. She did her best to focus on the snowy sidewalk to avoid falling on her face in front of him.

"So how's the new office so far?" she finally asked.

"Good. We're still settling in. I imagine I'll only be here one or two weeks out of the month, the way my schedule is right now. I'm going to be heading out of the country in a month or so, which will complicate things."

That was *something,* at least. "I haven't had a chance to

talk to Sage much this week, but in the few conversations we've had, I can tell she seems to be enjoying the work."

He slowed his steps slightly, and she adjusted her own pace to match his. "Actually, I'm glad you brought her up," he said. In the old-fashioned streetlights, his eyes suddenly looked troubled. "I wanted to talk to you about her anyway and was planning to drop by the bookstore tomorrow."

Maura frowned, aware of a complicated little tangle of emotions. She wanted things to go well between Sage and Jack, for her daughter's sake. For her *own* sake, on the other hand, she wouldn't mind a little distance between the two of them, especially if it meant she could avoid these sudden encounters with him that left her off balance and unsure of herself. "Is there a problem?"

"Not with her work. She's been great with helping me set up the office, and she's very efficient and eager to please. The perfect employee, really."

"That's great."

"She's got natural instincts too. The other day she pointed out a couple of problems with a building I'm working on that I hadn't even considered."

Every mother liked to hear good things about her children—but why did she have the feeling a big "but" was coming? "What did you want to talk to me about, then?"

He was silent as they stepped down off the curb and crossed the street, and she felt as if they were picking their way around the conversation as carefully as she was trying to navigate through the ice in the road.

"I don't know how to ask this without just blurting it out, bald and unadorned," he finally said. "Is there any chance Sage has a drinking problem?"

Sage? *A drinking problem?* For a brief moment, she thought she must have misheard him. This was their *daugh-*

ter he was talking about. Sage—funny, bright, giving Sage. On the heels of Maura's shock came the low thrum of anger.

She jerked to a stop. "What kind of question is that? You're asking me if my daughter is…is some kind of drunk? Why the hell would you even *think* such a thing?"

He stopped alongside her and held up his hands. "Calm down. I'm just asking. I was a college student. I know kids her age can sometimes take things to excess. Maybe party a little harder than they planned."

"Not Sage," she bit out.

"Well, I don't know what else to attribute it to. A couple of mornings since we opened the office, she seems almost hungover, out of it and pale when she shows up. This morning I heard her throwing up in the bathroom. She was better in the afternoon, but she still didn't seem like herself."

How did he know what Sage's real self was like? He barely knew their daughter! She wanted to snap the words at him, but she remembered her own concern for Sage since she'd moved her things home from her dorm. She had to agree her daughter had seemed very under the weather, but Maura would never believe she was abusing alcohol. Sage didn't even like the taste of beer. She had admitted as much after her first year of college, when Maura had probed about the notorious Boulder party scene.

"I think she might have a bug," she told Jack now. "I can promise you, she's not out partying. For one thing, she's still underage. For another, since she came back from school, she's been in bed before *I* am every night. Even over the weekend."

"That doesn't mean she's not drinking by herself."

Just the idea of that shook her to the core. Sage *had* been struggling since Layla's death. Was it possible she was drowning her grief in alcohol? No. She wouldn't believe it.

"I know my daughter, Jack. That's not her. If nothing else, she would never want to ruin her chances to work with you by coming in with a hangover. I think she has a bug," she said again. "I had planned to take her to the doctor in the next week or so if she doesn't start feeling better, but if it's affecting her work, I'll try to get her in earlier. She needs to be working on her online courses."

"She's doing her job. I have no concerns in that area. I was only worried about her health." He studied Maura in the streetlight's glow. "I shouldn't have said anything. Now I've upset you."

"No. I'm glad you did. It's my job as her mother to worry for her."

"And mine now as well," he said, as if she needed that reminder of the strange turn her life had taken the past month, with Jack now a major part of their lives after all these years.

"I'll push her to go to the doctor," she promised. "If you see anything else unusual, please let me know."

"I'm not sure how Sage would feel about me snitching on her to her mother."

"Why not? Fair is fair. She tells me everything you do," she lied.

To her surprise, he laughed. "In that case, I'll be sure to drop a dime if I see her doing anything crazy. Which one is your car?"

They had reached the parking lot, she realized, without her having much recollection of the actual journey. "That SUV there on the back row."

The wet snow of earlier had frozen to the windshield, leaving the worst kind of mess. She sighed. Apparently she wouldn't quite be able to end this long day yet.

"Go in and turn on the defroster and heater. I'll scrape for you."

"I can take care of it."

"So can I. Where's your scraper?"

Arguing with him would only make her sound ridiculous. She reached inside the door on the driver's side and pulled out her ice scraper.

"Thanks," he said, taking it from her and immediately starting work on the windshield. "Go inside and get warm."

She didn't answer, just grabbed the second scraper that—like any good mountain dweller—she kept in her vehicle as a backup.

"You're as stubborn as ever, aren't you?" Jack said when she joined him at the windshield.

She gave him a cheeky smile. "Parenthood has only made me better at digging in my heels."

"I'll keep that in mind."

The words weren't sexual at all, but for some crazy reason, she felt a ridiculous heat spread from her stomach to her thigh muscles. *Grrr.* She ignored it and put her back into making sure she scraped more ice off the window than Jack did. He'd grown soft living in California, where he only had to worry about a little fog, while she had spent twenty winters honing her ice-removal skills.

They didn't say much as they worked, only the occasional comment about how he had forgotten how cold it could get once the cloud cover moved off, and how this winter had been mild compared to some. When they'd finally cleared off the last window, he shook the remaining snow off the scraper before handing it back to her.

"There you go. You should be able to see now."

"Thank you. I generally find that useful when I'm trying to drive. Shall we do yours?"

"I think I'm good." He gestured across the parking lot to one of the few other vehicles there, an SUV that looked brand-new, judging by the temporary plates hanging inside the disgustingly frost-free back window.

"How did you manage that?"

"I had errands this afternoon after it snowed and I brushed it off then. Thanks for the offer, though."

She shrugged. "You're new in town. Well, if you don't count your first eighteen years, anyway. I wouldn't want you to think we're not neighborly to our architects, brilliant or not."

He chuckled and reached in front of her to open her driver's-side door, in an astonishingly sweet gesture. She gazed at him. This whole thing would be much easier if he would act more like a jerk instead of doing these kind things that left her flustered and off guard.

She brushed past him to climb inside her SUV again, too aware of him to pay as much attention as she should to her footing. Her boot slipped on a patch of ice just outside the vehicle, and to her mortification, she felt herself falling. In an instant, Jack released the door and grabbed for her instead, clamping his hand around her upper arm and catching her.

She managed to find her balance, but her good sense seemed to have completely deserted her. She couldn't seem to look away from the sudden flare of heat in those blue eyes, the pulse beating along his jawline, the warm air that emerged in a cloud with his exhale.

She should move. Right now. The warning whispered through her like a cold wind, but she instinctively blocked it out. He was warm and sweet and gorgeous. Why would she possibly want to move?

CHAPTER NINE

SHE HELD HER breath as he lowered his head to kiss her, his mouth warm against the winter night and tasting sweetly of cinnamon.

She shouldn't respond. If she stood here like an ice sculpture, he would probably take one quick taste and then move on. Some part of her brain knew that was the wisest course, but the rest of her apparently didn't want to listen. He was warm and delicious and she hadn't known the sweet seduction of a man's kiss in *forever.*

His arms wrapped around her, pressing her against the door, and she thought he murmured her name, low in his throat. That sexy sound apparently was all her foolish body needed to ignite. She wrapped her arms around him and kissed him back, lost in the heat and the wonder of it, all tangled with memories of so many other kisses.

He had always been a fantastic kisser. Even as a young man, he had known just how to taste and tease and explore. Now, age and experience gave him a laser-sharp focus on her mouth that left her weak and achy and wanting much, much more.

Why had they bothered scraping all the snow when the heat they generated would have done the job?

She had a sudden memory of their first kiss. After weeks of hanging out together, talking and laughing and helping each other through their respective family crap, she had been dying inside, waiting and waiting for him to finally take the next step and wondering if she was going to have to paint a big red X-marks-the-spot on her mouth to clue him in that she wanted him to kiss her.

Finally, one evening they had gone hiking up in Silver Strike Canyon. They had been sitting on a boulder enjoying the twilight and the picnic she had packed and, suddenly, out of the blue, he had grabbed her sandwich out of her hand, tossed it into the grass and devoured her mouth until neither one of them could think straight.

The memories were all tangled up with the present. She was no longer that seventeen-year-old girl. She was a mature woman with needs she had ignored far too long, but right now, in Jack's arms, she wanted to be that reckless, wild girl, throwing caution to the wind in the arms of the boy she loved.

His kiss deepened, heightening the aching hunger, and she kissed him back, pressing against his hard strength.

For all she knew, they might have stood there all night, kissing until their toes went numb with frostbite. She wanted to, but suddenly the sound of a car's engine out on the street pierced the haze of desire. Before she could pull away, she heard a loud honk, then a bunch of whooping and catcalling, then teenaged voices grew more distant as the car passed them.

Oh, good grief. What was she doing, standing out here on a frigid January night, tangled in Jack Lange's arms? She felt as if she had been in hibernation for twenty years, just waiting for him to return and wake her....

She jerked out of his arms and sank down sideways on the driver's seat, wishing she could shove him out of the way, slam the car door and squeal out of the parking lot. But she was thirty-seven years old, not some foolish teenage girl. She was certainly adult enough to face up to her mistakes.

Jack looked down at her, his ragged breathing sending out little puffs of condensation. "We always could generate enough flames to burn down the whole Silver Strike forest."

"Winter nights at this high altitude can do crazy things to people's judgment," she said, her voice as prim as her maiden aunt Gertrude's underwear.

He looked amused. "So you're saying the cold and the altitude are to blame for my overwhelming urge to slip into that backseat with you right now and see just how crazy our judgment can get?"

Her whole body felt flushed, tingly, and she couldn't quite catch a full breath. "Have a little originality, Jack. You mean you haven't changed your technique at all in twenty years?"

His smoldering look had a wouldn't-you-like-to-know flavor to it. "Oh, I've definitely branched out. But I have to say, once in a while there's something to be said for the tried and true."

She almost had to close her eyes at the jittery hunger his words evoked. Thirty-seven, she reminded herself sternly. Much too mature and centered to be tempted into necking with a guy in the backseat of a car—especially when the man in question was the only one with whom she had ever enjoyed the activity.

"You'll have to try that particular walk down memory lane with someone else. I'm tired and I'm going home. Good night, Jack. Thank you for helping me scrape my windows and for keeping me from cracking my tailbone on the ice. I'll be sure to watch my step more carefully from now on when I'm around you."

He laughed again. "Good night, Maura. Sweet dreams."

At last—about ten minutes too late for her peace of mind—he closed the vehicle door behind her. Maura drew in a deep, cleansing breath, aware of the tremble of her hands and each pounding heartbeat. She shifted into gear and drove out of the parking lot, wondering how the heck a January night in the high Rockies could turn so steamy.

"WOW. THIS IS A SURPRISE. You brought me lunch. Thanks, Mom!"

Maura forced a smile for her daughter, who sat behind a tasteful oak desk in the reception area of the Hope's Crossing branch of Jack's firm. The reception area wasn't large, perhaps twelve feet by fifteen feet, but it was decorated with comfortably sturdy mission-style furniture, and a couple of Arts and Crafts–era lamps with shades of bronze glass that looked as if they belonged in a museum somewhere.

Sage wore one of the blazers she had purchased at her favorite thrift shop. She seemed as polished and cool as the office, until Maura looked closer and saw the circles under her eyes, the pale cast to her features.

"We need to talk, and I couldn't figure out another way to pin you down. Eat your turkey wrap. Dermot Caine fixed it especially for you. I think he always adds extra yellow peppers because he knows you love them. Go ahead. Eat."

Sage studied her for a moment, then obediently untwisted the paper around her sandwich and took a small bite. Maura took a bite of her own, though she wasn't very hungry. Parents needed to lead by example, right? Anyway, it was no big sacrifice. Dermot's sandwich wraps were always delicious, even when she wasn't in the mood to eat.

Her gaze kept drifting to the closed door behind her daughter, and she finally had to ask. "You said your, er, Jack is out of town?"

"He had meetings in San Francisco for the rest of the week. He's supposed to be back on Saturday night, though."

Maura told herself she'd only asked because she didn't want to be interrupted for this long-overdue discussion with her daughter. She certainly wasn't interested in his whereabouts for her own sake.

She wasn't avoiding him. Or at least she didn't want to *admit* she was avoiding him. Ever since that stunning kiss the week before, she had gone out of her way to park in the opposite direction from his office and to make sure their paths didn't have any reason to cross.

She couldn't help it if the memory of his mouth, hard and determined, and his hands slipping inside her coat left her breathless. Okay, maybe she had spent far too much time this past week reliving that kiss. She was quite sure that was just a case of the winter crazies and would pass soon enough.

"This is nice," she said, dabbing at the corner of her mouth with one of the napkins Dermot had included. "I've hardly seen you since you moved back. It seems like you're always studying or over at one of your friends or here at the office. I think I saw you more when you were living in Boulder."

"I guess things *have* been a little hectic," Sage said.

"Right." She took a deep breath and set down her lunch. "That's probably why you haven't gone to the see the doctor like you promised me last week."

Sage shifted and looked away. "I didn't promise anything. I said if I needed a doctor, I would go."

"But you haven't. And you're still not feeling well, are you? I didn't tell you this last week, but even Jack has noticed. He even asked me if you have an alcohol abuse problem. I told him you had a bug you couldn't shake."

"I don't have a drinking problem and I don't need a doctor, Mom. Back off, okay? I'm fine."

"You're not fine, honey. Since you came home, you're always pale and you don't have any energy. I'm worried about mononucleosis. It runs rampant on college campuses, from what I understand."

"I don't have mono."

"You might! How do you know? It takes a blood test before you know for sure."

"Jeez, Mom. Did you seriously do a Google search for 'mono'?"

"I was just looking up your symptoms," she said, trying not to feel defensive. She was a mother worried for her child. Nothing wrong with that. "Admit it, you haven't felt well since you came home. Even during the holidays you weren't yourself."

"Give me a break. I had just discovered the identify of the ultrasecret father you always claimed didn't exist."

"I never said Jack didn't exist. I only told you he wasn't a part of our lives and tried to stress you still had Chris, who was—and still is—an excellent stepfather. The point is, you're not yourself. We need to make sure you don't have something contagious."

"It's not contagious," Sage muttered.

"How do you know? I made an appointment with Dr. Harris. She has one last opening today at five. I'm sure Jack would understand if you closed up the office a little early in order to make it."

"No."

And Jack called *her* stubborn. She ground her back teeth and wondered why her daughter's strong will always took her by surprise, even after nineteen years of coming up against it. "You're going to the doctor," she said as sweetly as she could manage, "even if I have to get your uncle Riley to come in here, handcuff you and stuff you in the backseat of his patrol car."

Sage snorted. "As if he ever would."

"He might. You never know. What's the point of having a brother who's the chief of police if you can't take advantage of the badge once in a while?"

Sage shook her head. She fidgeted with her turkey wrap for a moment, then placed her hands flat on the desktop. "Mom, I don't need to see Dr. Harris."

She sighed. "You need to be examined by *somebody*. Is there another doctor in town you would rather see?"

"I saw a doctor at student health services when I went back to clean out my dorm room." Her daughter spoke the words like a confession, fast, with the syllables all blurred together.

Maura stared. "Why didn't you say something? Did they give you any medication? What was the diagnosis?"

"Well, the good news is I don't have mono." One corner of her mouth lifted as if she were trying to make a joke.

Was it something more serious? *Cancer?* Maura felt as if every internal organ had frozen. Her heart surely had stopped beating, her lungs couldn't draw air, her blood was no longer pumping. "What? What did the doctor say?"

Sage sighed. "I didn't want to tell you like this. I don't know *how* I wanted to. The truth is, I *didn't* want to, but… well, not like this, here in the office over turkey wraps."

Her face was frozen now too, and she could barely form any words through the sudden panic attack overwhelming her. She couldn't lose Sage too. She *couldn't*. "Tell me! What's wrong?"

Sage chewed her lip the way she used to when she was working on her times tables. "I'm pregnant."

Maura sank back in her chair as everything started working again in triple time. She couldn't have heard correctly. She was hyperventilating, her breath coming fast and shallow, and her stomach gave a sickening curl. "You're… what?"

"You know. Preggers. Knocked up. Bun in the oven."

She couldn't think. She could only stare at her pale daughter sitting in this elegant office that represented everything Sage had ever wanted.

"How?" The word scored her throat.

"The usual way, Mom," Sage said, her tone dry. Still she didn't meet Maura's gaze, but resumed fretting with the paper wrap on her sandwich.

So many things made sense now. Sage's exhaustion, her sudden emotional outbursts, the upset stomach. Why hadn't she said anything? All through the holidays, she hadn't so much as given away a hint. Had their relationship become so superficial and strained since Layla's death that Sage felt she couldn't confide in her anymore?

"I didn't know you were even dating anyone," she whispered. "Not since Michael Jacobs in high school."

Sage didn't lift her gaze from the desk in front of her. "I'm not. Not really. It was…just one of those things."

"Who is the young man?"

"I don't want to talk about that right now, Mom, if you don't mind. I haven't figured out what I'm doing yet."

"What are you *thinking* about doing?"

"I don't know. I really don't." Sage sighed. "I guess I'm just stupid, but I didn't even suspect I might be pregnant until Christmas. I wasn't having my period, but I just thought… I don't know, that my cycle was all messed up because of stress and school and Layla and everything. When I went to the health center, they—*we*—figured out

I must be about fifteen weeks along, which kind of eliminates some of my easier options, you know? I'm not sure if I could actually *use* those options, but I guess it can be harder to get a second-trimester abortion."

This couldn't be real. Her daughter talking about abortions and trimesters as if she were discussing the latest movie trailer. Maura felt by turns icy cold, fiery hot, then completely numb.

"You're looking pale. Are you ready to kill me now?" Sage whispered.

"No. Oh, no. It's a…shock, that's all."

She suddenly remembered being seventeen and pregnant and alone and having to tell her own mother. Mary Ella had been just months away from James McKnight walking out on the family. She had *hated* adding to her mother's stress and had put off telling her as long as she possibly could.

"It was a shock to me too. We, uh, used protection, but I guess it failed. Obviously."

Sage gestured to her abdomen, which now Maura could plainly see was bulging. A baby. Her daughter was going to have a *baby*. She still couldn't wrap her head around it. She was only thirty-seven years old. Certainly too old to be a *grandmother,* for heaven's sake.

"I'm sorry," Sage said, her voice small. "I know this changes everything."

"Yes. Yes, it does."

Sage looked so defeated, so small, that Maura did what she should have done in the first place, what she *would* have done if she hadn't been reeling from the concussive grenade her daughter had just thrown in her lap. She leaned across the desk and wrapped her arms around Sage.

Her daughter smelled of wool from her sweater and watermelon-scented shampoo. When Sage was first born and they were living in the little apartment above String Fever she had rented from Katherine, Maura used to hold her daughter for hours, her face buried in her neck as she savored the scent of baby powder and breast milk and a world of possibilities.

"You're not mad?" Sage asked.

She hugged her more tightly. "No, honey. How could I be? I would be the world's worst hypocrite to yell at you about an unexpected pregnancy, wouldn't I? I just wish you had told me."

In her ear, Sage sniffled a little, which made Maura sniffle as well. Sage eased away to grab a tissue from the box on her desk and handed one to Maura too.

"I've been trying to figure out the best way to tell you," she admitted. "I just… With everything I've been dealing with—Jack and working here and my online classes—it just seemed easier to put it out of my head. I guess I figured I would deal with everything later."

She had vivid memories of having the same instinct. For a long time after she finally figured out she was pregnant with Sage, she had wanted nothing more than to hide in her bed with the covers over her head and pretend none of it was real, that Jack was still there, that she wasn't pregnant, that she wasn't alone and terrified.

"You can't do that, not when you have a pregnancy to consider. Deal with everything later, I mean. Somebody else is now depending on you to make sure you're filling your body with proper nutrients and doing everything you can for a healthy baby. Are you taking prenatal vitamins?"

Sage nodded and tucked her hair behind her ear. She looked impossibly young for this conversation. "The clinic doctor prescribed them for me, and I've really been trying to eat better since I found out. I also made an appointment to follow up with a doctor over in Telluride to start on all the prenatal visits. It's next week. Now that you know, would you…could you come with me?"

"Yes. Of course." Maura squeezed her daughter's hand. "I'll do whatever you need."

"Thanks, Mom. That…means a lot."

How much more stress could she endure in a month? First having Jack come back, then Sage leaving school and now this, all on top of the grief that seemed her constant companion.

"I know you said you didn't want to talk about it, but have you told the baby's father?"

"No. I haven't talked to him since…that night. I told you, it was a one-time thing. Nothing serious."

Again she felt constrained from offering advice in this arena. How could she tell Sage she shouldn't withhold this information from the child's father when Maura had done just that for twenty years?

She glanced at the closed door. "What about your, uh, Jack?" For a crazy, fleeting moment, she wished desperately that he were here to help her know what to say, how to respond. Theoretically they were supposed to be a team now.

She hadn't wanted him back in Sage's life, but since she couldn't change that now, it seemed only fair that he help her face this now, after twenty years when she had to shoulder every crisis on her own.

With inordinate care, Sage wrapped her mostly uneaten sandwich and tucked it back into the bag. "I haven't told him yet. I wanted to tell you first. I thought that was only right. I mean, I like Jack and everything but…it's different than my relationship with you. I still barely feel like I know him. I'm not quite sure how to sit down with him and say, *hey, looks like history is about to repeat itself. Funny, isn't it?*"

But Sage would eventually have to face her father with the news, no matter how difficult. Maura's heart ached a little, remembering well the strain of knowing she was disappointing so many people who had different expectations for her.

"My family was here for me when I was pregnant with you, Sage. My mom was a pillar of strength, and my older sisters were wonderful. They all backed me up and supported me. Even Riley. Rumor had it he got in a fight at school once when somebody called me a particularly nasty word."

She didn't feel compelled to add that Riley was always on the lookout for any excuse to fight in those days. That wasn't the point anyway.

"I hope you know I love you. Nothing will change that. I'm…concerned about the difficulties ahead of you and the choices you'll have to make, but I love you and trust you to do what's best for you and the child."

"Thank you. Thank you so much." Sage sniffled again and wiped at her eyes with the tissue. "Sorry. You know I'm not usually such a baby, but lately it seems like I cry at everything."

"It's the hormones. Get used to it. You've got twenty-something weeks to be an emotional wreck."

"I've been so worried about telling you. I thought you would yell and scream and tell me what an idiot I've been."

"We've got time for that too," Maura said with a wry smile.

Sage smiled back, and Maura was happy to see much of the tension she had sensed in her daughter over the past few weeks seemed to have seeped away. "I just never thought you'd be so…cool about this."

There she was being cool again. This was definitely an Academy Award–caliber performance. Apparently these past months of pretending she had her life together had given her serious acting skills useful in other areas of her life.

She wasn't *cool* with her daughter's unwed pregnancy. She was sick, physically sick. Sage had such natural talent for architecture. Jack had told her so, and he would know. Sage had dreams and goals for her future, and Maura didn't know how any of those were attainable now, with another life to consider.

CHAPTER TEN

"THANKS AGAIN FOR coming with me, Mom. I didn't think I needed moral support, but now that we're here, I'm so glad you came."

"So this is it?"

"I think so. Aspen Ridge. He's in unit twelve."

The town-house development was one of the more luxurious in Hope's Crossing, all glass and cedar and river rock, set on an exquisitely landscaped sprawl of land that provided a beautiful view of the town and the mountains beyond.

How was he adjusting to living here? Was it difficult for him to look out that picture window toward Silver Strike Canyon, a vivid reminder of all the reasons he had left?

She pulled into a visitor parking lot near his town house. "Are you sure you don't want me to wait in the car?"

"Do you mind coming in?" Sage asked.

Yes. She really didn't want to be part of this conversation with Jack. Sage was here to tell her father about her pregnancy, an embarrassing discussion for any girl, not to mention one who hadn't known her father existed a little over a month ago.

Maura preferred to stay right here instead of having to face him with the inevitable awkwardness. How could it be anything else? *She* hadn't told Jack about her own pregnancy. How weird was it to find herself here with Sage while their daughter told him *she* was pregnant?

"I don't mind," she lied. "I'm here, aren't I?"

"Thanks, Mom." Sage smiled nervously and Maura reminded herself this wasn't about her. It was about Sage and her fledgling relationship with Jack. "I thought about waiting until tomorrow at work, but after his text this morning while we were at breakfast it just seemed like a sign that I shouldn't procrastinate something so important. I'll feel better when it's done, right?"

"Have I told you how proud I am for the way you're facing all of this? I know telling Jack is going to be hard, just as it was rough when you told your grandmother last night, but you're confronting it head-on and trying to make the best of it. It's exactly the right way to handle this."

"Thanks, Mom."

Sage still seemed reluctant to open the door, and Maura made sure it was unlocked, then opened her own. Though the day was mild for early February, the outside air rushing in was still much colder than her climate-controlled vehicle interior, and she shivered a little but forced a smile anyway.

"You'll do fine. What's the worst that could happen?"

"He could shove me out the door and tell me he doesn't want anything to do with me. I mean, come on. What father wants to find out his daughter is knocked up?"

Maura tried not to think very often about her own father, who had betrayed and abandoned his family to pursue his own dreams. When she had found she was pregnant, James McKnight had been so self-involved, so entranced with his new life as a fancy-free bachelor and award-winning archaeologist, that he hadn't seemed to care about the lives of any of his children. She could count on one hand the number of times he had even *seen* Sage before his death.

"Jack seems like a decent guy. I haven't had much to do with him since he came back—but that alone should be proof. He's here, isn't he? Despite his personal feelings about Hope's Crossing, he came back for you, to establish a relationship with you. I don't think he's going to shove you out the door, not when he has made such an effort to make sure that door is in the same general vicinity as you."

Sage nibbled her bottom lip, looking about ten years old again. "I guess you're right. He didn't *have* to move back to Hope's Crossing and open an office here. I figured out the first day I worked for him that everything we're doing here in town probably could have been done more efficiently from San Francisco."

"Right. He's here for you, and I don't think this pregnancy will change that. You need to trust him now more than ever."

Sage sighed. "Even though I know that intellectually, it doesn't make telling him any easier."

Maura forced another smile. "You'll do fine. Come on. Let's get this over with. Rip off the Band-Aid and all that."

"Thanks, Mom."

Sage finally opened her SUV door and climbed out, then headed past snow-covered ornamental pine trees toward Jack's town house. Maura followed more slowly, making her way carefully up the curving path. The temperature was still cold but above freezing for a change, one of those teaser days that made her long for spring.

Sage waited until she reached her on the doorstep before she rang the bell, then tucked her arm in the crook of Maura's elbow as if they were taking a casual stroll along the parkland trail that ran parallel to Sweet Laurel Creek.

They stood that way, arm in arm. The two of them

against the world, as it had been from the moment she was born and again the past year since Layla died.

Jack answered the door in jeans and a casual tan shirt with the sleeves rolled up to his forearms. He had reading glasses on, and his wavy dark hair was slightly messy, as if he had just absently run one of those strong, long-fingered hands through it as he read.

Despite her tension, she was aware of a completely inappropriate—and unwelcome—stir of attraction. Drat the man for still twanging her strings after all this time.

"Hello. This is a surprise." He quickly removed the reading glasses and tucked them in the pocket of his shirt, and she tried not to be charmed by his embarrassment.

"We were in the neighborhood, sort of. When you sent your text, we were just finishing up brunch with Grandma up at the resort at Le Passe Montagne. Have you tried it yet?"

"I haven't."

"Well, you need to," Sage said. "It's really excellent. They have these crepes on the weekends that are just fantastic. Melt-in-your-mouth fantastic. All these weird fillings you wouldn't think would be good but are, like asparagus and sweet potatoes, truffles, artichokes. Any combination you can think of. I love the savory ones, but my favorites are the sweet. They make a blackberry crepe that is totally delish."

Sage ground to a halt as if she had suddenly remembered their purpose there. "Sorry. We're letting all your heat out. Can we come in?"

Curiosity flickered in his blue eyes, but he opened the door wider. "Of course. Please."

They walked inside and she was astonished at the size of the townhome. Most of her house could probably could fit in the great room, with it's sweeping post-and-beam ceiling and two-story river rock fireplace.

"Let me take your coats," Jack said. Sage quickly shrugged out of her fluffy parka and handed it to her father. Maura dug her curled fingers into the pockets of her wool coat, driven by the ridiculous urge to clutch it around her in some sort of feeble protection. He was waiting for her, though, his head curiously turned, and she finally pulled her arms free and handed it over.

His hand brushed hers as he took it, and a little spark jumped between them. Just a current, she knew, but his gaze seemed to catch and hold hers until she couldn't breathe. She saw a flicker of heat there, as if he were remembering their kiss too, but he turned away to hang their coats on a rack made of entwined elk antlers near the entryway.

"Sit down," he said when he returned to them, and gestured to the rustic leather sofa and chairs arranged in front of the fire.

Sage took one edge of the sofa and sent Maura a silent plea to sit next to her. She couldn't ignore it, as much as she might have wanted to pick a chair halfway across the room, away from Jack.

Sage reached for her hand. Her fingers were trembling and Maura squeezed them for support and comfort.

"We don't want to bother you. You're probably working, aren't you?" Sage said.

"Just trying to catch up on a couple of projects. It's fine."

"Well, we won't stay long." She was silent for several beats while Jack continued to watch them curiously. Finally Maura squeezed her fingers again, and Sage drew in a sharp breath.

"I…need to tell you something. That's why we're here. I should have told everyone earlier but, well, everything has been so crazy. I just… I needed to figure things out on my own first."

Alarm replaced the curiosity in his eyes. "What is it? Are you okay?"

The concern in his voice and expression touched something deep inside Maura. He hadn't intended to be a father, but she couldn't deny he was trying hard here to do the right thing by Sage and seemed to genuinely care for her.

"I am. I will be, anyway. No, I am." She curled her fingers in Maura's.

"You're worrying your father," she said gently. "It will be easier if you just tell him."

Sage sighed. "This is hard. Really hard. But you'll, uh, figure it out soon enough. I guess I just need to come out and tell you. So… I know you've been worried about me the last few weeks and even told my mom you thought maybe I had a drinking problem."

"I didn't know what to think."

"I don't have a drinking problem or the mono or the flu or anything like that. The truth is, um, I'm pregnant."

Jack's features turned blank for perhaps five seconds, and then his eyes widened and his gaze shifted—inadvertently, she was certain—to Sage's midsection, then quickly back to her face. For once, she shared a moment of complete accord and sympathy with him. She completely understand how flummoxed he must be feeling right now.

"You're… Wow."

"I know. It's a shock for me too. It wasn't planned, obviously. And it wasn't even like you and Mom. You guys were in love and everything."

Jack met her gaze, and she felt heat seep into her face at the memory of just how desperately she had once loved him. Something flickered in his eyes, something soft and almost tender.

Oblivious to the sudden tension, Sage continued, "I wasn't even dating the guy, really. I mean, I liked him and everything but he was…is, well, seeing someone else."

This was more than she had told Maura. Apparently Jack merited a little additional information.

"But he was still willing to screw around on her with you? He sounds like an ass." His voice was hard.

"He's not. He's… We were friends and…"

"More than friends, it sounds like."

Sage's cheeks turned pink. "Well, things went a little too far, obviously."

His daughter. This young woman he had only barely discovered was now going to bring new life into the world. How the hell had his world become so complicated in a matter of weeks?

"Is he stepping up to take care of his responsibilities?"

She looked down at her hands. "I, um, haven't told him about the baby yet."

"Now, that sounds familiar." The words came out with more of an edge than he intended. Maura winced and Sage gripped her mother's hand more tightly.

"It's early days yet," Maura murmured. Her cheeks looked as pink as Sage's, and he wondered what she was thinking.

A child. His daughter, barely older than a child herself, was pregnant. Some bastard had knocked her up and walked away, leaving her alone to deal with the consequences.

This whole thing seemed like the echo of a particularly nasty nightmare.

How was he supposed to react? He didn't know the first

thing about babies or pregnancies. His only experience with either had been through a couple of his employees—a receptionist who had worked there through two pregnancies, until she was eight or so months along, and a really talented young associate who had ended up leaving to do consulting from home after the birth of premature twins.

With each pregnancy, it seemed like baby talk had taken over the office. Everybody who came in seemed to want to talk about ultrasounds and baby names and *circumcision,* for Pete's sake.

All that opulent fertility had left him more than a little uncomfortable. When the office chitchat had started to revolve around swollen ankles and breast-feeding, he had struggled to find any safe, politically correct thing he could say as the male employer that wouldn't be misconstrued. He had finally decided he would be wise to just ignore the pregnancies as much as possible.

He wasn't the employer here, though, and he couldn't ignore this. Sage was his daughter—and he had no more idea of what he should say to her than he had known what to say around the office.

He finally settled on something he thought was relatively innocuous. "Are you, uh, feeling okay?"

"Yeah. I'm feeling pretty good. I've been so tired the last few months, but I'm starting to get some energy again."

She mustered a little smile. It struck him again how very pretty she was, this child he and Maura had created together. Her smile was almost heartbreakingly sweet, with that little dimple that seemed to peek out at opportune moments.

In the next few months, her life would change completely. Did she have the first idea how very much? He wasn't sure *he* did, he just knew Sage didn't look nearly mature enough to be a mother.

"This has got to be a shock for you, right?" Her dimple peeked out again. "I mean, it's got to be weird finding out you're a father and going to be a grandfather, all in the space of six weeks. Two for the price of one."

A grandfather. Good Lord. He was only thirty-eight years old. He stared at her and then shifted his gaze to Maura, who didn't look any more thrilled about that than he was.

"It's certainly…unexpected. A baby. Wow. I'm still reeling."

"I am too, if you want to know the truth. And I've known for several weeks."

"Why didn't you say anything?"

"That seems to be the question of the hour," Maura said.

Sage sighed. "I didn't want it to ruin things between us. It won't, will it? I mean, I know everything's different now but… I would still like to continue working for you as long as I can, if you'll let me."

He frowned. "Did you think I would fire you and throw you out on the streets just because you're pregnant?"

"No. Not really. I was pretty nervous about telling you, until Mom reminded me that you came back to Hope's Crossing when you didn't want to, only because of me. She told me I needed to trust you."

"Did she?" He glanced at Maura and saw another hot tide of color wash over her cheeks. Good to know she didn't think he was a complete jerk. "Of course I want you to continue working for me. I would have to be stupid to let a thing like an unplanned pregnancy rob me of the best office manager I've ever had."

"Thanks. That means a lot to me. I just don't want things to be…weird."

He laughed roughly. "I'm not sure my life could possibly get any more weird, unless an alternate life form suddenly comes swarming out of my fireplace."

Maura and Sage laughed, and he couldn't help but notice both of them looked more at ease than they had when he let them into the house. "Thank you for coming in person to tell me this. I'm sure it wasn't easy for you."

He directed his words to Sage, but he had a feeling Maura hadn't exactly been thrilled to come to his house to break this news—yet she had stepped up and supported her daughter anyway, despite her own personal misgivings. He considered that very much a mark in her favor.

"It was totally the right thing to do," Sage answered. "Talking to you about this in the workplace somehow didn't seem right."

Wherever she had decided to tell him, he could only imagine the courage it must have taken her to face him. What had it been like for *Maura* after he'd left town, having to tell her family and her friends she was pregnant? Twenty years ago, that couldn't have been an easy task in a small town like Hope's Crossing, which could be insular and closed-minded.

The old biddies who had been so cruel to his mother, who had shunned her because of the inappropriate outbursts and wild mood swings caused by her mental illness, might be dead by now but he could still remember them clearly.

He had one particularly vivid memory of going grocery shopping at the small store on Main Street that had been the only place to buy fresh meat and produce before the chains had moved in. He would have been maybe eight or nine at the time, old enough to begin to have some awareness that his mother wasn't like the pretty women in their perfectly matched polyester pantsuits who pushed their offspring through the store sedately, not with hair-raising twists and circles that made him laugh but scared him at the same time.

Frances Redmond, a particularly cranky lady, had been working at the checkout. When Bethany finally picked out her groceries and pushed the cart to the checkout, he remembered Mrs. Redmond making snide comments about every item.

"Nuts? Bananas? Can I get you some crackers to go with the rest of your crazy-lady food?"

It seemed benign now, just somebody trying to make a stupid joke about something they feared and didn't understand, but his mother had turned red as the package of Kit Kats he had wanted, and he had realized this was one of her bad days.

"You don't know anything. I am *not* crazy, you stupid bitch," she had yelled, far too loudly, and had grabbed his arm tightly and dragged him out of the store, leaving her groceries on the belt while all the pretty ladies and their perfect children watched with horrified fascination.

Maura had faced that den of vipers on her own. The wagging tongues like Laura Beaumont and Frances Redmond and Elsie Whittaker. That must have taken great courage on her part.

Why had she stayed here in Hope's Crossing? If he had been in her shoes, he would have run as far and as fast as he could.

Hell, that's exactly what he *had* done, at the first opportunity.

Her mother would have helped her. He couldn't picture Mary Ella, his favorite English teacher, being deliberately cruel to any of her children. He was fiercely glad for that suddenly, grateful she could have someone in her corner when she was a frightened teenager.

She would do the same for her own daughter. Somehow he knew without question Maura would be a loving, supportive mother during the challenges Sage now faced with this pregnancy.

"Where are you two off to today?" he asked, suddenly loath to send them quickly on their way.

"Home," Maura answered with alacrity. "I've got laundry and grocery shopping to catch up on. Really exciting, isn't it?"

Sage wrinkled her nose. "I should do homework. I have a paper due in my ancient-history class at the end of the week."

"Feel like taking a drive with me first?" he asked on impulse. "I need to head up to the site Harry wants to set aside for the recreation center to do some measurements. I could use a couple of assistants. I actually wanted to give you a call today, Sage. That's why I texted you, to find out what your plans were."

"Oh?"

"I know you mentioned you wanted to observe a project from the outset. This might be your best opportunity."

"I would love that! My homework can probably wait until later this evening. How about you, Mom? Think you can you put off the laundry and shopping for a while to help us?"

"Do you really need two assistants? Wouldn't I just be in the way?" She was plainly reluctant to join them. "I can pick Sage up later, or you could just drop her by the house on your way back here."

Obviously she didn't want to spend any more time than necessary with him. He could understand that, he supposed, but after their kiss the other night, he was unwilling to let her slip away so easily.

"Any chance I could persuade you otherwise?" he pushed. "You've lived in Hope's Crossing a long time now. You run a business that has become one of the community gathering spots. You would have a unique perspective about the town and the people who live here."

"Oh, I don't know about that."

"Sure you do, Mom." Sage turned to him. "She's being modest. One of the reasons the bookstore survives and even still thrives in this market is because my mom has an uncanny way of knowing which books people in town are going to want to read, which coffee blends are sure to be hot, events people will fall all over each other to attend."

Maura looked both flustered and pleased at her daughter's praise, but he could still see lingering reluctance. He jumped in before she could refuse again. "That's exactly what I need. That instinctive knowledge of the town and the people who live here. To be honest with you, one of the toughest things about any new project is letting go of my own perceptions to focus on the needs of the client. I have many preconceived notions about Hope's Crossing, as you may be aware."

"Most of them wrong," she muttered.

Not all of them, though. He remembered that scene at the grocery store and a dozen more, incidents where people had shunned his sweet, troubled mother. He wasn't quite willing to forgive everyone in Hope's Crossing yet. Despite that, he would work his tail off to make sure the town and its citizens, biddies or not, had the best damn recreation center their money could buy.

"Come with us, Maura. I need to figure out what the town wants out of this project. I need you."

She scrutinized him, her gaze narrowed as if she were trying to ascertain what game he was playing. If she figured it out, he had to hope she would decide to let him in on it. He didn't quite know what was going on himself. He only knew he was still fiercely drawn to her, just as when he had been that stupid kid desperate for the peace he found only with her.

More than a week after their kiss, he couldn't forget the softness of her mouth, the sweetness of her response.

He wanted more. Foolish as he knew that was, he wanted to see if that moment outside her car had been a fluke, or if they could still generate that same kind of heat.

"I suppose I could spare an hour or so," she finally said. "The laundry will still be there tomorrow. Unfortunately. And the grocery store too, for that matter. Watching you work will be…interesting."

"Interesting? I'm not sure about that. I'll only be taking pictures of the site and a few measurements. Nothing too exciting."

"But probably better than laundry," she said.

"I guess that would depend what's in your laundry."

She laughed and shook her head, and he was entranced by her all over again. He had seen her smile too seldom since he had returned to Hope's Crossing, and a laugh was a rarity indeed. He wanted more of that too.

At the same time, now that she was agreeing to go with them, he found himself conversely uncomfortable with the idea of her observing him.

He had a sudden memory of sitting on a blanket in the canyon with her, describing in detail the judicious development he wanted to create there, homes that blended into the landscape, recreational opportunities that benefited the entire town and not only the elite who could afford exorbitant ski passes. He also suddenly remembered how heady—*erotic,* even—he had found her rapt attention.

He cleared his throat. "Just give me a few minutes to grab some supplies and my coat."

Trying to shake that seductive image, he headed quickly to his office to find his camera and a fresh battery pack for it, a sketchbook and his laser distance meter.

He thought water bottles might come in handy and headed for the kitchen to take some from the refrigerator. To his surprise, he found Sage standing at the stove, stirring something on one of the burners. Maura was nowhere in sight.

She grinned at him. "I hope you don't mind, but I found all the ingredients for cocoa in your cupboards. Even though we just had brunch like an hour ago, I thought that would taste delicious on a cold day like today. Look, I even found a thermos in the pantry!"

"I had nothing to do with that," he admitted. "I paid a service to stock the kitchen with the basics for me. I've barely even had time to look through the cupboards."

"They're really efficient, whoever you found. I've got everything I need. I just need five more minutes for the milk to come to a boil."

"Not a problem. I'm not on any kind of timetable here. Do you need help?" Not that he would be much, but it seemed only right to offer.

"No. I've got this. Why don't you go in and keep my mom company? I wouldn't let her help either."

Sage seemed determined to exert her independence at every turn. He wondered if she had been that way before her sister's death, or if that pivotal event had changed her in some fundamental way.

When he walked into the great room, he found Maura

perched on the edge of the sofa, leafing through a coffee-table book about the American West.

"This is interesting," she said when he walked in. "Did you know the only survivor of the Battle of Little Bighorn was a horse named Comanche?"

"I did not. Thanks for sharing."

She laughed a little. "What's the point of having all these fascinating books if you don't look inside them?"

"Here's the thing. All those books? The decorator picked them all. I haven't read a single one."

"Did you hire Vanessa Black with Design West Interiors? That must be why she came into the store and placed a huge order a few weeks ago. Thank you for that."

"You're welcome." He decided not to mention he had insisted to Vanessa that any books be purchased from her store, even if she could have found them cheaper somewhere else.

"Don't you think it's wrong to use books as props?"

It suddenly struck him as a pretty sad commentary on the state of his life that he hadn't had time to look at any of his own books yet—and that he had to pay someone else to create a home for him in the first place.

"I prefer to think of them as carefully chosen design elements. Who knows, I might leaf through them at some point."

"You should. You've got some great titles here. What is Sage up to in the kitchen?"

"Making hot cocoa. The old-fashioned way, apparently."

"That's how she prefers it when she has the chance."

"She's handy in the kitchen, isn't she?" More than a month since meeting Sage, he still felt as if he knew so little about her.

"She's always loved to cook. Cleaning up, now, that's

another story, but she loves creating new dishes. She and Layla used to come up with the most amazing Sunday-morning breakfasts, all while I slept in. Let me tell you, it's a little disconcerting to wake up to delectable smells filling your house when you have no idea where they're coming from."

She paused, a soft smile playing at her mouth. "I would stumble into the kitchen and find the two of them in there laughing and giggling and having a great time together."

"It sounds like they were close."

"Yes. They hardly noticed the four-year age difference between them. Layla missed Sage so much when she went to college."

He was sorry again for the grief both of them had endured at the loss of someone they had loved. Before he could say anything, Maura quickly changed the subject.

"What about you? Spend much time in the kitchen these days?"

"Hardly any," he admitted, after a pause. If she didn't want to talk about her daughter, he wouldn't pry. "I make the occasional soup and omelet, but I usually hire a meal service."

"I must tell you, Jack, I'm a little surprised you're not married. A wife seems like an even more handy accessory than a pile of coffee-table books."

"Last I checked, you can't buy one of those on Sky-Mall, though."

"That *is* an inconvenience. Can't you find a service to help you with that too?"

He was silent before he confessed to what he considered his second biggest mistake, after leaving Maura alone and pregnant here in Hope's Crossing. "I was married once for about five minutes, before she decided she wanted a little more out of a marriage than an empty chair at the dining room table."

He thought of Kari, elegant and lovely and completely the wrong woman for him at a time when he had been totally focused on building his business.

"I'm sorry."

He shrugged. "Our divorce was amicable and easy. And almost completely my fault, as you probably already assumed."

"I don't believe I said anything of the sort."

He had chosen poorly to begin with, but he hadn't handled their difficulties at all well. "You don't have to say it. I've said it enough myself. I was a lousy husband. Selfish and thoughtless and focused only on my ambitions."

"Rather like your father?"

He stared at her, caught completely off guard by the comparison. He wasn't at all like Harry. His father had been a stone-cold bastard.

"Sorry. I shouldn't have said that," she said. "I always knew your dreams were bigger than Hope's Crossing. Even if not for your feud with your father, I think I knew you still would have needed to leave in order to reach them. I'm happy for you, Jack. It's inspiring to see someone who nurtured a dream as a young man and worked and struggled and fought to make it happen. You must be pleased."

Gut-check time. He sat back in his chair. Was he pleased at his success? Yes, he enjoyed the awards and the recognition, but when was the last time he remembered feeling excited about one of his projects? Whenever he started a new project, when all the possibilities lay ahead of him, he welcomed the challenge but he always wanted more.

Before he could figure out how to answer her, Sage came in holding two thermoses. "Okay, the cocoa is finally ready.

I made two kinds, cinnamon and regular. Cinnamon's my favorite, FYI."

"Good to know." Maybe he had passed that particular gene to her. He was a sucker for cinnamon drops and cinnamon cookies. He even liked cinnamon schnapps.

As he helped the women into their coats, he reflected on his conversation with Maura. What would she say if he told her this project in Silver Strike Canyon, where he had once built so many ideas in his head, was the first thing in a long time to stir his blood and spark his creativity?

CHAPTER ELEVEN

MAURA FOUND IT fascinating to watch Jack work. Watching *Sage* take in everything Jack did with big eyes and an eager expression was even more so. Sage followed him like Puck followed her at home, writing down measurements and snapping pictures where he directed her.

Her mother used to talk about how, when her older twin sisters were learning to talk, they shared a language between them that only they seemed to understand. By the time Maura came along a few years later, her sisters had mostly outgrown it, but she could still remember they called juice *juba* for a long time and couldn't eat a pancake for years without calling it *cakee.*

As she watched Jack and Sage discuss the site, she imagined this was how her mother had felt watching her toddler daughters play—a little on the outside of their private communication and not quite sure how she fit in.

"Where is the north boundary?" Sage asked.

"Just there at the ridgeline, but beyond that it's abutted by Forest Service land," he answered. "With proper covenants and usage permits, we could possibly utilize that for a network of trails."

They were so alike, it was almost painful to watch them together, especially knowing she had kept them apart all these years.

"How big is the original property?" Sage asked.

“Three hundred acres, give or take an acre or two. It runs from the streambed on the west to that fence line on the east, then from the road to the ridgeline.”

Maura looked at the dimension of the lot, set perfectly in the trees and with a stirring view of the ski resort, farther up the canyon. “And Harry’s just *giving* it to the town?”

“As far as I understand. But don’t believe for a moment he’s doing this out of the goodness of his heart. He doesn’t have one, remember? I’m sure he’s looking for some kind of tax break.”

“Still. This is a prime building lot, don’t you think? Whatever tax break he might receive, he could probably make twenty times that by building condominiums here.”

“No doubt he has a hundred tangled ulterior motives. If memory serves, he always did. Harry’s reasons don’t really matter to me, frankly. My job, if I win the contract, is to design a recreation center that meets the myriad needs of the community.”

From what little she had seen, especially that look of naked longing she had spied in the old man’s eyes just before Harry fell in the bookstore, she couldn’t help wondering if most of Harry Lange’s motivations had to do with the man standing in front of her.

“Now that you’ve had a good look at the site, you’re welcome to wait in the warm car. No need to freeze your feet off out here in the mud while we finish surveying.” Jack must have clued in that she was feeling a little excluded by all the lingo he and Sage were throwing back and forth.

The idea of a heater was not without merit, but she could see a freshly groomed snowmobile trail that snaked off through the trees. Suddenly the idea of stretching her legs a little seemed extraordinarily appealing.

“Since you’re busy here, I think I’ll take a little walk

to gain a different perspective of the site." She gestured to the trail, clean and enticing in the pale afternoon sunlight. "I should have a good view back this way. Don't worry. I won't go far."

Jack gave her an absent nod as he and Sage set up another measurement. Neither of them seemed to pay much mind to her. She sighed a little, reminded strongly of how Sage and Layla used to collude together in the kitchen over spinach-mushroom quiche or sugar-drizzled pear cake.

She walked through the trees in a quiet hush broken only by the river down below and the occasional throb of an engine on the roadway beyond that. A few fresh inches of snow covered the packed snowmobile trail, but she wore sturdy winter boots with good tread.

The sunshine filtered through the trees in lacy patterns, and she was struck by the beauty of the bare, spindly red branches of the dogwoods against the starkness of new snow. A few pine siskins flitted among the currant bushes in search of any leftover berries, and she watched them for a moment before continuing on her way.

She needed to get out more. Maybe she ought to ask Evie if she could tag along on one of her cross-country ski excursions into the backcountry. Every time she walked outside, she was reminded of her glorious surroundings and her connection to Mother Earth.

The trail gained a little in elevation, making the way a little more strenuous. She decided to walk only as far as an interesting-shaped pine tree ahead, which made a V where two saplings had grown next to each other but sprawled out to seek sunlight in opposite directions.

Much to her chagrin, she had to pause at the top to catch her breath, even though the hill wasn't very steep. Wow. She was really out of shape. When was the last time she had gone to the gym? Before Christmas. Probably even before Thanksgiving and the onset of the holiday rush. Apparently she needed a new recreation center in town worse than anyone else.

She leaned against one of the angled trees—only for a moment, she told herself—and gazed down at the silvery river trickling through mounds of snow. Past it, she could see the roadway gleaming black in the sun.

A blue SUV came around the corner much too fast, but the driver managed to regain control and speed on down his merry way. She watched it for a moment, shaking her head at the heedless idiot.

When she turned back, her breath caught. Though it was probably a few hundred yards away at a downward angle, she saw something she should have noticed immediately.

A huge Douglas fir grew alone perhaps four feet off the roadway and had been turned into a makeshift memorial. Purple-and-pink plastic ribbons fluttered in the breeze. Around the base of the tree—just below a pale portion of the tree trunk where the bark had been scraped away ten months earlier—she could see stuffed animals, plastic flowers, a white cross, all protected from the snow by a small awning someone had erected.

Blood rushed from her face and she braced against the bent tree here to keep her balance. She hadn't realized the recreation center site was so close to the accident scene, down the canyon only a few hundred yards. She had been here, of course. After the accident, she had asked Mary Ella to drive her here, and the two of them had held each other and wept.

She drew in a breath now, unable to take her eyes away from that benign-looking tree. Her brother Riley, who had studied the accident report in great depth, had given her his solemn vow that Layla died immediately upon being thrown from the vehicle, that she didn't suffer. It was a comfort of sorts, but she couldn't help wondering if Layla had known even an instant's fear as the vehicle rolled out of control.

She didn't know how long she stood there in the ankle-deep snow, gazing across the road at the place where her world changed forever. She couldn't seem to make her feet move back down the little hill toward Jack and Sage, and so she stood listening to the resilient song of the pine siskins and the wind in the trees and the endless trickle of the river.

"Everything okay?"

She jerked her head around at the words and was shocked to see Jack standing only a few feet away. Her feet were cold, she realized. Her face was too.

"Yes. Fine. Why wouldn't it be?"

"You seemed lost in your own thoughts. I called out twice."

The heat seeping into her cheeks was almost painful against the cold. "Sorry. I was, uh, sort of meditating." A wind had risen while she stood on the hillside, and it knuckled its way under her coat. "Are you and Sage finished?"

"We wrapped things up a few minutes ago. Sage headed back to the SUV to get warm and I…came looking for you."

"You didn't need to do that. I was just about to turn back." Maybe. If she could have managed to wrench her gaze away from that makeshift shrine.

"No big deal. I needed to stretch my legs anyway." He looked over her shoulder, his gaze following the direction she had been facing. "What were you looking at?"

"Nothing." She tried to distract him by starting to head back down the trail, but Jack was no fool. Unfortunately for her.

"That's where your daughter was killed."

She sighed. At least her face probably wasn't blotchy and red and tearstained. She had cried so much these past months, she figured she had worn out her tear ducts. "Yes. I hadn't realized how close it was to the building site until I reached this spot. I…didn't come looking for it out of some morbid obsession, if that's what you're thinking."

His blue eyes seemed softer, somehow. "I wasn't thinking that at all. Even if you had come for that reason, I would find it perfectly understandable."

"Is it?" She paused. "I keep thinking I'm making progress, you know, putting my life back together. But I still feel like I'm paralyzed. Like my feet have been frozen in the snow for months and everyone else just keeps moving on around me."

He reached a hand out and briefly brushed her fingers, then dropped his hand again as if he wasn't sure whether he had the right to offer comfort. She wanted to grab his arm and hold on to the warmth as tightly as she could. "I can't even imagine the depth of your pain and what you've been through this last year."

For once, she felt comforted by someone's compassion instead of asphyxiated. "It sucks, if you want the truth. It really, really sucks. I keep expecting the pain to ease a little bit. I don't want it to, you understand, everybody has just been telling me it will. Once in a while I'll have a day that almost feels normal, you know? I'll find myself looking forward to something, and then I have to stop and remind myself Layla isn't here and I shouldn't be looking forward to anything. How terrible is that? Sometimes I have to remind myself."

He was silent and the cold wind ruffled the edges of his hair a little. "Call me crazy, but I can't imagine that a daughter who got up early with her sister to surprise you with breakfast would have wanted you to feel guilty for trudging forward with your life."

Okay, she was wrong. Her tear ducts still worked, apparently. She could feel a hot tear trickle out and she quickly brushed it away with the finger of her glove.

"Intellectually, I know you're right. Layla was life and laughter and joy. If she could see me like this, she would have dumped a handful of snow down my back and told me to get over myself. Either that, or she would have dragged me down beside her on the couch with a pen and paper and made me sit there until we came up with ten or twenty nice things we could do for someone else to shake me out of my funk."

"She sounds wonderful. I'm sorry I didn't know her."

"You would have liked her. Everyone did. She probably would have asked you where the hell you've been all these years and how you could possibly think you were good enough to be Sage's father, but eventually I think she would have liked you too."

She offered him a smile—shaky and a little lopsided, but it was the best she could manage without bursting into sobs. He gazed at her for a moment and then he muttered an oath. Before she realized what he intended, he reached out and wrapped his arms around her, tugging her against him.

She should probably resist. The thought penetrated somewhere in the recesses of her brain but, quite simply, she didn't want to. Unlikely though it might be, Jack offered warmth and strength and comfort and she wanted to soak up every drop.

She nestled her head under his chin, her arms around his waist, and he did nothing else but hold her.

Twenty years ago, she had turned to Jack for safety and comfort as well, during that crazy time after her father had walked out. He had been grieving after his poor mother had committed suicide and they had turned to each other, two lost souls looking for a little peace together. She had shared *everything* with him and had trusted him with her deepest pain.

The years since had taught her to be much more wary with that trust.

Though she wanted to stay right here soaking up the comfort of his embrace, she forced her arms from around his waist and took a step back, and then another. "I think I'm okay now. Thank you."

He studied her, those blue eyes intense and unreadable. "You're a strong woman, Maura," he finally said.

Strong? Ha. "I don't feel like it most of the time, but thank you for saying it and for allowing me to vent. Apparently I needed it. But we should probably head back to Sage."

He looked as if he wanted to say more, but he finally nodded and led the way back down the trail toward where he had parked. The wind now whistled a mournful cry through the trees and blew some of the powdery snow in cold crystals against her face.

"Did you find what you needed at the site?" she asked when the silence between them began to feel awkward.

"I think so. My brain is already spinning with ideas. There are definitely a few challenges to contend with, but that's one of the things I love most about what I do—figuring out how to work around all the obstacles to attain the vision the client and I would like for the site."

"What are some of the challenges?" she asked, mostly to hear more of his passion for his work.

He seemed only too willing to talk about it and, as they

walked through the trees, he talked to her about drainage problems and the unwieldy grade of the site.

"How will you address the issues?" she asked.

"No idea," he admitted. "But I'm sure I'll come up with something."

"Of course you will," she said, earning a look of surprised gratification from him.

When they reached the SUV, a few hard, mean snowflakes began to spew from the quickly moving iron-gray clouds. Through the window of the vehicle, they could see Sage stretched out on the backseat, her eyes closed and her cheek pressed against the leather upholstery.

"Look at her. Sound asleep," Jack murmured. He gazed at their daughter with a tenderness and affection that, absurdly, made Maura want to cry again.

"She's brilliant at sleeping anywhere. When she was six or seven, she once fell asleep in the middle of the Silver Days parade, curled up in a lawn chair right there on Main Street."

He chuckled softly at the image, and she was struck with great force by the full realization of how very much she had taken away from him. He had missed out on twenty years of Sage's life and she was beginning to wonder if her motives for not telling him about their child had been as altruistic as she had told herself.

"She looks so young."

"I know. I still can't believe she will be twenty in the spring."

"And *I* still can't believe she's pregnant. What jackass could do that to her? Look at her. She's not even out of her teens. She looks like she should still be playing with dolls."

Sage was two years older than *Maura* had been. And Jack hadn't been a jackass. He had been an angry, grieving young man looking for a little peace, and they had both found that together. If they had used a little more effective birth control, they wouldn't be standing here together looking at their sleeping daughter.

"I agree. She has a huge, bright, promising future ahead of her. I'm terrified we'll have to stand by and watch that future disappear in a puff of smoke."

"What can we do?" he asked.

The moment seemed surreal, somehow, of shared concern and cooperation for their child, and she found it both unexpected and sweet. "Right now, I'm not sure we have any power at all in this situation. I think adoption is her best option. If we present a united front on that, we might have a little more impact on her decision."

He raised an eyebrow, and the capricious sun chose that moment to peek through the clouds. "Is that what you want? For her to give the baby up for adoption?"

"Are you kidding? It would rip my heart out. But don't you think that would be best for her and the baby? Sage isn't in any place to raise a child by herself right now. How will she finish college?"

"You would know that better than anyone. You were in exactly her place."

She gazed at Sage, so pretty and bright. "I wouldn't trade a moment of my life as her mother, even those terrifying early days when I didn't have the first idea what I was doing. The first time I gave her a bath by myself without nurses or my mother there, I cried the whole time, afraid I was going to drop her or drown her or give her pneumonia or something."

She smiled a little at the memory of her own foibles and found him watching her with that unreadable expression again.

"You didn't, though."

"I didn't drown her, at least. I'm sure I made a thousand other mistakes. But you know, despite all the mistakes and the challenges and the...*pain,* being a mother has been an incomparable blessing."

She loved both of her daughters. Without them, her life would have been as sterile and cold as, well, Jack's appeared to her. "I want Sage to know the joy of being a mother, but not this way and not now. Not before she has the chance to at least *try* for the goals she's been setting since she was that little girl designing elaborate houses for her dolls."

"I'll do whatever you need. I'm here for her now too, Maura."

She smiled, finding immense comfort in his promise. Jack might have left all those years ago, but he was here now. That was the important thing. For Sage's sake, she told herself. Not for her.

CHAPTER TWELVE

"THIS WILL BE SUPER FUN. Thanks for inviting me, Mom."

Maura smiled across the String Fever worktable at Sage, making good inroads on the roast beef and arugula sandwich from the brown-bag lunch she had packed for her that morning. Maura took a bite of her own and set it back down amid the bead idea magazines scattered across the worktable.

"We live in the same house, but it seems as if we hardly see each other. And with spring finally on the horizon, I've been desperate for some new jewelry to wear. This seemed like a perfect way to kill two birds and all that. Beading and lunch with you. Two of my favorite things."

"I know, right?" Sage smiled. "I've been meaning to come over to the bookstore on my lunch, but there are some days I'm so busy I don't have five minutes free."

"Is this going to be a problem with, er, your father?"

Sage snickered. "Not at all. And have you noticed you call him *er, your father* every time you happen to mention him?"

"I hadn't noticed. Sorry. I'll try to stop."

Jack had been back in their lives for nearly three months now. Would she ever be completely comfortable with the whole situation?

Not that she had much interaction with him. His job kept him so busy, she had only seen him a few times in the past six weeks since the day when the three of them had made a visit to the recreation center site and he had held her and offered quiet comfort.

Sage swallowed a bite of her sandwich. "I wasn't complaining, just pointing it out," she said. "I think it's kind of funny, if you want the truth. He does the same thing, except he uses *um, your mother* instead."

Why would they have reason to talk about her? And why should the idea of Jack discussing her leave her flustered and off balance?

"How is Jack?" she asked, to hide her reaction.

"He's good. Great, actually." Sage dipped a carrot in the small container of low-fat ranch dressing Maura had packed knowing it was her favorite. "We're hearing good things about his chances for winning the recreation project bid."

"I'm not particularly surprised," she answered, trying to keep the dryness from her tone. "I would be more surprised if he *didn't* get it."

According to Katherine, who was on the city council, Harry Lange had told Mayor Beaumont and the rest of the council that his donation of the land was conditional on the city choosing his son's bid. Without Jack on board as the project architect, there would be no recreation center.

She would never tell Jack *or* Sage that, however. Contrary as he was—much like his father in that regard—Jack just might choose to walk away rather than give Harry something he obviously wanted. If he found out about it, Jack likely wouldn't appreciate his father pushing his weight around town on his behalf.

She had to wonder what Harry was up to, whether he was simply manipulating everyone in his own unsubtle way, or if he genuinely wanted his son to stick around Hope's Crossing so badly.

"So you're still enjoying working there?"

"Absolutely. Jack is…fantastic. He's a genius, Mom. I'm learning more from watching him work than I could from years and years of classes."

"That's great." Her answer was even mostly sincere. For Sage's sake, she was pleased to see them developing a relationship.

"If you want the truth, I still can't believe that Jackson Lange is actually my father, even after all these weeks of working with him. I studied his work in some of my early-level architecture classes and never once had any inkling he might be related to me. It still all feels so weird, you know?"

Maura couldn't argue with that. Definitely weird. "Did you see I left you another message from that Gunnison adoption attorney?"

"Yeah. Thanks. I've got a stack of attorneys I need to call back when I have more time. I'm planning to set aside a day next week. Hey, I forgot to get a drink. Can I grab you something from Claire's stash in the fridge?"

She didn't miss how quickly Sage changed the subject. She suspected Sage didn't want to talk about the adoption because she was having second thoughts. Maura had to pray that wasn't the case.

"I'll get us both something to drink. I wasn't thinking. You stay off your feet. What did you want?"

"Well, I'd really love a Mountain Dew right now, but I'd better just stick with a bottled water."

"Still staying off the caffeine?"

"Yes. Everything else has been easy. I don't smoke or drink, but the caffeine thing is going to kill me."

"You're doing great, honey. It will go by so fast, you won't even remember being without Mountain Dew for a few months."

"If you say so."

"I'll be right back."

She headed to the front of the store. Claire was just finishing ringing someone up, and Maura waited until the customer finished and headed out the door, not willing to interrupt a sale.

"Hey, can I bum a couple of bottled waters from you? We forgot to pack them in our lunch. I'll add it to your tab over at the store."

Her friend grinned. "You can have whatever you want from me as long as I can still grab my morning coffee at your shop."

"Of course. I keep the Sumatra–French roast blend just for you," she answered.

"I'm so glad the two of you scheduled the worktable today. It's great to see you together. How's Sage feeling?" she asked.

"She seems to be doing fine."

"Second trimester is such a blessing, as I remember it. I'm praying she'll have a gentle, uneventful pregnancy for the remaining months. It…might make what comes after a little easier to bear."

She was grateful for her friend's compassion—but as much as she loved Claire, she really didn't want to talk about Sage's adoption plans, especially when she hadn't come to terms with another loss herself.

"Thanks, Claire."

"Go ahead and grab a water bottle. Have you figured out what you're going to make today?"

"Maybe just some new earrings. Neither of us has a lot of time."

"I just got in some new wooden beads. Have you seen those yet?"

She shook her head. "Where are they?"

"Go grab whatever you want to drink, and I'll bring back some samples while you two finish your lunch."

"Thanks."

As at home in String Fever as she was in her own store, she headed into Claire's neatly organized office, where the minifridge was tucked under a counter. She grabbed a couple of water bottles and heard the phone ring and Claire answer it, just as the bells chimed out front, heralding new customers.

With water bottles in hand, she headed for the door of the office, then cringed for Claire's sake when she spied the newcomers out in the store.

"Hello!" sang out Genevieve Beaumont, her arm tucked into the crooked elbow of her fiancé, Sawyer Danforth.

The two of them together looked like Barbie and Ken, tall, gorgeous and perfect for each other. Gen, with her gleaming smile and classically beautiful features, always seemed to make Maura feel short and grubby, the crazy-haired naked troll in the toy box.

Claire gave Gen a practiced smile that hid any sign of the exasperation Maura knew she must be feeling. She held her hand over the phone. "Hi, Gen. I'll be with you in a minute," she said.

For more than a year now, the rest of Hope's Crossing had been forced to accommodate Gen's various wedding whims. She was Bridezilla on steroids, demanding and unreasonable and sometimes petulant as her wedding was scheduled and rescheduled. It was now less than a month away, much to the relief of all the local merchants under pressure to make sure everything turned out perfectly for Gen's marriage to Sawyer Danforth, son and heir apparent to a politically powerful Denver family.

Claire had been unlucky enough to be dragged into the wedding preparations when she had agreed to complete custom beadwork on Genevieve's gorgeous wedding dress. She had finished it beautifully—twice, actually, since the first dress had been violently destroyed by Layla and Taryn Thorne and the other teenagers involved in the car accident during their incomprehensible vandalism and robbery spree.

Maura really didn't want to talk to Gen, Charlie Beaumont's older sister. Relations between the two families had been strained, to say the least, since Charlie had pleaded guilty and been sentenced.

She slipped through the store as unobtrusively as she could manage. At least the worktable was tucked into the back corner of String Fever, the view obscured from the front by display racks. Maybe Gen wouldn't even notice them here.

Much to her dismay, she found Sage looking pale, her hands flat on the worktable as if she needed it for support.

"Here's your water. Sorry I took a little longer than I'd planned."

Her words seemed to jerk Sage out of her trance. She blinked and curled her hands into fists, then stood up so abruptly her chair nearly tipped backward. "I need to get out of here."

Maura stared. "What's wrong? Are you feeling sick."

Sage shot a look toward the front of the store, where Maura could see the happy couple looking at Claire's extensive chain collection. She shoved her arms in her coat and wrapped it around her tightly. "I just…really need some fresh air. And I should be heading back to the office. I forgot Jack wanted me to fax some papers to the San Francisco office."

"What about the earrings we were going to make?"

"I can't. Not right now. I'll… Maybe we can do it another day. Sorry. I just… I need to go."

She whirled around to the front of the store with another look that bordered on panic before she scooped up her backpack and rushed to the back door, which led her out in completely the opposite direction from the shortest route back to Jack's office.

At the sound of the slamming door, Claire looked up from her conversation with Genevieve and Sawyer, her brow furrowed. For just a moment, Maura wasn't sure how to respond. A dark suspicion took root, but she wasn't ready to look at it yet. She quickly gathered up the remains of their lunch and returned the beading magazines to the rack on the wall. They had only pulled down a few findings, and it was easy for her to return them to the displays. When she finished, she pulled on her coat and walked reluctantly toward the trio, still talking by the front desk.

She still didn't want to talk to Gen or Sawyer but also couldn't be deliberately rude to Claire by leaving without a word.

"Sorry to interrupt," she said. "I just wanted to let you know we apparently only came for the use of your table and the free water bottles. Thanks for that."

"You're not making anything?" Claire asked, clearly disappointed.

"Not today, I guess. Sage wasn't feeling well. She said she needed some fresh air."

Sawyer stiffened almost imperceptibly. She wouldn't have noticed if he hadn't been standing next to her, in all his perfectly handsome glory—at least she would find him handsome if she were the kind of woman who went for someone ten years younger and fairly plastic. Which she wasn't.

"Sage? Was that… Sage McKnight?"

"Yes. She's my daughter."

"Is she okay?"

"I'm sure she'll be fine. I'm sorry. I didn't realize you knew her."

"Oh, I don't. Not really. Well, just a little. We met at a party last summer when I was in town for a few weeks working on your dad's reelection campaign—remember that, Gen? We went to that party at the reservoir? A friend of a friend, I think, but it turned out to be mostly college students."

"Of course. Rachel Zeller's birthday party."

"Right. We were trying to get a donation out of her father so we went, but the crowd was a little young for us. Sage and I went out on the wakeboards while you were working on your tan, remember that?"

"Look at you, with your memory for names and faces. That will come in so handy when you're back in Washington, won't it?" Genevieve's smile was rather tight, Maura thought.

"Tell Sage we said hello." Sawyer gave that charming smile of his that seemed to make every female heart flutter helplessly like a moth with a singed wing, and that dark suspicion dug its claws in more sharply.

"I'll be sure to do that."

"Let me know if everything's okay," Claire said, her pretty features furrowed.

"I'm sure she's fine. Thanks, Claire. Sorry to ditch on you."

"Not a problem. That only means I'll get to look forward to having you both in again."

Claire had an uncanny way of turning any obstacle into a positive. It was pretty darn annoying sometimes.

"Right. See you later."

She walked out into the cool March afternoon and headed down the street toward Jack's office. Worry for her daughter was the reason for these butterflies jumping around in her stomach, she told herself. She was absolutely *not* nervous to see Jack again.

When she arrived at Lange & Associates, she could see through the window she had guessed correctly. Sage was sitting behind her desk staring down at her hands. She didn't even register awareness when Maura pushed open the door.

"All right, spill. What's going on?"

Sage finally looked up, her features pale and set. She blinked when she saw Maura. "Mom. You didn't have to follow me."

"You ran out of String Fever like you were about to throw up on the sidewalk. Forgive a mother for being worried for her child. Now, what's wrong?"

"Nothing. I'm just… I'm being stupid."

"Why don't you let me be the judge of that?"

"No, I am. I've been stupid for months. Everything is so messed up."

She started to cry, sloppy tears that leaked out of her eyes and dripped down her cheeks, and Maura reached for her, her heart aching for her daughter. "It's Sawyer, isn't it?"

Sage drew away a little to stare at her. She didn't answer, just let out a little sob that confirmed everything.

"Oh, honey." Maura held her closer and Sage wrapped her arms around her mother and held on as if she were five years old, afraid of the monsters under her bed.

"I know. You don't have to tell me. I'm such an idiot."

Sawyer Danforth was the father of Sage's baby. How on earth had this all become so complicated? He had been engaged to Gen for longer than a year. They were supposed to have been married last fall, but the wedding had been postponed after the accident. His family was wealthy, powerful and connected—and would not be at all thrilled at their scion for fathering an out-of-wedlock child with someone they would consider a nobody.

She could see nothing but a vast sea of heartache for her child and didn't know the first thing she could say or do to help Sage wade through it.

"Can you tell me what happened between you? Were you…dating?"

Sage sniffed. "It's not like I was in love with him or anything. Well, I thought I was, a little. But even at the time I knew how stupid that was. I mean, how can I possibly compete with Gen Beaumont? She looks like a supermodel and I'm like a Keebler Elf."

Despite her own broken heart, she had to smile a little at the imagery, so similar to her own troll comparison. "You could kick Genevieve Beaumont's skinny little butt in any kind of head-to-head competition, especially if it called for brains and personality."

For a moment, Maura thought Sage might smile at that. Though her mouth twitched a little, her eyes still looked bleak. "We all went to a birthday party this summer. Rachel Zeller, Josie's big sister. I guess she was a sorority sister of Genevieve's or something. She and Gen—and Josie, for that matter—spent most of the day lying out, working on their tans. Gen wouldn't even get in the water. I'd never been wakeboarding, so Sawyer was showing me what to do. We had a lot of fun together, but it was…nothing."

She clenched her hands together. "So we were on the

boat and we were talking about music and stuff, and he couldn't believe it when I told him Chris was my stepdad. I guess he's a big fan of Pendragon. I told him they were coming to Boulder in August, right when school started, and I could probably get him and Gen backstage."

Maura usually attended all the Pendragon concerts when they played anywhere in Colorado, but she had made an excuse for that particular one. Her relationship with Chris had been more than amicable since the divorce, but his current girlfriend struggled with their friendship, and Maura had decided she couldn't cope with the drama this year.

"Sawyer was really excited about the concert, so we exchanged emails and cell numbers," Sage went on. "We kept in touch, nothing serious, just fun. Maybe a little more flirty than we should have been, given his engagement, I guess, but we were just messing around."

She sighed. "So I got him the tickets from Chris for the concert, but it turned out Gen had something else that night. He didn't want to miss it, though, especially after I had gone to the trouble to get the backstage tickets for him, so he asked if he could hang with me. I just... We went to the concert and backstage. It was a crazy night. We hung out with Chris and the rest of the gang, and we went back to Sawyer's hotel and, well, one thing led to another, I guess."

Sage looked so miserable, Maura's heart broke all over again. "I knew he was engaged to Gen, but we had so much fun together, even before, you know. I guess some part of me thought maybe he really liked me."

"I'm sure he did."

She shook her head. "No. He used me, for everything. He left first thing in the morning. *Thanks for the fun night. See you around.* That's all he said and then he never returned any of my texts or calls. I was so *stupid*."

Sawyer was gorgeous and charming and much older than Sage. He had already passed the bar, for heaven's sake. What did he want with a nineteen-year-old girl in her second year of undergraduate work? They were not only in different social strata but completely different stages in their lives.

Maura could absolutely believe he had used Sage for whatever he could get out of her, and Sage had probably been a starry-eyed girl, overwhelmed that someone like Sawyer wanted to be with her.

"What am I going to do?" Sage whimpered.

Maura released a heavy breath. "You're not going to like this, but I think you need to tell him."

"I can't! He's getting married in a month!"

This was the reason Sage had been so evasive all these weeks when they'd pressed for the identity of the baby's father—she had to have known the storm that would result.

"I think that's exactly why you should tell him now. He has to know. It's only fair to him and to Genevieve."

If possible, even more color leached out of Sage's cheeks. "Genevieve? Why? She doesn't have anything to do with this."

"Wrong," Maura said gently. "Be fair. Wouldn't you want to know if the man you were preparing to take vows with could father a child with someone else during the engagement, when he's supposed to be head-over-heels, can't-think-of-another-woman in love with you?"

"It was just a mistake," Sage wailed. "We…he had too much to drink and he wasn't thinking. This wasn't supposed to happen."

She folded Sage's fingers in hers. They were cold and trembling and Maura wanted to tuck them against her heart and warm them. So much pain because of a few foolish moments between two young people who should have known better.

"Listen to me, Sage. You and I, we have a unique perspective on this, don't we? I can see as a woman who's been exactly in your shoes the choices I should have made twenty years ago. I should have told Jack, no matter the consequences. All my rationalizations and excuses are just that. My way of making myself feel better for my cowardice in not telling him. I regret it now, more than I can tell you. I can see now how much you needed him in your life from the beginning. If I had only had the courage, I would have told him. He may still have chosen to stay out of your life, but at least he would have had the choice. I took that from him and it was wrong—for him and for you."

She hadn't admitted that out loud before, but the words still resonated with truth—so loudly in her head that she must have completely missed the sound of the office door opening. Behind Sage she caught a flicker of movement and turned.

Jack. Of course. How much had he heard? Judging by his expression, he must have been standing there for some time. He gazed at her for a long, charged moment and she couldn't think what to say to him.

She wouldn't call her words back, even if she could. They were truth and she should have admitted it a long time ago. She had committed a grave injustice against him and she didn't want to see Sage do the same thing.

Sage hadn't noticed him. She had her face pressed to Maura's shoulder. "What's going on?" he mouthed.

"I'll explain later," she mouthed back, holding up a finger, before turning back to Sage and pressing her point. "I don't know what you're going to do about the baby, whether you plan to keep it or place it with an adoptive family. Judging from your evasiveness with the attorneys who have called, I think you're not quite sure yourself. Either way, I think you owe it to yourself, to Sawyer and to the child you both created to involve him in the decision."

"He's going to hate me. I'll ruin everything for him."

"You didn't create this mess on your own, honey. He's a grown man. He made his own choices all along the way."

"But the wedding. It's next month."

She might not particularly like Gen Beaumont—or any of her family, for that matter—but that didn't mean she wanted to ruin the young woman's wedding, which so many people had worked tirelessly to pull off.

But putting her grief aside, she knew this was the right thing. Better for Genevieve to know now than to find out after they exchanged vows that her fiancé had been unfaithful to her.

For all she knew, maybe Genevieve wouldn't care. It was no secret around Hope's Crossing that Sawyer Danforth had political aspirations even greater than his father's, who had once been the president of the state senate.

Maybe, like a good political wife in training, Genevieve knew all about any extracurricular activities—going on the logical assumption that Sage hadn't been his only indiscretion—and had chosen to look the other way.

"I don't want to," Sage said in a small voice that reminded Maura of the time Sage's appendix had burst when she was nine and she had to be rushed into emergency surgery, scared to death and fighting the whole way.

"I know, honey." She hugged her, aware of Jack standing behind Sage. "It's your choice, of course. I've told you what I think you should do, but you're an adult. You can decide to say nothing if you want."

Sage grabbed a tissue from the box on her desk and

sniffled into it. "When…when I tell him, will you come with me?"

A tremendous rush of pride burst through her. "In a heartbeat."

"Do you have room for one more?" Jack asked in a low voice. Sage whirled around and turned pink at the sight of her father behind her.

"I guess you heard."

"Only the last bit. I'm surmising you encountered the, uh, sperm donor and you're trying to decide whether to hand him a cigar."

"It's a little more complicated than that, but, yeah," Sage said.

"He's supposed to be getting married in a month to the mayor's daughter, Genevieve," Maura explained. "It's only the biggest social event to hit Hope's Crossing since the original Silver King Ball."

"Ah. I don't know how much my opinion is worth in this situation, but I agree with your mother. Telling him is the right thing to do, even though it's going to be tough and probably ugly."

Sage sighed. "Why does everything have to be so *hard?*"

"If doing the right thing were easy, wouldn't everybody just naturally do it?" Maura said.

Her daughter didn't seem to appreciate that bit of maternal wisdom, but Jack smiled a little.

"I guess we should get it over with. Find him tonight while I can still manage the nerve."

"Do you want me to make a few calls?" Maura offered. "I can at least find out if he's staying at the Beaumonts or at one of the hotels while he's in town."

"No. I still have his number, unless he's changed it. I'll try to text him. Ask if I can meet him somewhere. I'd rather tell him without Genevieve there at first. Then he can decide whether to tell her or not."

Maura wasn't sure she agreed with that, but she had meant her earlier words—Sage was an adult and could make her own decisions about how to handle the situation.

CHAPTER THIRTEEN

"READY OR NOT, I guess." Sage opened the passenger door of Jack's SUV and a rush of cold air flowed inside from the wind tunnel created under the porte cochere at the sprawling Silver Strike Lodge.

"Are you sure you don't want us to go inside with you, honey?" Maura leaned up from the backseat, where she had insisted on sitting so Sage could take the front seat next to him. Her features were twisted with worry as she watched their daughter.

Sage tucked a stray hair tossed by the wind back behind her ear. "I really think it would be best if I go the rest of the way by myself. It means a lot to me that you both came this far. I'm not sure I could have made it here on my own, but I think I should talk to Sawyer first alone."

Jack wished he could make this easier for her. Was that a universal parental sentiment, this desire to make the world straighten itself out around his child so her path was always smooth and even? Intellectually, he knew that was not only impossible but would create someone unable to cope with life's inevitable challenges, but that didn't stop him from wanting to ease her burden.

"I'll find a parking space and we'll wait in the lobby for you, okay?"

"You really don't have to do that. I can call you when I'm done and you can just tell me where you parked."

"We'll be waiting for you in the lobby." He spoke almost sternly, determined to do this, at least. He hadn't been here through most of her life and all the other tough things she'd had to deal with, especially losing her beloved little sister. He wouldn't let her down now that he had the chance to offer support in whatever small way he could manage.

"Thanks, you guys." After a pause, she leaned into the car and kissed him on the cheek, then did the same to Maura.

"I'm sure I'll be out soon. I mean, come on. How long does it take to ruin a man's life?"

She gave them both a quick, nervous smile, then closed the door, squared her shoulders and walked into the lobby.

If Maura hadn't been there, Jack probably would have pounded his fist on the steering wheel. At the very least. "Damn it. Why won't she let us go with her? I'd like to have a word or two with the son of a bitch myself."

"Maybe that's why she insisted on talking to him by herself at first. She didn't want you pulling the outraged father act."

"I *am* outraged. It's no act. The man is twenty-six years old. He's a full-fledged adult. She's not even twenty yet and as green as a field of clover, a vulnerable kid dealing with loss and uncertainty. He had no business messing with her."

Maura touched his arm, just a soft brush of her fingers, and some of his wild anger seemed to ease away. "She's knows what she's doing. Let her handle this her way, okay?"

"What else can we do? She's a stubborn thing."

"I'm afraid she gets that from both of us. Poor girl was doomed from the beginning."

He smiled a little. While he was tempted to use the valet parking, he had the feeling Sage might want a quick getaway when they were done, and wouldn't want to wait out in the cold for the valets to find his car, so instead he pulled a short distance away to the parking lot.

Maura was quiet as he opened the back door for her and reached a hand to help her out. "Careful. It's icy," he said, and maintained his hold on her arm, telling himself it was only out of concern for her safety.

After a pause, Maura pulled her arm away but slipped her hand into the crook of his arm for more stability. Despite his lingering worry for Sage and his sharp anger at Sawyer Danforth for being the catalyst for everything Sage was going through, a sweet tenderness seeped through him at this small indication of her trust.

The night was clear and beautiful. The mountains soared overhead, commanding and powerful. He had forgotten how vivid the stars could be up here. Even with the ambient light from the resort and all the development around it, he could see their vast, glittery pattern overhead.

None of this was here in his memories. His mother often used to paint the meadow that had been here. In the summer it would be filled only with flowers and birds, the occasional curious mule deer. He could clearly remember playing in the grasses, confident in the knowledge that she was nearby.

Now it was a cramped parking lot. Amazing what changes twenty years could render.

"Looks like the lodge is doing a good business this weekend."

He glanced down at Maura. "You sound surprised."

"The resort keeps the ski lifts running until April, usually, but business slows down once March hits. The shoulder season will be here before we know it."

"How much of your business is tourist dependent?"

"Not as much as you might think. The locals make up

about seventy to eighty percent of our customer base. When the skiing is lousy, though, it still hurts all of us on Main Street."

"Good thing it's not lousy very often."

She smiled. "That's both the beauty and the curse of living here in the high Rockies. We can pretty much count on snow from October to April."

They walked in silence toward the lodge for a few moments. The building loomed above them, big and commanding and oddly elegant. It reminded him of one of the old national park lodges, with the dark pine and soaring glass windows.

"Have you had a chance to try any of the restaurants up here yet?" Maura asked. "They're all very good."

He shook his head. "Want to know something funny? This is actually the first time I've even seen the lodge."

Her eyes widened. "Seriously? You've been back in Hope's Crossing for months. Weren't you at all curious in that time about what your father has done up here?"

"Not really." The scent of her, lemony and sweet, drifted to him and he was strangely comforted by her presence and by the heat of her brushing against him as they walked. "I didn't need to see it. I knew whatever had been done up here wasn't at all what my mother intended when she left the land to me."

His mother had been a direct descendant of Alice and Harvey Jackson, who along with the Van Durans had been the original silver barons here. Bethany had been the *last* descendant, actually, of her generation. When she gave birth to him, *he* had become the last descendant. Now that honor went to Sage, he supposed.

Even when her family had lost most of their wealth after the silver mines played out, the Jacksons, unlike the Van

Durans, had managed to hang on to most of their land and had even managed to buy more. As a result, his mother had inherited thousands of acres up here, where the original mines had once dotted this canyon.

Bethany had left the land in trust to him, but Harry and William Beaumont had conspired together to break the trust, claiming his mother's undeniable mental illness had left her unfit to make those decisions for herself before she committed suicide. The land rightfully should have gone to her husband, not to a teenage boy, Harry had successfully argued in court.

That final betrayal from his father after a lifetime of distance and disappointments had been the last straw for Jack. Driven by fury and pain and a vast, aching helplessness, he had walked away from Hope's Crossing for good.

Only recently was he beginning to realize all he had left behind.

"It's not as terrible as you'd feared, is it?" Maura asked. "At least we don't have any Las Vegas–style casinos right in the middle of town."

"No. It's actually quite…pleasing." It was a grudging admission but he meant it.

"I've always thought so. For all his faults, I can't deny that Harry has pretty good taste. For what it's worth, he's also the one who insisted on the zoning restrictions that help the downtown maintain its historic flavor instead of turning everything into strip malls and big-box stores."

He didn't want to hear anything good about his father. As far as he was concerned, Harry was a cheat and a liar and had manipulated and schemed his way to defrauding his own son.

The doors opened soundlessly for him, and he and Maura walked into the lobby, dominated by a massive fireplace and hanging ironwork chandeliers that probably weighed as much as his SUV. The Silver Strike Lodge—named for the original mine—apparently appealed to a well-heeled crowd, judging by the designer après-ski apparel worn by those in the lobby.

"Speak of the devil. Your father is here, just to give you fair warning," Maura said in a low voice.

He jerked around in time to see Harry walk out of what looked like a steak house off the lobby, along with a couple of men who had the same well-fed look of prosperity.

"Warning duly noted."

"I don't mind waiting alone for Sage here in the lobby if you want to get out of here. You could wait out in your car."

He raised an eyebrow. "I'm a grown man. You really think I need to run away from my father?"

"Wouldn't be the first time."

Oh, ouch. He winced a little as the arrow hit home. No doubt that was just how she saw things—that he had chosen to leave instead of sticking around to fight for what had rightfully been his. If only the whole situation had been that simple, but he had been an eighteen-year-old kid with no power, influence or money to hire the huge team of attorneys it would have taken to defeat Harry.

He had tried to convince somebody to take on his case on its merits, but nobody in the entire county—or the next, or the one beyond that—had been willing to go up against Harry and his consortium, especially when the developers had started to break ground only minutes after the judge broke the trust.

Beyond that, Jack had finally decided his mother's memory had suffered enough through the judicial system. Harry had trotted out every single diagnosis, every manic episode, every delusion as fodder.

By the time his attorneys were done, all of Bethany's actions had appeared insane to everyone in that courtroom. Including him. Instead of the sweet, funny, creative soul he remembered, who used to take him up into these mountains to hunt for blackberries and pick wildflowers and identify birds, Harry had tainted Jack's own picture of his mother.

He hated his father for that more than for taking the land.

"I think he saw us. He's coming this way."

Despite himself, he was amused at Maura's exaggerated stage whisper. She always used to make him laugh, he remembered, even when his life had seemed completely miserable.

"Quick. Maybe we can duck down and hide behind the sofa," he stage-whispered back.

She frowned but didn't have time for a sharp retort before Harry joined them.

"This is a surprise. Are the two of you dining at the lodge tonight?"

Jack's spine stiffened and he felt the hot rush of adrenaline churning through him, as if his body was gearing up for a fight. His reaction annoyed the hell out of him, but he supposed it was no different than a person instinctively brushing away a fly. What *did* surprise him was the realization that Maura had come to stand next to him, shoulder to shoulder. He glanced down and found her giving Harry a look that reminded him of her little dust mop of a dog going to battle against a mountain lion.

"We're waiting for our daughter," he answered. "She had a matter of…business to discuss with one of your guests."

Harry pursed his lips. "Rumor has it she's pregnant."

Beside him, he could feel Maura tense, but he couldn't see any good in lying to Harry. No doubt he already knew more about the situation than Jack did. "For once, the grapevine has it right."

"She have any plans to marry the father?"

"Absolutely not," he and Maura said in unison. When he met her gaze, he thought he saw a little spark of laughter in her eyes before they both turned back to Harry.

"Of course not. Nobody gets married these days," Harry muttered. Jack waited for him to make some kind of asinine comment in the mode of *like mother, like daughter* so he could deck him, but Harry wisely refrained.

"I would like to get to know this young lady. She is my granddaughter, after all. You—" He turned to Maura. "Bring her to my house tomorrow for dinner."

"I'm afraid we have plans tomorrow." She'd answered calmly enough, but Jack was suddenly completely convinced she was lying.

"Then Sunday evening around six. You may come as well," he told Jack peremptorily, then turned and walked away before either of them had time to come up with another lie.

Jack stared after him, shaking his head. "You know you really don't have to go," he said to Maura. "Contrary to popular belief—especially his own—he's not lord of all he surveys."

She shrugged. "It probably won't be *completely* miserable and I'll probably be hungry anyway around then. If it means I don't have to cook, then, yay."

"I would be willing to cook for you if that's the only way you'll agree to go."

"I thought you could only fix omelets and cheese sandwiches."

"Maybe, but they're delicious omelets and cheese sandwiches. Better than the swill you could probably get from Harry's Cordon Bleu–trained chef."

She smiled. "Don't ever tell him this, but I've been dying to see the inside of that mausoleum of his. Word has it he owns a dozen original Sarah Colville paintings, and nobody ever sees them but Harry. That's just criminal. Sarah has a vacation home here in Hope's Crossing and I've been a huge fan for years."

"Okay. How about this? You take Sage and enjoy your French feast and the priceless art, and then afterward you can come to my place and tell me all about it while we roast marshmallows in my fireplace?"

"You never mentioned roasting marshmallows was another culinary skill."

"I like to keep a woman guessing. Save a few impressive accomplishments in reserve, just in case."

She laughed outright at that, and he was completely entranced by her. "An enticing offer indeed, but I'm going to have to regretfully decline. If *I* have to go have dinner with Harry, *you* have to go."

He sighed. Yeah, he was afraid of that. He could imagine few things more miserable than sharing a meal and being forced to make conversation with the old bastard.

On the other hand, he and his father had been circling around each other like a couple of bull elk on either side of a meadow since he'd arrived back at Hope's Crossing, each waiting for the other to charge first so they could tangle antlers.

"Well, maybe Sage will decide she wants nothing to do with Harry, and we'll both be off the hook," he suggested.

Maura shook her head. "Nice try. I would think you know our daughter better than that by now."

Our daughter. He was pretty sure that was the first time

she had ever said those words together. How could a couple of simple words leave him breathless?

"I guess we're stuck then," he said, his voice a little raspy.

She flashed him a look, and he saw something warm flicker in her gaze before she looked away. "Don't worry, Jack. I'll hold your hand and help you through it."

She was flirting with him, he realized through his shock. He wasn't even sure she was aware of it.

"I'll hold you to that," he answered, beginning to think he, at least, was caught by much more than the prospect of dinner with his father.

HARRY WALKED THROUGH the lobby of the lodge, his heart pounding in his chest—not the scary, call-the-paramedics kind of pounding. This was something he wasn't very accustomed to—anticipation, joy and an aching regret for the years he had lost through his own greed.

Every time he saw Jack, the yearning to permanently have his son back in his life ate away at him like a lousy case of acid reflux. As far as he could tell, Jack still wanted nothing to do with him. Could he blame him? Harry had made stupid choices twenty years ago, had picked power and influence over what was right, and now he was paying the price for his shortsightedness.

He was alone and had discovered in recent years he didn't like it one damn bit.

He didn't like thinking about how very afraid he had been after his heart attack, lying in that hospital room by himself and knowing that there was not one single person who cared whether he lived or died, except maybe his attorneys. Even they would probably prefer their commission managing his estate to actually having to deal with him.

The way things stood, Jack didn't want to allow Harry back into his life. So Harry would just have to knock all those obstacles out of his way and earn his way back in, whatever it took.

He headed for the elevator toward his owner's suite on the top floor of the lodge. Though he had a home not far from here, the biggest private residence for twenty square miles, tonight he couldn't face the echoing emptiness of it. He pushed the button for his floor, grateful nobody else came in to force him into conversation right now. He might not enjoy being alone, but that didn't mean he was gung ho to talk to a bunch of idiots, just for the sake of hearing another human voice.

To his chagrin, the elevator stopped at the third floor. The doors swung open, and a young woman in a bulky parka walked in and quickly turned around to face the front, but not before he saw her face, blotchy and red, and identified her.

His granddaughter.

He knew all about Sage McKnight. Since the moment he had learned she was his granddaughter in that bookstore, he had made it his business to discover everything he could about her, from her interest in astronomy, to her first boyfriend in high school, to what she got on the SATs. He knew she was an architecture student in Boulder and that, since Christmas, she had been working as Jack's office assistant.

What he *didn't* know was why she was so upset.

"What's wrong?" he asked, instantly on alert. He might be an old man with a bad ticker, but he could still kick some serious ass.

She turned slightly and he saw recognition in her eyes, which were huge and bruised-looking in her delicate face. "What are you doing here?"

"It's my hotel. What's wrong?" he repeated, hitting the emergency-stop button.

She closed her eyes and sagged against the wall of the elevator. "It's just been a really shitty day and I want to go home. Do you mind starting this thing again?"

"Who hurt you?"

Her laugh was hoarse and ragged around the edges. "I got myself into this mess. I can't blame anybody else. Do you mind?" She shot a pistol finger at the control panel.

He hit the emergency button again to start the elevator up. "I've got an apartment here. You look like you could use a drink."

She placed two hands on her abdomen, pressing her shirt down and showing off the bulge there. "I'm knocked up, Gramps. Not to mention that I'm still underage. But thanks for the gesture."

Gramps. She'd called him Gramps. He found the nickname particularly abhorrent but not the sentiment behind it. "Come on up anyway. I can get you a glass of water and you can wash your face, get a tissue. Whatever you need."

"Are you saying I'm a wreck?"

"I didn't say that. I only wondered if you wanted a drink of water."

She swiped at her cheek with a rough chuckle. "It's a nice offer, but my parents are waiting downstairs."

"I know. I just spoke with them. They can wait a few more minutes for you to pull yourself together. A Lange would rather die than show weakness."

"Nice. You have that embroidered on a pillow somewhere?"

"Not yet. Maybe you can stitch something up and give it to your kindly old grandfather for Christmas."

She snorted a little, and he was glad to see some color

had returned to her cheeks. "Yeah, all right. I could use a few minutes to gather my thoughts. And I really need to pee. That's one of the worst things about being pregnant. I can't be more than ten feet from a bathroom."

Information he didn't need, thanks, but he wasn't going to argue. He swiped his card and the elevator door opened into his penthouse suite. She looked around, but he didn't see any hint that the grandeur of the place impressed her in the slightest.

"So where's the bathroom?"

"Down the hall. First door on the right."

"Thanks."

While she was gone, he headed into the kitchen and tried to see if he had anything in the Sub-Zero refrigerator suitable for a pregnant teenager. He settled on a bottled water, but then had second thoughts and thought she might enjoy a soothing cup of tea.

The fool housekeeper usually kept an assortment for his rare guests, but where the hell did she store it? He rummaged through the cabinets and finally found a clever little basket by the spice rack he didn't know he had.

One thing he *did* know he had was a hot-water dispenser at the sink that produced near-boiling water in an instant. A moment later, he had a tea bag steeping in a cup.

He met her in the living room and handed it to her. "Here you go. It's lemon balm tea. Supposed to be soothing."

"Thanks." She sat down on the edge of the sofa and held the mug between her hands. "I suppose you're curious about why I look like I just walked into poison ivy."

"No. Not really," he lied. He had a feeling keeping the mood light might set her at ease. Sure enough, she laughed roughly.

"Yeah. It's a girl thing. You wouldn't want to know."

He waited a beat, wondering what to say yet terrified that, if he said nothing, she would find the silence too uncomfortable and would leave.

"I just told my baby's father about the pregnancy," she finally blurted out. "It…wasn't pleasant."

"Oh?" he kept his tone low and nonthreatening, as if she were a stray kitten he was trying to lure with a bowl of milk.

"Needless to say, he's not throwing a parade down Main Street. He's got a girlfriend. A fiancée, actually. She doesn't know anything about what happened with us, and he doesn't want to tell her."

Now that she had started, she didn't seem to want to stop. "It was…ugly. He doesn't believe me. Said there's no way he can be the father. We used protection, FYI. I was a virgin, not an *idiot.* But I guess it failed, because, you know, here we are."

Again, too much information, he wanted to tell her, but he couldn't interrupt the flow of words that seemed to be gushing out of her like air from a ripped balloon. "He accused me of getting pregnant on purpose to extort money from him and his family. As if I want or need his stupid family's money. He even had the nerve to accuse me of staging the whole thing. The concert tickets, the backstage passes, all of it was apparently designed so I could get him to be my baby daddy and ruin his wedding next month. Can you believe it?"

"Did he threaten you?" he asked, his voice deadly calm.

He knew just who she had to be talking about. He made it his business to know who was staying in his hotel and, as far as he could tell, only one person fit the bill. Sawyer Danforth. Hell, he'd just had dinner with the bastard's future father-in-law.

"He didn't hurt me. Just yelled and threw things around like a two-year-old having a tantrum. I can't believe I ever liked him enough to, well, you know."

Right now he didn't want to think about *you know* in connection with the granddaughter he had just discovered. Instead, he sipped at the one drink a day he allowed himself and tried to figure out how he could kick Sawyer Danforth out of his hotel on his bony, privileged little ass.

"I've ruined his life, apparently. He wants me to get an abortion, even though I'm five months along already."

"What are you going to do?"

"Not get an abortion. That's for sure." She finally sipped at the tea and apparently liked it well enough to take a second sip, which gave him a completely ridiculous sense of accomplishment.

"I don't know what I'm going to do yet. That's the question of the hour, isn't it? Am I keeping the baby or giving it up for adoption? It's a little more weighty decision than trying to figure out whether to take Math 1060 this semester or put it off until my junior year."

"True."

She sighed. "Well, anyway, it's done. I told him. My mom and Jack were certain it was the right thing to do, but now I'm not so sure. It might have been better if he didn't know."

"If you decide to keep the baby, you don't need his help, do you? Your mother did an okay job raising you by herself."

She sipped at the tea again. The longer she sat quietly on his sofa, the more tension seemed to seep from her shoulders, he was happy to see. "I'm not my mother. I love her like crazy, but I don't think I'd be happy here in Hope's Crossing going to playdates and PTA meetings. I want all that, sure. But not yet. Not until I've had a chance to do a few other things first."

Either way, she was going to hurt, all because of a few foolish moments with the wrong person. Life was nothing but pain. If he had learned anything the past year, simply by opening his eyes to the world around him, it was how helpless one person can feel trying to hold back that unrelenting tide of sorrow.

"You'll figure it out. You're a smart girl."

She made a rude sound. "How would you know? You don't know anything about me."

He decided not to tell her just how much he had learned about her. She might think it was creepy, not just an old man intensely curious about this unexpected progeny.

"It's in your genes. You're my granddaughter, aren't you?"

"Well, I can't exactly be *too* brilliant. I got myself into this mess, didn't I?"

"And you'll come up with a plan to deal with it. That's what you and your father both do. You plan and plot and figure out the angles. It's why you're going to make one hell of an architect, just like he is."

She cocked her head, squinting at him, and he wondered just how much he had revealed with that particular statement.

"I hope so. I better go. My parents are probably ready to call hotel security to go look for me. Uh, thank you for the tea. And the conversation. They both helped."

"You're welcome. Anytime. And I mean that."

She blinked a little, then gave him a tentative smile that seemed to arrow straight to his damaged heart. "Okay. Thanks. I might take you up on that."

He rose, grateful his almost seventy-year-old bones hadn't creaked too loudly, and walked her to the elevator, wishing he knew how to protect this vulnerable, wounded child and take away the pain he knew was coming.

"If you want me to, I can kick Sawyer Danforth out of his room right this minute and bar him and his snooty parents from ever staying at my lodge."

Her jaw dropped and her eyes filled with horror. "How did you… I never said it was Sawyer."

"Didn't you hear what I said about good genes? You're not the only smart one in this family, missy. I know what's going on in my own hotel."

He regretted saying anything when her shoulders went tight again and she gazed in panic at the elevator and then back at him. "You can't say anything. Please!" she begged. "He said he was going to tell Genevieve himself when the time is right. If word gets out to her before he has the chance, he's going to be so pissed."

It would serve the little prick right for not keeping his business in his pants. He didn't care about hurting Danforth, but he didn't want to cause his granddaughter any more distress. "I can keep my mouth shut," he promised. That didn't mean he couldn't drop a hint in his housekeeper's ear about putting the scratchiest sheets on his bed and substituting his shampoo for itching powder.

"Thanks. Thanks a lot."

"In return, you can do something for me."

She instantly looked wary. "What?"

"I invited your parents and you to dinner at my house on Sunday. I doubt either of them is inclined to accept that invitation. You can make sure they do."

"The rumors are true, then. You *are* a crazy old man. How am I supposed to do that when Jack hates you and you're not on my mom's list of favorite people either?"

"You're a smart girl," he repeated as the elevator doors

opened. "Lange genes, remember? I'm sure you'll think of something."

She shook her head in exasperation, but to his eternal shock, she stepped out of the elevator and kissed him on the cheek.

"Thanks for the tea and sympathy," she said, then slid back inside just as the doors closed behind her.

He stood for a long time gazing at the elevator with a finger pressed against the skin she had kissed, feeling foolish that he thought he could still pick up the scent of her in the air, of lemons and tears.

His granddaughter needed him, damn it. And her parents did too, for that matter. He had become very good at subterfuge this past year. Now what could he do to help the three of them?

CHAPTER FOURTEEN

"YOU'RE GOING *WHERE?*"

Maura sighed and straightened a line of books on a shelf in the home-improvement section, aware of Mary Ella's horror-stricken expression beside her. "Yes. You heard me correctly. As much as I would vastly prefer taking you up on your offer to catch a movie tonight, I have plans. We've been invited to Harry's for dinner. I tried desperately to get out of it. I mean, who wouldn't? But Sage pulled the poor, pitiful *I just want to get to know my grandfather* card, and now I'm stuck."

"I don't care *what* card she pulled. I would have sliced off two or three fingers if it meant I didn't have to share a meal with That Man."

Despite her own internal struggle over the impending evening, Maura had to smile at her mother's dramatics. "But, Mom, you have so much in common. You both love art and music and books, and now you even share a grandchild!"

"Oh, thank you very much for that reminder."

"Seriously, why do you hate Harry so much? You're nice to everyone else in town, even grouchy Frances Redmond, but you treat Harry like he ran over your dog or something. What did he ever do to deserve this gargantuan grudge you hold against him?"

Mary Ella leaned back against the bookshelf, pensive. "You can thank Jack for it."

"Jack?"

"He was one of my favorite students. Oh, I know all about how teachers are supposed to see the good in all our students and not pick favorites, but that is sometimes easier said than done when you're teaching literature and composition to moody teenagers. I've taught hundreds of young people. Maybe into the thousands. But something about Jack just…touched me. He was so wounded and he tried desperately not to show it. I knew what his childhood must have been like, growing up with an…unstable mother like Bethany Lange."

"She was more than unstable, Mom. She suffered from schizophrenia."

"Yes. You should have known her before her mental illness started to manifest itself. She was just one of those beautiful spirits, you know? Everyone loved her."

She seemed wistful here, and Maura let the silence continue until her curiosity swelled. "Your feud with Harry?" she finally prompted.

"Oh. Right. Well, I had Jack in my English class that terrible spring when Bethany committed suicide. I tried to go easy on him with assignments, but he insisted on filling every one. My heart was just breaking for him. Do you know, he only missed one day of class, to go to her funeral."

"I don't doubt that." Something soft and tender fluttered in her chest as she pictured him lost and grieving for his mother but determined to focus on his goals.

"In one of our last assignments, I allowed the students to write an essay about anything they chose. Jack wrote this really heartbreaking piece about watching a beautiful bird trapped in a thicket of thorns, trying desperately to free itself, beating its wings bloody in the effort. He had tried to help but the bird had pecked and pecked at him and refused to let him close—obviously a metaphor for his relationship with his mother. He seemed so troubled that I decided—foolishly now, I can see that—to show it to Harry. I thought maybe he would, I don't know, make sure Jack received grief counseling or something to assure him Bethany's suicide wasn't his fault."

"I'm guessing he didn't respond well."

Mary Ella scoffed. "He laughed. Can you believe that? The essay fairly *dripped* with his son's pain and sadness, and that bastard laughed. He said it was a good thing Jack didn't fancy himself a writer and had an architecture scholarship instead, because it was a bunch of sentimental garbage. The bird was weak and would never have survived anyway, even if Jack could have figured out a way to help it."

And Maura had to sit across the dinner table from the man. She fought anger and revulsion. "And you've hated him ever since."

"Jack was a kindhearted boy. He took after Bethany in that respect. It broke my heart, the way Harry treated him. Everyone in town knew that, to build his ski resort, he shamefully used her mental illness to break the land trust she had set up for Jack."

"Why didn't anyone do anything about it?"

"Without Jack here to fight for himself, what could we do? He walked away from the whole situation, and nobody else had any legal standing to reinstate the trust. And if you want the truth, most everyone took the cowardly way and let Harry and William Beaumont do what they wanted. Hope's Crossing was dying, our young people leaving, and people were eager for any way to keep that from happening. Like it or not, Harry offered salvation of a sort."

At what cost, though? Good or bad, Hope's Crossing

had been forever changed by the ski resort and the resulting growth and development.

Before she could answer her mother, Mary Ella's expression sharpened on someone who had just entered the store at Maura's back.

Maura turned at the sudden puzzlement in her gaze, and tension suddenly coiled inside her. Laura Beaumont, Genevieve's mother, was stalking toward them and she did *not* look like she was shopping for the latest bestseller. Her usually perfect hair was sticking out in strange directions, and she was missing the immaculate makeup that was as much a part of her as her own skin.

As she drew closer, she seemed to wobble a little, and Maura picked up the definite odor of eau de liquor.

She drew in a breath. She had no fight with Laura, she reminded herself. For months after the accident, she had hated the whole Beaumont family, but after Charlie's sentencing hearing, when the whole twisted truth about the accident had emerged, most of her fury had abated. She tried to tolerate Laura during their brief social interactions, mostly by not dwelling on the fact that Laura had wanted her son to completely escape punishment for his impaired driving, which had caused Layla's death and Taryn's severe injuries.

"Hi, Laura. Can I help you find something?"

"Yes. Where's the little tramp?" she demanded loudly, her words slurred at the edges.

Beside her, Maura could feel Mary Ella tense, and any hope she might have stupidly held that she could avoid a confrontation with the Beaumonts flew out the window. This was going to be a scene, and probably an ugly one.

"The brilliant Charlie Chaplin silent movie?" she asked in a bright voice, deliberately misunderstanding. "I don't carry it. I'm sorry. Our DVD section is pretty small. Perhaps you can find it online. Just so you know, it's actually called *The Tramp,* not *The Little Tramp,* though many people get confused."

Mrs. Beaumont blinked at her, trying to process that. "I'm not looking for a movie, you idiot. I want to talk to your whore of a daughter. She's ruined everything!"

And there went her temper. Maura dug her nails into her palms to keep from smacking the other woman and tossing her out into the rainy afternoon. "Okay, this is the part where you're going to apologize for calling my daughter ugly names, and then leave my store."

"I won't! Where is she? I hope she's proud of herself. Three weeks. Three more weeks and my Genevieve would have been Mrs. Sawyer Danforth of the Denver Danforths. Do you know how long we've been planning this damn wedding?"

Apparently Sawyer had found the stones to tell Genevieve about his indiscretion. And apparently Gen had found the even *bigger* stones to either postpone the wedding—again—or back out of it altogether.

For Genevieve's sake, Maura hoped she had broken it off completely and sent Sawyer "Keep It In Your Pants" Danforth on his merry way. She understood indiscretion and that people made mistakes, but if a man couldn't be faithful during an engagement—when he was supposed to be completely enamored with his chosen bride to the exclusion of all else—what were the chances he would remain faithful after the vows were exchanged?

"Wait. The wedding's off?" Mary Ella asked, her expression wholly befuddled.

"Yes, it's off! How could she go through with marrying him after she found out he supposedly got the stupid little bitch pregnant?"

Mary Ella's jaw sagged, and Maura felt a twinge of guilt for not having told her, but she hadn't felt it was her secret to share yet. Not even with her mother.

"Last I heard," she said coolly, "he was claiming he couldn't be the father and that Sage must have slept with dozens of men at college."

She didn't add that, when Sage had reported that part of their conversation, Jack had wanted to climb the stairs at the lodge and rip his head off. It had taken both of them to talk him down.

"I wouldn't be a bit surprised," Laura Beaumont snarled. "But the fact that he *might* be the father was apparently enough for Gen to call off the wedding. Where is she? I want to ask her what the hell she was thinking to ruin my daughter's life! She knew he was engaged, the sneaky little bitch. I bet she slept with him on purpose, didn't she, and probably poked holes in the condom too. She recognized a money train when she saw it, and she didn't give a rat's ass who she might hurt in the process."

So much for the gracious society matron, doling out her patronage around town like freaking Queen Elizabeth. Apparently Laura was a mean drunk. Who knew?

As Maura saw it, she had a couple of choices. She could take the other woman on right now—and probably chew her up and spit her out. Or she could try to deflect Laura's anger and in the process protect her child.

Sage was the important one here. She wouldn't put it past Laura to track Sage down at their house or, worse, at one of her friends' houses for a confrontation, and that was the last thing Maura wanted. Better to nip this in the bud now by using the power card—the only person Laura Beaumont and her husband feared.

"Sage isn't here right now. I'm sorry. She's probably at home dressing for the dinner we're having shortly with her grandfather. You know Harry. He's so impatient. He wouldn't want us to be late."

She blinked like a big, crazy-haired owl. "Harry?"

She deserved to be struck by lightning for shamelessly using Harry this way, but just now she would do anything necessary to protect her child. "Harry Lange. Oh, I just assumed everyone in town knew. Harry's son, Jackson, is Sage's father. They've recently reestablished their relationship. It's really been heartwarming to see."

Beside her, Mary Ella cleared her throat, and Maura prayed she wouldn't say anything.

As for Laura, she stared at the two of them, brow furrowed as if she had just stumbled onto a stage and discovered she was the star of a play she'd never rehearsed. "Uh, really? I…hadn't heard."

"Oh, yes. It's not something we've necessarily been trying to keep a secret, but we haven't exactly put an ad in the paper or anything. Harry and Sage are becoming quite close." This was a blatant lie, though Sage *had* told her and Jack about going to his penthouse apartment the other night at the lodge. If this would protect her daughter, she didn't care how many lies she had to tell.

"I…see."

Laura visibly withered, all her bluff and bluster trickling away. For one brief, preposterous second, she actually felt a little sorry for the mayor's wife, used to pushing her weight around town and making everyone accede to her wishes. Harry was the only person she couldn't afford to offend.

Though she had little reason to be compassionate to the

other woman, she decided perhaps a little sympathy was called for in this situation. She called these little impulses toward unsolicited goodness her *What Would Claire Do?* moments. Her new sister-in-law was the most sincerely generous person she knew, almost to a fault.

Maura always figured she couldn't go wrong if she tried to guess how Claire would behave in a given situation and then attempted to emulate that. Right now, she figured Claire would dig deeply for a little kindness, no matter how difficult.

After an awkward moment, she reached forward and squeezed Laura's fingers. "I'm very sorry about the wedding. I know how much effort you and Genevieve have put into making it perfect. From everything I've heard, it was going to be exquisite. Perhaps she and Sawyer can still work things out."

Laura closed her eyes, her chin trying its Botox-tight best to wobble a little. "I doubt it. She's so livid with him. I've never seen her like this. Her father and I talked to her until three in the morning, and she just won't listen to reason. She said she won't marry a man she can't trust, and she's convinced she'll never be able to trust Sawyer now."

Good for Gen, she wanted to say, but she didn't think Laura would appreciate the sentiment. She thought of the few times she had seen the happy couple over the past few months, and the random vibe she thought she had picked up that perhaps Genevieve Beaumont wasn't as thrilled about her upcoming nuptials as everyone else.

Maybe Gen had been looking for an excuse to derail the wedding crazy train. Sage had given her that, in spades.

"We have to let our children make their own decisions, don't we?" Mary Ella said softly. She stepped forward to pull Laura into an embrace that was much more genuine than anything Maura could have provided right then. "As much as we might wish we can hold their hand and guide everything they do, a good mother knows her job is to arm her children with the courage and the capability to make the tough choices for their own lives, even if we don't think they're the best ones for them."

"It's so *hard,*" Laura wailed.

"I know, my dear. I know. Did you drive here? Why don't you let me give you a ride home. Once you've had time to rest and talk to William, I'm sure things won't seem so dark."

"I s'pose that would be okay."

"Sure it will. Come on."

"Thank you," Maura mouthed to her mother.

"Oh, you're going to make it up to me," Mary Ella murmured in a voice that likely didn't carry to Laura. "Apparently you left a few juicy tidbits of information out of our conversation earlier. I expect a full report after dinner tonight. You can even text me *during* dinner if anybody starts throwing knives."

"What knives?" Laura asked in confusion.

"Nothing, my dear," Mary Ella said, as she tucked her arm around Mrs. Beaumont and walked her to the door of the bookstore. "Let's get you home. There's a girl."

After her mother and the mayor's wife left the store, Maura stood for a moment, watching them walk to Mary Ella's car, wondering whatever had happened to her quiet life.

WHY WAS SHE always late?

She heard on the radio once that a person who was perpetually tardy was trying in a passive-aggressive way to control everyone around him or her. She didn't care about controlling anybody. She just figured she had too blasted much to do in a day.

After Laura's little scene at the bookstore, Maura had to scramble to catch up with the rest of her day, and she finally managed to leave the store about twenty minutes past the time she should have in order to get ready for Harry's dinner.

She drove home just a little faster than strictly legal and pulled into the driveway with fifteen minutes to spare before Jack was due to pick them up.

"I'm home," she called out when she raced inside, and dumped her bag and her keys on the hall table. "Just give me a second and I'll be ready."

Her only answer was Puck jumping around her feet. "Hey there, sugar. Where's Sage? Hmm? Where's our Sage?" she asked the dog, who yipped at her and licked her face.

"Sage?"

Her daughter didn't answer and Maura frowned, more concerned than she probably should have been, given that any potential threat from Laura had been effectively neutralized. A moment later, she picked up the sound of the shower running down the hall. No wonder Sage hadn't answered. Apparently Maura wasn't the only one in the family running late.

She carried the dog into her bedroom with her, grateful for the ridiculous comfort she always found from the small, warm weight in her arms. "You can help me figure out what to wear," she told the shih tzu, who gave her a cheerful little grin and plopped belly-first onto the carpet at the foot of her bed.

As she had spent all day fretting about what to wear and had mentally tried on and discarded a dozen outfits, it didn't take her long to pull out what she had settled on, a tailored white blouse over slimming tan slacks and a chunky red-

and-umber necklace-and-earring set she had made a few years ago at String Fever.

How could she be old enough to be someone's grandmother? she wondered as she quickly touched up her makeup. She didn't have a single gray hair or wrinkle. She had just finished running a brush through her hair when she realized the shower was no longer running.

She headed out into the hall, Puck trotting merrily at her heels, and knocked on the door. "Sage? Everything okay?"

Her daughter opened the door, a towel wrapped around her expanding middle and her wet hair sticking out just as wildly as Laura Beaumont's had earlier. "No. Not really. Jack's going to be here any minute and I'm miles away from being ready. I lay down for a nap this afternoon and must have slept through the alarm I set on my phone, and now I still have to dry my hair and everything. I must have turned the stupid phone off when I lay down."

"That must be why you didn't answer when I tried calling a few times this afternoon."

"Sorry," Sage said, turning back to the bathroom just as the doorbell rang. "Oh, no! That's probably Jack."

Maura did her best to ignore the stupid little skitter of her heartbeat. "No worries. Just finish getting dressed. I can stall him until you're ready."

Puck, of course, had scampered to the door the minute the bell rang, always eager for someone else to love. Maura gave one quick glance at the mirror hanging above the console table in the hallway. She smoothed down a flyaway strand of hair and reminded herself to breathe, then she opened the door.

"Good evening."

"Hi, Jack. Come in." There. Good. That sounded halfway coherent and not the gibbering fool she felt on the inside at the sight of him, sexy and gorgeous in a cotton shirt the color of fir needles and a tan sport coat.

He walked into the entry, and Puck immediately yipped a greeting and brushed his little head against Jack's leg.

"There's the little guy," Jack said with a smile, reaching down to the ground and scooping up the dog with one hand, much to the dog's delight.

"Sage isn't ready yet," Maura said, while her silly insides melted into mush like Puck's. "Sorry. We were both running behind. She shouldn't be long, though."

"She can take as long as she needs. I don't mind being late."

"I wondered if you would show at all."

"I promised her I would," he said. "I didn't *want* to promise her that, mind you, but this daughter of ours can be fairly persuasive."

"I believe I'm aware how persuasive she can be." He'd called Sage *ours*. Was that the reason for this little flutter in her chest? Or was it the scent of him, of cedar and bergamot and something sexy and outdoorsy and very much Jack?

"I guess I lack imagination. For the life of me, I couldn't figure out a good way to wiggle out without disappointing her."

"After you've had time to adjust to being a parent, you'll figure out we spend half our lives disappointing our children. It's part of the job description."

He laughed and rubbed a gleeful Puck's head. "So far I'm at least filling that part of this new role."

"I don't think so. Sage already adores you, Jack." It was a tough admission, but she decided if he could overcome his animosity toward his father for Sage's sake, she could be generous and tell him the truth.

"The feeling is mutual," he answered.

She was becoming far too fascinated watching those long fingers scratch behind Puck's ears. "Yes. Well, would you like something to drink? I've got beer, some white wine, ginger ale or soda."

"Ginger ale. Thanks."

"Sure."

If she hadn't been ridiculously on edge, she should have invited him, as a proper hostess would, to take a seat on the comfortable living room sofa. She didn't even think of it until he had already followed her into the kitchen—and then the impulse deserted her completely when she spied a massive, colorful bouquet dominating the work island and sending out sweet aromas that reminded her of a moonlit tropical beach.

"Wow. Gorgeous!" she exclaimed, admiring the birds-of-paradise, heliconia and red ginger.

He set down a wriggling Puck, who headed immediately for his food bowl. "A secret admirer?"

Didn't she just wish? "I doubt they're for me. Sage would have said something when I got home. They must be for her."

He narrowed his gaze, looking very much like any other protective father. "You think that bastard Danforth sent them? After the way he treated her last night? There should be a card, right?" he said, sifting through the stems.

"Stop that! You can't just read the card without her permission," she exclaimed. "The message might be private."

He raised an eyebrow as he plucked a card out from the center of the vivid bouquet, so incongruous on a Rocky Mountain evening in March. "Then she shouldn't have left it out here for anyone to see, right?"

She laughed despite herself and shook her head. "Put it back."

"I certainly will, after I make sure Danforth isn't trying to pick up where he left off."

The card wasn't in an envelope and she supposed there was some truth to what he'd said—that Sage would have hidden it if she had wanted to keep the contents private. She shouldn't be so nosy, but she had to admit she was intensely curious. "Well? Who is it from?"

"No idea. It's not signed."

She frowned too and tried to read it upside down, but she couldn't make out the words at the angle he held it. "What does it say?"

He read the card with a puzzled look. "'John Wayne said courage is being scared to death but saddling up anyway. You've got some grit, young lady.'"

"What?"

"That's what it says. And no signature. Just a doodled angel."

"What? Let me see that!" She snatched the card out of his hands and read the words for herself. "Oh, my word. The Angel of Hope sent Sage flowers!"

"Maybe they're for you."

"I'm not a young lady anymore, in case you hadn't noticed."

"I've noticed," he murmured, his voice low in the kitchen. Her gaze met his, and her foolish toes wanted to curl at the intensity there.

She straightened them out quite firmly and looked away, turning back to the bouquet and rubbing a hand over one of the waxy blooms. "I think the Angel must be psychic. Seriously, how else could anyone know Sage is going through a rough time right now?"

"There were plenty of people in the lobby of the hotel

last night," he said after a slight pause. "Someone might have seen her come down looking upset."

"True." Her mother now knew after the scene with the mayor's wife at the bookstore. For that matter, any number of people might have found out. She didn't imagine Laura would be particularly discreet as they started canceling wedding arrangements, despite her and Mary Ella's best efforts to calm the situation.

She rubbed a thumb over the flower again and inhaled some of the sweet scent, wishing she were on a pristine beach somewhere on Kauai right this moment, instead of here dealing with unplanned pregnancies and Harry Lange and this treacherous softness for Jack she didn't want.

A drink. She had come in here to get him something to drink, she reminded herself, and went to the refrigerator to grab the ginger ale. "Genevieve Beaumont called off her wedding to Sawyer today," she said, reaching into the cabinet for a glass.

"How did you hear that?"

"Mrs. Beaumont came into the store a few hours ago calling Sage all kinds of horrible names for ruining her daughter's life."

"And she was able to walk out again without help from the paramedics?"

She had to smile at his quite correct assumption that she would fight to the death in her daughter's defense. "I felt a little sorry for her, if you want the truth. All her plans for her daughter going down the drain. I think I know a little about how that feels."

With a sigh, she handed him the glass. "The implosion of this wedding is going to be a huge scandal in town, without question. Word is going to trickle out, if it hasn't already started. I just wish I knew how to protect Sage from the fallout."

"I don't see how you can, Maura. Maybe that's what the flowers are about. Somebody is trying to buoy her up a little before the storm."

"It's a lovely gesture, if that's the reason, but I hate that she's going to have to endure the gossip and the whispers."

She knew all too well what that was like. At least she hoped she would be able to teach her daughter to hold her head up and face down the gossips, as Maura had done.

With a sigh, she poured herself a glass of ice water from the filtered pitcher in the refrigerator. "This whole thing seems terribly unfair. She's been through so much already this year."

"So have you."

"Yes. And to be completely honest with you, Jack, I'm not sure I have the strength for more."

"The scandal?"

"You should know me better than that. I don't care about any petty scandal." She paused and sipped at her water before setting her glass down on the counter. She shouldn't be revealing so much to him, but somehow the softness in his gaze, the quiet compassion, in the wake of her stress the past few days, had her spilling all the secrets she had barely admitted to herself.

"I don't know if I can endure more loss," she said, her voice low. "I think she's made her mind up to give the baby up for adoption. It's the right thing for Sage. I know that. For Sage *and* the child. But...it's going to rip my heart out."

The last was almost a whisper, and he gazed at her for only an instant before he set his glass down and reached a hand out to tug her against him. His arms wrapped around her tightly, enfolding her in his solid strength, and she sagged against him, relishing the heat.

"I know," he murmured. "I know."

She fought tears for several reasons—including the completely silly one that she didn't want to have to redo her blasted makeup before their dinner with Harry on account of scary mascara streaks all over her face.

"What's so wrong with hiding out in the bunkhouse for a few months?"

"You won't. You'll face this just like you've faced everything else."

She shook her head, the urge to cry gone as she stood in his arms. He was so solid, his muscles hard against her curves. She wanted to stand here forever, just borrowing that strength a little.

"Thank you," she murmured.

"You're welcome." His voice was low, intent, and when she met his gaze, heat glittered in the blue depths. She waited, holding her breath, a curl of anticipation inside her, and then finally he lowered his head and kissed her on a long sigh.

His mouth was cool from the drink and she shivered at the glide of his tongue against hers. Everything inside her went weak, hungry. For weeks, she had wondered if she would ever taste his kiss again. Now here it was, when she was nervous for their dinner with Harry and sick with worry for Sage.

Somehow, unbelievably, kissing Jack was like slipping into the hot tub on a cold winter's night. Calming, comforting, relaxing. Despite this hunger for more, he calmed something edgy and tight inside her.

She was falling in love with him all over again. She probably had been since he'd returned.

She pushed that unwelcome realization away, focusing instead on how wonderful it felt to be here in his arms again, to tangle her mouth with his, to feel the welcome heat seeping into all the cold places inside her.

"Okay, I think I'm finally ready," she heard Sage call out. "Where are you guys?"

The words pierced the soft haze around her and she blinked to the awareness that their daughter was going to walk in on them any moment. Somehow she managed to find the strength to step away from him, her breathing ragged and her heartbeat racing in her ears.

He looked just as stunned as she felt, his pupils dilated and his hair slightly messy where her hands must have played in it without her being conscious of it.

"In the kitchen," she answered. Her voice came out husky, thready, and she had to cough a little to clear it. "In the kitchen," she repeated more loudly.

Sage burst through the doorway just a second later. "What are you doing in *here?*"

"A drink. I was, uh, thirsty, and Maura was pouring some ginger ale for me," Jack said, looking around a little blankly for his glass. When he found it on the counter, he picked it up with an air of triumph and sipped at it, then coughed as it apparently went down wrong.

"O-kay," Sage said. "Well, sorry I made you both wait for me."

Jack shot a glance at Maura. "No problem. I didn't mind at all."

She could feel herself flush and dearly hoped Sage didn't notice. "You look lovely, honey," she said. It was true. Sage wore a maternity blouse Maura hadn't seen before, a soft rose. She had pulled her wavy hair back into a loose knot and wore a pair of dangly silver-and-rose earrings Maura had made for her birthday a few years earlier.

"I guess you saw my flowers."

After a few more deep, cleansing breaths, she almost felt as if her brain had received enough oxygen for the synapses to start firing again. "They're lovely. Your own gift from the Angel of Hope. That's certainly something to treasure."

A sly, secretive smile played at her mouth for just a moment. "Isn't it?"

"But how did the Angel know about what was going on? It really makes me wonder again if it's someone we know."

Sage shrugged, but she still had a knowing sort of look in her eyes. "The mystery is half the fun. That's what you and Grandma McKnight always say." She glanced at her watch. "We'd better go. I wouldn't want to keep Harry waiting too long."

"Oh, no. We certainly wouldn't want that," Jack said drily.

Sage led the way through the house toward the front door, and Jack, of course, insisted on helping them into their coats. When his body brushed hers from behind, Maura shivered and had to hope he didn't notice—though from the sudden intake of breath, she guessed she wasn't as good at concealing her reaction to him as she would like to be.

At least she wasn't worried about meeting with Harry anymore. She was much more concerned with fretting about what she was going to do about Jack and this very inconvenient and ill-timed hunger—and preparing herself for yet another loss when he left Hope's Crossing once more.

CHAPTER FIFTEEN

THAT KISS.

Wow.

As Jack helped them into their coats and then followed Sage and Maura down the sidewalk to his SUV, heat seethed and churned through him. He was eighteen years old again, in a sun-drenched alpine meadow, convinced he was the luckiest bastard in the world to have the most beautiful girl at Hope's Crossing High School in his arms.

No, actually. He was much smarter than he'd been back then. Now he *knew* it was much more than luck that she had actually kissed him back, had trembled in his arms and wrapped her own arms around him and pressed her softness to him.

It was nothing less than a miraculous gift.

He felt a little as if he had been wandering alone through some bleak wilderness all these years, convincing himself he was happy and had everything he wanted or needed. Being back in Hope's Crossing, being with her again, showed him just how foolish he had been. He hadn't been happy. Something fundamental and beautiful and *right* had been missing all this time.

Maura.

He had feelings for her. They were tangled and complicated and he didn't know what the hell to do about them.

At his vehicle, Sage brushed past her mother to immediately take the backseat, leaving Maura to sit in the front.

"I can sit back there," Maura said. "You're the pregnant one. You need the legroom, don't you?"

"There's plenty of room back here. I'm perfect. Get in, Mom. Seriously. We're going to be late!"

She really must have been a stubborn little thing when she was a kid. Once more, when he thought of all he had missed, he was hit by a familiar pang. This time, he embraced the ache. It forced him back to reality. He had missed so much of Sage's life, because of Maura. As much as he was drawn to her again, how could he fully trust her after such a huge betrayal?

The night was cool and clear. Hanging over Woodrose Mountain was a huge full moon that reflected a pearly glow on the dusting of snow that still lingered on the ground. None of them spoke much as he drove through town to the mouth of Silver Strike Canyon, where he turned on the GPS he had already programmed with the coordinates for Harry's place. He refused to acknowledge the strange reality that he had no idea how to get to his own father's house.

"We could have told you how to get there," Maura commented as the sultry female voice gave its automated directions. "Harry's house is a little hard to miss up the canyon."

"I suppose that's true," he said, embarrassed to realize he hadn't even thought of asking her and Sage for directions. "I guess I'm just used to using the GPS."

Counting on himself and circumstances he could control. Figuring out his way. That's what he preferred, his modus operandi since he'd left Hope's Crossing. He had learned early he couldn't count on anyone else. Bethany had been in her own world half the time, and Harry… Well, Harry hadn't given a damn about his son.

For a brief time, he had leaned on Maura. Maybe one of the reasons he had made such an abrupt break between them was that he had started to realize he was beginning to rely *too* heavily on her.

"Sweetheart, I need to tell you something before you hear it from someone else," Maura said to Sage when the GPS indicated about a mile to go to Harry's house. "For all I know, Harry might mention something and I…want you to be prepared."

"What's wrong?" Sage sounded scared. "Is it Grandma?"

"No. Grandma's fine. Everyone's fine. It's just…" She drew in a breath and spoke in a rush. "Genevieve called off the wedding."

Sage didn't answer for several beats. When he checked the rearview mirror, he saw she was huddled against the seat, her arms folded across her small baby bulge. "She… did?" Her voice was small, disheartened.

Maura nodded. "I'm sorry, honey."

"So he must have told her, then. After the other night, I thought for sure he would wait to tell her until the baby was born and he could get a DNA test."

"That's the way many guys would have handled the situation," Jack said. "Why totally disrupt your life if the baby's not even yours?"

"I guess. I know it's his. I've never been with anyone else, either before or since. I'm not sure I ever want to be again, since I'm apparently Fertile Myrtle. Who would ever want to be with me now that I've ruined another guy's life? And I'll probably have stretch marks and everything."

He didn't quite know how to respond to that. Fortunately, Maura stepped in. "Why don't we not stress about everything at once tonight? How about we deal with tonight's dinner first, the remaining months of your pregnancy after that, and we can worry about stretch marks and future relationships way down the line?"

Sage sighed. "Yeah. I know. You're right."

How did she do that? Take a potentially explosive situation and defuse it so effortlessly? He wondered if that was a skill one picked up automatically as the parent of teenage girls.

The voice on the GPS announced they had reached their destination, and Jack pulled up in front of a set of forbidding black gates. Someone must have been watching, because they slid open instantly. With no small degree of trepidation, he drove through the gates and up a long drive surrounded by trees and what in a month or so would be exquisite landscaping, when it wasn't covered in snow. The well-lit driveway circled around in front of the house, which looked to be about three stories and probably twenty-five thousand square feet.

It was more modern than the lodge, a style he would have called Western contemporary. The most distinctive feature was a curving, multistory wall of glass windows that offered views in every direction.

The house was sprawling and grand—all in all, a far cry from the modest home of Jack's childhood.

"Here we are, then," he said. "Are you sure you wouldn't rather turn around now? The gates have closed behind us, but I'm pretty sure I could ram them."

"I'm in. Let's do it and hope your air bags work," Maura said quickly.

Sage just rolled her eyes at both of them, but he was glad to see some of the sadness had left her expression. "We're here. We might as well eat, don't you think?"

"I suppose. Plus the car's pretty new. I wouldn't want to

raise the rate on my insurance policy. Front-end damage might be a little hard to explain to my agent."

Given his mixed emotions about this upcoming dinner with his father, a rate hike might be worth it, he thought as he climbed out and opened the doors for both of them. Maura climbed out quickly before he could help her, stubborn thing, but he reached inside and grabbed Sage's arm to help her slide from the backseat.

"Be careful. There might be ice."

"Do you really think Harry would allow that?" Maura asked. "The driveway is probably heated."

Yes, that could make sense. Still, he took Sage's arm and held his other out to Maura. After a long moment of hesitation, she slipped her arm through and he escorted them to the door.

The wide, carved-oak double doors leading to the house opened before they could reach it, and Harry stood framed in the light. He looked far different from the cardiac patient Jack had seen only weeks ago. Instead, he appeared bull chested and strong in slacks and a sweater that probably cost more than the monthly payment on Jack's new SUV.

"You're late."

"My fault, Grandpa," Sage said with a cheeky smile, though he could still see shadows in her eyes. She must get that skill from Maura, the ability to put on a show and pretend everything was normal.

Much to Jack's shock, she slid her hand away from his arm and leaned in to kiss Harry on the cheek. "I lay down for a nap this afternoon and slept through the alarm on my phone. I'm really, really sorry."

Harry was obviously no match for Sage when she put on the charm. "Don't worry for a minute. You're not *that* late. Come in. Come in."

Sage smiled warmly at him and moved inside the massive living room, followed by Maura.

"Hello again, Mr. Lange," she said with a tepid smile.

"Call me Harry."

"We'll see. I think after all these years of calling you Mr. Lange, that's what I'm more comfortable using."

"I'm sure that's not the only thing you've called me over the years."

"But I'm trying to be a better person and teach my daughter not to emulate my bad language."

Harry laughed out loud and didn't seem offended. "Fine. Call me whatever you'd like."

"That's what I'd planned."

Still chuckling, Harry led the way into the house. "Would any of you like a drink before dinner?"

"Mineral water, please," Maura said.

"That sounds good." Sage smiled.

"Nothing for me," Jack said.

Harry looked as if he wanted to say something but seemed to change his mind. He moved to a side table and opened a cabinet to reveal a clever minirefrigerator, from which he pulled a small bottle of Evian for Maura and handed it to her.

They made small talk for a few moments—well, Maura and Sage and Harry made small talk, actually. He was still trying to adjust to how surreal it felt to be in his father's house after all this time.

"Dinner is probably close to finished. Shall I let my chef know we're ready?"

"That would be great. I'm starving," Sage said.

Harry left for a moment, presumably to give orders to his chef. In his absence, Jack walked around the great room, admiring the art on the walls.

"That's one of Sarah Colville's works. Exquisite, isn't it?"

He studied the oil on canvas, a rich and detailed plein air of a valley he recognized from Snowflake Canyon, one of the offshoots of Silver Strike.

"It's lovely," he said.

"She's brilliant. I wonder where your father keeps the rest of his collection."

"Scattered around the house," Harry answered for himself from behind them. "I've got one in my office, one in the den. There's even one in my bedroom, though if you tell the old biddy that, I'll cut out your tongue and serve it to one of my dogs."

"She's not an old biddy. She's a lovely woman."

"You would think so, I suppose? She and your mother are peas in a pod."

He waited for Maura to snap at Harry in defense of her mother, but she merely gave him a cool smile. "I'm surprised you're willing to have Sarah's artwork in your home if you dislike her so much as a person."

"I can separate the art from the individual. Her paintings are brilliant. I would buy more, but she refuses to sell me any more directly, out of sheer spite. I'm forced to find them where I can."

Jack thought he might just have to look into purchasing one of the woman's paintings if she was so discriminating in her patrons.

"The dining room is this way." Harry looped an arm through Sage's, which left Jack to walk in with Maura. Her shoulder brushed his as they walked, but she didn't meet his gaze. Still, he could feel the connection simmering between them.

The room Harry led them to was huge, with richly molded ceilings and a long table that looked as if it would seat twenty people easily. Did Harry entertain often? Somehow Jack didn't think so. Everything he had heard about his father since he'd been back in town indicated Harry was a bit of a recluse who kept himself distant, unapproachable to the people of Hope's Crossing.

Four place settings had been set at one end of the table. He might have expected Harry to sit at the head, where he could lord his position as boss of the world over all of them, but his father helped Sage into a chair and then sat beside her, leaving two places across the big table for him and for Maura.

As soon as they were seated, a small older woman with scraped-back dark hair entered carrying a large tray with their plated salad course, which she set down in front of them.

"Thank you, Mrs. Kingsley."

"You're welcome, Mr. Lange," the woman said softly, then disappeared into the kitchen.

"Wow. This looks fantastic," Sage exclaimed.

"I hope you like Italian food. I was in the mood. This is one of my favorite salads, *panzanella* with a champagne vinaigrette. Our *primo* course will be braised short ribs with pasta and the *secondo* will be lemon sole. I had the same thing during one of the best meals of my life at a great place outside Milan. Dante's."

Jack frowned. He didn't know what to say to that. He actually knew that restaurant. It was near the hotel and convention center he had worked on a few years earlier, and he had eaten there several times when he had been overseeing the project. What were the odds that Harry has just stumbled on the same restaurant?

The next few moments were spent enjoying the very delicious bread salad, which he had definitely developed a taste for during his time in Italy. The conversation was casual and polite, until just after the quiet woman in the dark clothing removed their salad plates and brought out the pasta and rib course, when Sage suddenly spoke.

"Oh, I almost forgot. Thank you for the flowers."

"You're wel—" Harry stopped with an almost comical look of horror on his face.

"I knew it!" Sage exclaimed, a look of triumph on her face that just now appeared very much like he remembered his mother. "The minute they were delivered, I knew they had to have come from you. You're the Angel of Hope, aren't you?"

Harry looked as if he were choking on his ribs. He chewed and swallowed, then took a quick sip from his wineglass, his face turning florid.

Maura, in the process of setting down her own wineglass, just about knocked it over, but she quickly righted it. "Harry? The Angel of Hope? That's impossible."

"And yet it's true," Sage said smugly, just as if she had suspected it all along. "You may as well admit it, Grandpa. You might have the reputation as the biggest crank in Hope's Crossing, but it's all a big act, isn't it? You're the one who's been going around all this time doing nice things for people. I think you're just a big old softy."

"Now you're being ridiculous," Harry said gruffly.

Jack would have joined in Maura's disbelief, if not for that stray memory of the night right after Christmas when he had been walking back to the B and B and had spied someone dropping something at a run-down house in the neighborhood. He remembered that brief moment of suspicion when he had seen the man rub at his chest, the reminder that just a few days earlier Harry had been in the hospital with heart problems.

"It has to be you," Sage said. "You sent me the flowers when nobody else but my mom and dad knew what was going on with Sawyer."

"Okay, this doesn't make sense." Maura actually looked horrified by this prospect. He remembered the way she and Sage had talked about the Angel of Hope, with almost a reverence. They had talked about how the Angel had helped to lift the mood of the town after the devastating accident.

He could imagine how much of a shock she must find it to even consider that Harry might be behind the secret acts of kindness.

"It makes *total* sense, Mom. Think about it. Who else has the time and the money and…*cojones* to pull off some of things the Angel has done. The Angel gave Caroline Bybee a new *car!* Who else would do such a thing but Mr. Lange?"

"You're all crazy. Every damn one of you," Harry blustered, and in that moment Jack knew that, as unbelievable as it might seem, Sage was right. The old bastard was the Angel of Hope. And he had thought the evening was surreal *before*.

"So I hear you got the bid for the recreation center project."

It was an obvious ploy by Harry to change the subject, and it worked surprisingly well. Beside him, Maura stiffened and sent him a shock looked under her lashes, while Sage gasped, her eyes widening.

"What?" she exclaimed. "You didn't say a word about it!"

"I received the notification Friday afternoon after you had left for the day. Later, we all had other things on our minds and I decided to wait for a better time."

"What about on the drive here? You could have mentioned it then!"

He had planned to, but he'd walked into Maura's kitchen and ended up kissing her until he couldn't remember his name, forget about the recreation center project. "Again, we had other things on our mind."

"This is wonderful!" Sage exclaimed. "That means you'll have to stick around town longer, doesn't it?"

Theoretically, he didn't really have to, but this provided as good an excuse as any to stay close to Sage. He figured he would try to stay at least until she had the baby. Depending on what she decided, he had planned to convince her to come to San Francisco for a while to make a new start. After talking to Maura earlier, though, now he didn't know what the hell to do. He couldn't do that to her right now.

"The idiot city leaders finally did something smart for a change," Harry said. "They picked the right man. You'll do a great job."

"I intend to," he said. He hadn't realized how curt his voice was until he saw pain flicker in Harry's gaze before he concealed it.

Yet another thing he didn't know what to do about. Judging by this dinner and a few other overtures Harry had tried since Jack's return, his father obviously wanted to extend an olive branch. He had no idea whether it was genuine or another of Harry's tricks. Either way, he wasn't at all sure he was ready to reach out and take it.

Why should he? Even if Harry *was* the Angel of Hope, that didn't mean he had suddenly become some kindly, misunderstood old man. He was ruthless and arrogant, and Jack couldn't see any evidence that that had changed over the years.

WELL, THIS NIGHT had turned into a total screwup.

By the time dessert was served—a fine chocolate

mousse with candied orange peels—Harry was ready to shove his guests out the door and retreat to his library with a cigar and the bottle of Bushmills 1608 he kept hidden from his housekeeper.

His son was one stubborn son of a bitch. He had sat in stoic silence most of the evening, answering questions that were asked of him but otherwise not doing one damn thing to contribute to the conversation.

As the minutes had ticked past, he could feel his temper edge higher and higher. Would it kill Jackson to try making a little small talk, for hell's sake?

And then the whole Angel thing. He was a first-class idiot. How had he let some smart-assed little girl trick him into slipping up and just blurting out what he had fought hard to keep a secret all these months?

Despite his protests, he could tell none of them had believed him, which meant the stupid jig was up. Next thing he knew, the whole town would be in on it, and he wouldn't be able to walk into a single store or restaurant in town without everybody pointing and whispering about him.

It was his own fault. If he hadn't started the whole Angel thing in the first place, this wouldn't have happened. The whole thing had blown up far beyond his intentions, until it had just about taken over his life.

After his first heart attack, he had been lying in that hospital bed with tubes connected everywhere and had never felt so damn alone. Jack was gone, had been for years, and the only other people in his life were business associates who didn't give a flying shit whether he lived or died.

He had all the money in the world, but it wasn't going to help him one bit if he kicked over in that minute, alone and, yes, frightened. He remembered lying in that hospital bed with the machines whirring and buzzing, the nurses bustling around him, and had come to what religious folks would probably call an epiphany. If he died, he had realized, no one would care, because somewhere along the way he had lost himself.

No. Not somewhere along the way. He knew when it was. During those terrible last years of his Bethany's life. To his vast shame, as the signs of her mental illness worsened and the medications became less effective, he had wanted nothing but to pretend none of it was happening. He had turned his focus away from his wife and his son and poured every bit of his energy and his time and his *life* into his development deals to make sure he didn't have to face his own failures at home.

He hadn't been able to "fix" her, so he had turned to what he *did* have power over, making money, and lots of it.

Once he had been a decent person, or at least he liked to think so, but in that hospital bed more than a year ago, he'd realized he had killed the last vestige of that decency when he had successfully managed to break the trust Bethany had left for Jackson, and subsequently created the Silver Strike Ski Resort and changed Hope's Crossing forever.

Plenty of other people had gotten rich along the way. The Beaumonts. A select group of investors. But something had been lost too, irrevocably. The peace and serenity of the town. Neighbors caring about neighbors.

He wanted to think his few paltry acts as the Angel had helped those ugly scars to heal a little. Even if he had been the only person who benefited, his efforts had been worth it. This past year had been the best he could remember since Bethany's condition had worsened.

When he came up with the idea during those days in the hospital, he had only intended it to be a short-term project, something to take his mind off this newfound mortality.

He had more money than he could ever spend and figured maybe if he gave a little of it back somehow, Whoever was keeping score might see it as his small effort to atone for all the mistakes he had made over the years.

He had enjoyed those first few visits by the Angel too much to stop. It had become as much a game to him as making money, figuring out who might be in need and how he could secretly help. Then he'd started hearing rumors about other efforts by the Angel, things he knew *he* hadn't been responsible for, and he discovered that others were following his example and giving credit to the altruistic mythical entity he had created out of fear and self-loathing.

Like it or not, the Angel would have to die an ugly death now. He didn't want everybody looking at him, assigning positive, saintlike motives to the little good he had done, when the whole thing had been selfish from the outset, aimed at helping to fill all the empty corners inside him.

It was a philosophical point he would have to remember to ask Reverend Wilson next time he saw him on the golf course. Hypothetically, of course. If people helped others because they craved that feeling of satisfaction and delight, was it really selfless? How could an act be considered altruistic if, in a roundabout fashion, somebody was just fulfilling a need inside themselves by helping someone else?

He didn't want to mull this over right now. He just wanted this dinner to be over so he could figure out his next move.

"Thanks for dinner, Harry. That was scrumptious." Sage smiled at him and he felt a ridiculous pang that the little scamp hadn't called him Grandpa.

"I'm glad you enjoyed it."

"Thank you for inviting us," her mother said, with that

calm smile that made a man wonder what was really going on inside her head.

Jack took a sip from his wineglass. "Yes, Harry. Thank you."

"You all made Mrs. Kingsley very happy to have someone else here to enjoy her food."

"Does she cook like that for you all the time? Because that was really superb," Sage said. "I'd love the recipe for that mousse."

"I'll make sure she sends it to you. And no, she doesn't. Cook like that all the time, I mean. This was a special occasion and her menu reflected it. I've got heart problems, as you may have heard, so most of the time I have to watch my diet."

"Are you okay eating all that rich Italian food?" Sage asked.

"I probably won't have a heart attack tonight, if that's what you're asking." He didn't like talking about his health, so he quickly changed the subject to one he knew would divert attention from him. "So now that you know what the little prick thinks about your pregnancy, have you figured out what you're going to do about the kid?"

Across the table, Maura and Jack both stiffened as if he'd stuck a poker up their respective bums.

What? Shouldn't he have asked that question? This was his great-grandchild. Didn't that give him some right to know?

To his satisfaction, Sage shot a quick look at both of them, then met his gaze with a directness that pleased him. Impertinent she might be, but he had meant what he'd had the Angel write her. His granddaughter had grit.

"I'm leaning toward adoption. The child ought to have

stable, devoted parents who can offer her all the things I can't. I think it's the best of all my options, don't you?"

"My opinion on the matter doesn't mean shit. You're the only one who can decide what to do."

She gave him a grateful look. "I know. The Angel gave me some very wise words about courage. I'll try to keep those in mind."

"You do that," he murmured.

So maybe the dinner wasn't a total loss. He might not be able to reach his son, no matter how hard he tried, but he was establishing some sort of relationship with his granddaughter. That had to count for something.

Sage slid back from the table. "Will you excuse me? I need to find a powder room."

"Of course. Go back the way we came, hang a left and it's the third door on the right."

Maura pushed her chair out as well. "That sounds complicated. It might take two of us, in the age-old tradition of females who are genetically programmed to insist on never entering a bathroom alone."

Only after the two of them had left did he realize this was the first chance he'd had all evening to be alone with his son, and he had to wonder if Maura had manipulated that particular outcome.

He faced his son directly. "Thank you for coming. I know you didn't want to."

"Sage can be persuasive."

This might be his only chance to achieve at least one of his goals for the evening, and he seized it. "I have something for you. I've been wanting to give it to you since you came back to Hope's Crossing, but the time has never seemed right. I invited you all to dinner because I wanted to get to know my granddaughter, of course, but also because I was hoping for a chance to give you this."

He half expected Jack to say he wanted nothing from him, but to his relief, his son only gave him a curious look. "What is it?"

"It's on the sideboard. One moment." He rose and had to flinch when his knees cracked. He wasn't quite seventy years old. Two young to be falling apart. For the first time in too long, he finally felt as if he had something else to live for. He had a granddaughter now, one who didn't seem to despise him, and he wanted to embrace every moment.

He reached the sideboard and picked up the small wooden chest that looked incongruously shabby amid the luxury with which he liked to surround himself.

"Here," he said, placing it on the table in front of his son.

Jack frowned. "What's this?"

"Some journals of your mother's and other keepsakes she treasured. Trinkets, mostly." To him, most of it looked like garbage, but he had to assume she kept the things inside there because they had meaning to her. Whether that was because of her mental illness, he didn't know, but he figured Jack could sort it all out.

"I don't know where most of it came from. Some colored rocks, a piece of petrified wood, a pressed flower or two."

"She loved the outdoors."

"Yes." He was quiet here, remembering the fey creature he had married, a woman who had loved art and music and being with her son. Even before her illness had progressed, some part of him had always resented their close relationship. He had always felt as if the two of them had a bond that excluded him.

"I loved your mother. I know you have some ridiculous notion that I didn't but…before her illness, before the voices in her head became so loud they drowned out the rest of us, she was…my angel."

"You locked her up. She loved being outside and you kept her locked in a room, sedated to her teeth until she was a zombie."

"She wasn't locked up, ever. She had full run of the house. Yes, I put locks on the doors of the house to keep her from wandering around. I had to. She was out of control. She might have hurt someone. Do you know how hard it was to keep her at home? The doctors wanted to put her in the state hospital, but I refused. She would have hated that. Instead I paid for round-the-clock care at a time when I could least afford it."

He didn't expect his son to understand. Jack had been a teenager with the idealism of the young, certain he could fix any problem in the world if only he set his mind to it. He had been busy with school and hadn't seen how Bethany was self-destructing.

"Is it completely impossible for you to believe that I thought what I was doing was best, for her and for you?"

Jack leaned back in his chair. "Mostly for yourself. Don't forget that part."

Yes. He couldn't deny that. As much as he had loved his wife in the beginning, when they were in their twenties and he thought she was the most beautiful thing he had ever seen, by the time she killed herself, he had felt trapped and angry and helpless, not a comfortable position for a man who had firm goals and ambitions.

"I made mistakes, with her and with you. No doubt about it. I'm sorry for that, son. And for…everything that came after. More sorry than I can ever say."

Jack gazed at him for a long moment, and Harry almost thought he might believe him. If he could only have his son back—whatever crumbs of a relationship Jack might be willing to throw at him—he would consider it fair repayment for his activities these past months as the Angel of Hope.

If he thought his son was going to run into his arms as if this was some dramatic made-for-television movie, he was destined for disappointment.

"Thank you for the mementos," Jack only said, his voice stiff and unyielding.

Harry fought the urge to rub at the ache in his chest, knowing this also had nothing to do with his A-fib. "You're welcome," he answered, just as Maura and Sage returned to the dining room.

"This house is awesome, Harry," Sage said. "I could throw a party and invite everybody in my dorm tower and the other three in the unit. That guest bathroom alone is bigger than my dorm room."

He forced himself to smile at her. He might not ever be able to pierce through the accumulated years of Jackson's animosity. He had this unexpected granddaughter now. If he treaded carefully with her, maybe, just maybe, he wouldn't have to be completely alone.

CHAPTER SIXTEEN

"SEE? THAT WASN'T SO miserable, was it?" Sage said from the backseat when they were finally back in Jack's Lexus. "Nobody poisoned anyone, at least."

"As far as *you* know," Jack answered. "Do you have any idea how many poisons don't show any symptoms until hours after ingestion?"

Maura laughed, as he had intended. "Always the optimist, aren't you?"

"So if I wake up dead, you can say I told you so," Sage teased.

The finely wrought tension in his shoulders from the ordeal of the evening seemed to ease with their lighthearted banter. He very much enjoyed their company. Both of them.

"You're right. It wasn't completely miserable. The food was good." What he'd been able to taste, anyway.

"Particularly that mousse. I'm definitely trying that sometime. Don't you think it was nice of Harry to track down the recipe from his housekeeper?"

Oh, yes. Jack was sure it had been quite a sacrifice for him to call her in from the kitchen and order her to print out a copy for Sage.

"I think Harry is mellowing in his old age," Maura said. "I still can't believe he's the Angel of Hope. Of all the people in town I might have guessed, Harry Lange would have been dead last on the list."

"He denied it, remember?" Jack said. "Quite vehemently, in fact."

"You lived with the man for eighteen years. Couldn't you tell he was lying?"

The trouble there was half the things Harry had ever said to him were lies, and he had never been very good at sorting through what was truth. In this, he had to agree with Maura, however. Harry had obviously been lying about his secret identity as the town's mysterious benefactor. He had evidence from his own eyes—that brief moment he had seen the Angel near Maura's house after Christmas and had wondered.

"I don't think the three of us should tell anyone that it's Harry," Sage said. "Can it be our secret?"

"I think you're right." Maura surprised him by agreeing. "He's worked really hard to keep his identity under wraps all these months. We should keep it a secret among us."

"Why?" Jack asked.

"Just the idea of the Angel, some secretive being who goes around doing kindnesses, has been good for this town. Knowing it's just a grumpy old man trying to atone for the sins of his lifetime kind of ruins the fun and beautiful mystery of it, don't you think?"

Was that what Harry was trying to do by sneaking around helping people with their troubles? Trying to atone somehow?

"Are you going to tell anybody Harry's the Angel?" Sage asked him.

"I can keep a secret if that's what you think best. Who would I tell, anyway?"

"Thanks." His daughter beamed at him. "I'll let Harry know we've all agreed to a conspiracy of silence."

Jack wasn't sure how he felt about that—sharing a secret about his father.

"He's done a lot of good around Hope's Crossing," Maura said. "I still can't really believe it's him."

"Maybe he just wants you to think it's him in order to deflect attention from the *real* Angel," Jack said, though he didn't really believe that himself.

"I would find that a little more palatable, to tell you the truth, than the idea of Harry Lange sneaking around town giving out packets of money and paying people's utility bills. It's a little disconcerting. Sort of like trying to picture Katherine Thorne and my mom suddenly having a hair-pulling catfight in the middle of the café."

He had to smile at the incongruous image of the very ladylike city council member and his former high school English teacher, both in their sixties, battling it out, *mano a mano*.

Sage laughed out loud. "I would pay good money to see that. I bet lots of people in town would. Hey, maybe if we asked them nicely, the two of them would stage a mixed martial arts fight, with all proceeds to go to Layla's scholarship fund."

"Don't you dare even put that idea in your grandmother's head," Maura said with a soft chuckle. "I could just see one of them breaking a hip and blaming me."

Jack laughed along with both of them. As he pulled up into the driveway of Maura's house, he felt a funny little bubble of something expand in his chest. It took a moment for him to realize he was *happy*.

Now, there was an unexpected emotion. He had just spent two hours with his father, he was back in Hope's Crossing, a place he'd never wanted to find himself. But he was with two women who made him laugh and think and worry.

Two women he had come to care for deeply.

He turned off the engine and moved around to help them both out of the vehicle. Inside, they could hear a few random, excited barks from Puck.

Maura unlocked the door, and the dog rushed out with yips of glee. She picked up his little wriggly body and scratched under his chin. "There's my good boy," she murmured, and Jack had to smile. Sage had told him of Maura's initial resistance to keeping the dog. Apparently the little fuzzball had won her over.

If only he could do the same.

The thought left him shocked and more than a little unsettled. Did he *want* to "win her over"? He still had every reason to be furious with her for his lost years with Sage. Could he move past that to the soft, caring, courageous woman she had become?

"Thanks again for coming," Sage said. "I know it wasn't easy for you, and it means a lot to me that you did it anyway, Dad."

Dad. She had never called him that before. He stared at her, his chest filling again with that effervescent joy.

"You're welcome," he said gruffly. Sage reached out and hugged him in that open, generous way of hers and, after an awkward moment, he hugged her back.

Over Sage's shoulder, he met Maura's gaze and saw a thicket of emotions there he couldn't begin to untangle.

"You don't need to rush away, Jack," she said after a moment. "You're welcome to stay and hang out with Sage. I'll even get out of your hair. I'm going to take Puck for a walk, since he's been cooped up all evening by himself."

Sage pulled away and winced. "My friend Jennie texted

before we left and asked if I wanted to come over and watch a movie when we finished dinner. I already told her yes. I haven't had a chance to talk to her in ages, but I can call her and cancel."

"No. Don't worry about it. I don't want you to change your plans on my account."

He studied Maura and the leash, and thought of the empty town house waiting for him. He didn't want to go home yet, especially when they hadn't had a chance to talk about the kiss earlier in the kitchen that had sizzled between them all night. "I was actually thinking a walk would be just the thing after that chocolate mousse. Maura, do you mind company?"

Her mouth tightened slightly, but she quickly straightened it. "Not at all," she answered. "Puck would love to have you along."

But you wouldn't? he wanted to ask, but didn't want to risk the bluntness of her answer in front of Sage.

"I probably won't be that late, since I fall over by midnight these days, but if you get back before I do, don't wait up for me," Sage said.

Maura smiled and kissed her daughter on the cheek. "Good night, honey. If I don't see you when you come home, I'll talk to you in the morning before you go into the office."

"Thanks, Mom. See you guys. Have fun."

Maura looked as if fun was the last thing on her mind, but she said nothing as she hooked the leash onto Puck, who just about wriggled out of his fur in anticipation. Jack held the door open for her, and together they walked out into the cool March night.

THIS WAS A phenomenally bad idea.

Maura gripped Puck's leash as if the little eight-pound

dog might suddenly start dragging her down the street. Her shoulders already ached from the effort she was making to ensure she kept a nice, safe bubble around herself and didn't accidentally bump into Jack.

Walking through the quiet streets of Hope's Crossing with Jackson Lange wasn't exactly the soothing, Zen-like experience she had been seeking when she'd come up with the idea to take Puck out on the leash. She was almost painfully aware of Jack. All she could seem to think about was that kiss in her kitchen earlier and how she hadn't wanted to stop.

"Nice night," he said into the silence, after they passed a few houses on her street.

Oh? She hadn't noticed. She drew in a breath and tried to focus on the spill of stars and the huge full moon hovering above Woodrose Mountain, instead of this fierce attraction that seemed to grow with every step.

"Spring is on its way, I guess. We've still got a few stray snowstorms left in the year, but I think the worst of winter is behind us."

She wasn't sure she was ready for the change. Spring meant hope and life and new growth, things that represented the inexorable march of time. Like it or not, it was inevitable. Soon the sunny days would outnumber the snowy ones, the tourist season would ease and the mountains would turn emerald and new.

Were they really talking about the weather, with all these currents that sparked and hissed between them? She racked her brain to come up with something else to say and blurted out the first thing that came to her mind.

"What was in the little box you carried out of your father's place?"

He was quiet for a long moment, his gaze fixed on their

route, and she wasn't sure he was going to answer. Was that a rude question? No. Nosy, maybe, but not rude.

"A few mementos of my mother's, apparently. Journals and keepsakes. That's what Harry said it was, anyway. I only had a brief glance at the contents before you and Sage came back. For all I know, maybe underneath the few things of my mother rest the still-beating hearts of all Harry's business rivals."

Despite her scattered emotions, she had to laugh. "Look at that. You made a joke."

His mouth turned up at the edges. "I've still got a few jokes left in me."

"You always used to know how to make me laugh," she said softly. "I'd forgotten that."

"Lately I seem to be remembering a whole slew of things that have slipped away over the years."

His words were pitched low, intense, and a subtle sense of intimacy seemed to wrap around them like tendrils of smoke.

She knew she was being cowardly when she deliberately changed the subject. "When do you start work on the recreation center?"

"Right away," he answered. "The city council wants tentative plans within the next six weeks or so. I'm heading to Singapore this week and will work long-distance from there, then hit it hard when I return."

"This will be a really valuable addition to Hope's Crossing."

"You think?"

"Claire and the others at String Fever have tried to bring the town together through the Giving Hope Day and other fundraisers, but I'm not sure it's been enough. When the tourists overwhelm the year-round residents by ten-to-one some winter weekends, it's tough to form a community. A recreation center might be just the thing to help people connect with their neighbors."

"That's a pretty heavy expectation to put into one building."

"I'm sure you're up to the challenge," she said.

"I appreciate the vote of confidence," he said with a half laugh, just as he realized with some surprise that they had already reached Sweet Laurel Falls.

THEY COULD HAVE walked in any direction. Was this a conscious choice on her part? She wasn't sure, she only knew that the night she and Jack had walked here after Christmas seemed like the beginning of this sea change in their relationship.

The warmer temperatures of the past week or so had begun to melt the ice. Already the water was beginning to make channels and rivulets over the face of it, and in some spots the ice had completely cracked away, shattered by warmth and the force of the current.

She wasn't quite ready to face how very much like that spill of water she felt, half-frozen but beginning the painful process of thawing. Layla was gone. She couldn't change that, nor could she give such little honor to the memory of the vibrant girl her daughter had been by curling up and wishing to die along with her.

She took a seat on the small bench near the bridge that spanned the creek and gave Puck the deceptive freedom to wander at the limits of his retractable leash, sniffing at every rock and tuft of grass peeking through the remaining patches of snow.

She loved it here. The stars, the city, the sound of the trickling water. She inhaled the cool night air and tried to relax—an impossible effort, especially when Jack sat down beside her and stretched his long legs out. Loath to reveal just how much he unnerved her, she drew in a deep breath and worked hard to relax taut muscles.

"So," he said after an awkward moment. "How long do you think we should keep ignoring what happened before dinner?"

"Oh, I was thinking ten or fifteen years ought to do it."

He gave a rough, surprised laugh, shifting to face her. "It seems only fair to tell you I'm more attracted to you than I ever was when I was a stupid teenage kid."

Her stomach muscles contracted as she remembered the heat of that moment in the kitchen and, worse, that stunning, irresistible tenderness.

"Fair? What's fair about telling me that?" she muttered. "What am I supposed to say?"

In the full moonlight, his features looked vaguely saturnine. "You could tell me to go to hell. You could tell me not to waste my time or energy. You could tell me you were completely unmoved by what happened and it was like kissing that really ugly statue of Silas Van Duran in Miner's Park."

Now, there was an idea. Though it would be a blatant lie, maybe that's what it would take to discourage him, to keep him just beyond that nice, safe perimeter she had maintained since divorcing Chris Parker. The words wouldn't come.

"I can't," she whispered instead.

"You can't what? Tell me you didn't enjoy that kiss? Or let me kiss you again?"

Her heartbeat pounded a heady rhythm and she didn't answer, only gazed at him in the light of the moon. It seemed the most natural thing in the world when he reached out and pulled her against him. He was warm in the cool of the night, and she wanted to burrow into him and never move. Jack was the most solid thing in her world right now. How had that possibly happened?

"What are we going to do about this?" he murmured.

"Why do we have to analyze it? Can't you just kiss me?"

He gave that rough laugh again that seemed to sizzle through her. "Why, yes. What an excellent idea."

His mouth descended and he tasted sweetly of chocolate and orange with the sultry undertone of wine, and she felt like that waterfall, with currents swirling warm and strong through her, breaking away the ice of the past year in great chunks.

"I've been fighting this since I came back to town," he murmured, his breath stirring her skin. "Damned if I can understand the pull you have over me."

Should she be flattered or insulted by that? "What can I say?" she shot back, her voice husky. "I'm a femme fatale and spend hours a day trying to come up with new ways to lure men into my clutches."

"Whatever you're doing works, at least with this man. I haven't been able to get you out of my head for weeks."

"I've been the same since you came back," she admitted.

He gazed at her for a moment, heat sizzling between them, then with a low sound he pulled her back into his arms.

They kissed for a long time, there in the moonlight beside the waterfall, and Maura felt something else that had been missing for far too long.

Peace.

The yip of a dog finally brought her back to a sense of time and place, and she realized she was practically on Jack's lap. Puck, on the other hand, sat some twenty feet away, the retractable-leash handle dangling in the dirt beside him.

Had she really been so distracted by the kiss that she had completely let go of the leash, heedless of her responsibility to her pet? Sweet Laurel Creek wasn't very deep or wide here, but if a tiny shih tzu like Puck were to fall in, it might as well be the mighty Missouri. Beyond that, the dog could have wandered off into the night and encountered all kinds of dangers, and she would have been too busy making out with Jack to pay attention.

Though she really, really didn't want to, she managed to slide her mouth away from his.

"Puck, come back here," she ordered. "Right now."

The dog gave a quizzical look, as if he considered this a fun new game, and was gearing up to bolt, until Jack simply said, "Puck. Come."

The dog immediately scampered over to them, so close that Jack could scoop down and pick him up. He handed the dog to Maura, and she cuddled his cold little paws on her lap, suddenly grateful for the distance the dog provided.

He sat back on the bench, though his fingers remained entwined with hers.

"Logically, some part of me keeps telling me I should still be furious with you for keeping Sage from me all these years. When I think about everything I missed with her, I still sometimes want to pound my fist through a wall. But then the other part of me sees her now, pregnant and alone and facing all this uncertainty and all these painful choices, and I have to wonder how the hell you can even stand to look at me, knowing I left you to deal with everything by yourself."

She drew in a shuddering breath, stunned at the depth of emotion behind his words. "It's done, Jack. We both made mistakes. For what it's worth, I forgave you a long time ago for not…not loving me enough to stay."

He stared at her, and beneath her hand she could feel his heart beating strong and fast. "Not loving you enough? Is that what you thought? It killed me to leave. I punched in your number at least once a day that first month, but I always hung up before the call could go through."

"We would have been lousy together back then. Over the years, I've wondered what would have happened if you had ever returned my calls. You would have come back and insisted we do something stupid and shortsighted like get married, and we would have been miserable together. You would have dropped out of school to support us and probably gone into construction or something. You certainly never would have become an architect. Eventually you would have hated me for stealing that dream from you."

"Maybe."

"Anyway, we can't go back and change anything. I'm not sure I would, even if I had the chance."

He was silent for a long time, petting Puck almost absently.

"You know," he finally said, "one of my first jobs out of graduate school involved a lot with this really spectacular view of the ocean near Monterey, but also an ugly, dilapidated building that had been built right after the Second World War. It was poorly planned and constructed with shoddy materials. We figured out right away the structure couldn't be saved. But we also figured out the one good thing about the whole lot, besides the view, was the foundation. It was still sturdy and as strong as when it had been laid down decades ago. Do you know what we ended up doing?"

"No."

"We tore the whole structure down and rebuilt something new and beautiful on the same foundation, a boutique hotel that consistently wins design and hospitality awards."

"Jack—"

"I think we have something sturdy and strong here, Maura. I'd like to see what we could build on that foundation."

Panic began to filter through the soft haze of desire that surrounded them. She eased away from him a little on the bench.

"Or we could forget tonight ever happened and go back to the wary sort of peace we've managed to achieve since you came back to Hope's Crossing."

"Why would we want to do that?"

She sighed, feeling like an idiot. "I can't… I don't do this well." She gestured back and forth between the two of them.

He raised an eyebrow. "From my perspective, you do it very well."

"That's not what I mean. I've had two serious relationships in my life—what we had together all those years ago and then my marriage. I ended up making a mess of both of them."

"I can't speak for your marriage, but you certainly didn't do anything to mess up our relationship. We were both young and stupid. I blame that more than anything. How long have you been divorced again?"

She sighed. "Officially, eight years. But our relationship was rocky long before then. His touring was hard on us, but more than that, I wasn't the sort of wife I should have been, probably because…"

She stopped, horrified that she had almost revealed to him that her marriage hadn't worked out in part because some measure of her heart had always belonged to Jack.

"Because?"

"Chris and I were never a very good match," she said, which was true enough. Just not the whole story. "Logically, we were perfect for each other. We both loved music and poetry and talking about books. He was so great with Sage that I really thought we could make it work, but… I guess our marriage was never strong enough to deal with all the challenges of his life as a musician. We didn't have that strong foundation you were talking about."

She really didn't want to talk about Chris right now—and not with Jack. "That's not really the point here. We were…were talking about us."

"I would like there to be an *us,* Maura. I loved you once. Since I've been back, I'm beginning to remember all the reasons why."

She closed her eyes against the soft seduction of his voice, against the fierce need to lean into his words and into him. "It's been twenty years. We're totally different people. We're kidding ourselves if we think we can just pick up where we left off, as if all those years and all the mistakes and all the…all the *pain* never happened."

"I don't want to go back. What we had was exciting and wonderful, but you're right, we're different people. I'm not that moody kid with the mountain-size chip on my shoulder anymore. I'm a man who has suddenly realized he spent twenty years looking for something. It's one hell of a kick in the teeth to find out what I needed was right here where I started."

She trembled, seduced by his words in spite of herself. "There's the difference between us. I'm not looking for anything. I lost my daughter less than a year ago. My other daughter is in trouble in the most old-fashioned meaning of the phrase. I'm empty inside, Jack. This last year has been a fine and terrible hell I could never have imagined."

With the rapid-fire emotional swings of the past year, she could feel tears scorch her throat. She waited for them to pass, even as she recognized that tears only reinforced her point. "I'm still wildly attracted to you," she finally said, after clearing them away. "That's probably obvious. But I'm not sure I'm healthy enough to bring my best self to a relationship right now. It wouldn't be fair to either of us."

"Okay. I can be flexible," he said after a pause. "We don't have to tangle ourselves in a relationship. How about just meaningless sex?"

The words shocked a laugh out of her, and it took her a moment to realize that was what he had intended. She definitely was still an emotional train wreck if she could go from near tears to laughter and this wild heat in just a matter of seconds.

She bumped her shoulder against his. "It wouldn't be meaningless. I think we both know that."

Her words seemed to seethe and curl between them, and he said nothing for a long time, while the endless creek bubbled beyond them and the town lights glittered below and Puck snored softly in her lap.

"I'm willing to give you time, Maura," he finally said. "We've waited all these years. I can wait a little longer."

"Jack—"

"Look, I told you I have to leave town next week for a job site in Singapore. I'll be running back and forth for at least a month. Why don't we put this discussion on hold for now and reassess when I get back?"

She wanted to tell him there was no point. What would possibly change in a month? But then, if she had learned anything this past year, it was the inescapable fact that a person's life could shift in an instant.

"Yes," she finally said. "Okay."

Puck's paws had been muddy, she realized, as Jack took her hand to help her from the bench. Her clothes were covered in mud now from having him on her lap, and Jack's probably were too.

Spring was like that. Muddy and messy and hard. Rather like life. But once you made it through the rough patches, it could also be sweet and beautiful. Could she and Jack find their way into the sunshine? For the first time in months, she wanted to find out.

CHAPTER SEVENTEEN

SHE REALLY DIDN'T want to be here.

The third week in April, nearly a month after their dinner with Harry Lange and the night she had walked to Sweet Laurel Falls with Jack, Maura stood at a small, well-tended plot at the Hope's Crossing cemetery. Whoever had selected this spot for a cemetery back in the town's rough and wild mining days definitely had chosen wisely. On an easy, rolling foothill across from Woodrose Mountain, the cemetery was a place of quiet serenity, with a lovely view of the surrounding mountains and town.

Around her stood family members and friends, gathered along with her to remember the one-year anniversary of Layla's death. Nearly everyone Maura cared about was there. Her mother and sisters, April Herrera and a few of her other employees, some of Layla's friends from school, just about all Maura's friends from the book group.

Katherine Thorne was there with Brodie and Evie, married just a few weeks. Taryn stood beside them using only a small cane for support, which Maura considered nothing short of a miracle, considering how badly injured Layla's best friend had been in the accident.

Even Harry Lange stood on the outskirts of the crowd, there but somehow separated from the press of people.

Maura appreciated the outpouring of love and support. On some level it warmed her deeply to know so many people had cared about her daughter—and about those Layla had left behind.

Over the past year, though, she had come to accept that the tangled path through loss and grief was mostly a solitary one. No one could help her find her way through the briars and over the rocky screes. Others might lend solace along the journey, but in the end, she—and everyone else who grieved—had to take each long, difficult step alone.

If she'd had her way, she would have marked this anniversary in some other way. A hike into the mountains with little Puck, or gathering her friends together for some kind of service project, or even just throwing herself into work for the day and letting it pass unnoticed except in her heart.

Sage had wanted this celebration of Layla's life, though. She had insisted on it and had worked out every detail, from scheduling the time to sending out invitations. She had even arranged the small buffet luncheon at Harry's place, being catered by one of Brodie Thorne's restaurants.

Maura thought she knew why this meant so much to Sage. While Sage no doubt wanted to honor her younger sister's life, Maura suspected it was also a distraction, an excuse to think about something else for a while and put off worrying about her pregnancy and the impending adoption.

With that in mind, she had decided she would let Sage have this memorial service this year—and only this year. The town already had the Giving Hope day around Layla's birthday, a day when everyone gathered to help each other by painting fences, doing yard work for the elderly, road cleanup. Whatever needed to be done. To her mind, that was a beautiful way to honor her daughter's memory and celebrate her life.

In contrast to the day of the accident, when snow and ice in the canyon had left the roads slick and dangerous, today was beautiful and sunny, a lovely, mild spring day that was rare and precious in the high Rockies. Spring had come early to Hope's Crossing this year. Most of the snow in town was gone, except for little patches under the sweeping branches of trees and on the north side of structures that didn't see much sun.

A light breeze stirred Sage's hair as she began to speak to the crowd. At nearly seven months pregnant, she looked round and soft and pretty. "Thank you all for coming," she said, smiling nervously. "It would have meant a lot to Layla."

She went on to talk about her sister and the people whose lives she had touched. Even after her death, Layla was helping others, Sage said. The scholarship fund in her name had already provided one year of college education to three of her schoolmates at Hope's Crossing High School and a year at a tech trade school for another.

"I found this great quote online while I was preparing this that really touched me. I have to see if I can get through this." Tears swam in Sage's eyes, but she didn't cry. Maura wanted to hug her, but she knew if she did, Sage would lose her battle with tears.

She was deeply proud of her daughter when she drew in a breath and sniffled a little but quickly regained control.

"It was an epitaph in an Irish cemetery and it just seems to fit perfectly. It says, 'Death leaves a heartache difficult to heal. Love leaves sweet memories impossible to steal.' I would like you to remember your sweet memories of Layla. You've all been given an envelope containing a butterfly ready to be released into the wild. I picked a butterfly release instead of balloons because it's better for the environment and because Layla always loved them. She called them 'flutties' when she was a little kid. We have perfect weather for those flutties today."

She wiped a tear with one of Mary Ella's embroidered handkerchiefs. Maura saw her mother wipe one too. Even Alex, her youngest sister, looked teary. "I found this other saying online. I couldn't find who wrote it, but I thought it was perfect. 'Butterflies are symbols of hope. They land beside us, like sunbeams, and belong to us for a moment, but then they fly away. And while we wish they might have stayed longer to share their beauty, we feel blessed for having s-seen them.'"

Another tear trickled down Sage's cheek, and Maura finally squeezed her hand as she fought her own tears. This was a celebration of life and today she wanted to remember Layla with joy, not sadness.

"Now if you could all open your envelopes. According to the company where I ordered them, the butterflies might need a moment to wake up before they take flight."

The next few moments were filled with rustling paper as the butterfly envelopes Sage had handed out were opened by everyone.

Maura opened her own and watched the monarch butterfly climb out to the edge of the paper and cling there for a moment, its wings reflecting sunlight as they opened and closed a few times. Out of the corner of her eye, she caught a few flashes of orange-and-black as other butterflies took flight, but hers remained stubbornly on the paper. At last, when she had just about given up, it finally took off, straight into the air.

Her heart in her throat, she followed its path and watched it dip and soar, joining the hundred others. A few even landed on the headstone before taking flight again.

Those assembled at the memorial watched for a moment.

Her sister Angie snapped some pictures of the butterflies flying off in all directions.

"Thank you all again for coming," Sage said after a short time. "It means a lot to me and my mom. Feel free to stay and visit if you want, but remember we're going to Harry Lange's house for dinner. If anybody doesn't know where that is, just ask me."

Sage stepped back into the crowd to talk to her grandmother before Maura had a chance to tell her what a wonderful job she had done. She turned around to follow another butterfly's flight, and suddenly her breath caught when she spied a tall, dark-haired figure walking through the crowd toward her.

Jack.

What was he doing here? He was supposed to be stuck in Singapore for another few weeks, yet here he was, looking strong and *wonderful.*

How on earth had he managed it? A week ago, he had told her the office complex he had designed had run into some snags with the complicated permit process in Singapore and he would have to stay longer than expected, at least through the initial start-up process.

She stared, shock and a soft joy bursting through her. She hadn't seen him in *forever,* though they emailed several times a day and talked on the phone at least three or four times a week. Their phone calls had become a treasured part of her day. They laughed and talked, sometimes for hours. She felt like she was seventeen again, having to steal the landline receiver from one of her older sisters' rooms.

Anticipation curled inside her as she watched him make his way through the crowd to Sage. He said something to their daughter, pointing to her expanding abdomen. She made a face but threw her arms around him, and he hugged her tightly.

Right. That's why he was there. He was Sage's father. He was here for their daughter, probably because she had asked him.

"It was a beautiful remembrance," Mary Ella said beside her.

She smiled at her mother. "Yes. Wasn't it?"

"The butterflies were a really lovely touch. And weren't we lucky it was warm enough for them?"

"The company Sage purchased them from said it had to be at least sixty-two degrees. It was sixty-four on our way here. We just made it."

"I'm glad," Mary Ella said.

"Are you coming to Harry's?"

Her mother made a face. "That man! I still don't understand why we couldn't have it at my house or even Claire's."

"You have to admit, he's got a little more room than either of you."

"He's got enough room to fit the entire town if he wanted to."

"Which, of course, he does not."

"I see Jackson made it, after all," Mary Ella said.

She wondered if somehow some of the butterflies had made it to her insides, as they rolled and jumped. Jack had come halfway across the world. She still couldn't quite believe it. "Yes. I just saw him. I haven't talked to him yet."

"Here's your chance now," Mary Ella said softly. She stepped away just as Jack approached.

"You're here." It was a stupid thing to say, but in that moment, after these weeks of talking and coming to know each other again long distance, she couldn't think of anything else.

"I pulled some strings. Rearranged my schedule a little."

"Thank you. I'm sure it means the world to Sage." *And to me.*

"Wouldn't you know, for all my logistical maneuvering, I still missed most of the memorial. My flight into Denver was delayed."

"It doesn't matter. You're here. That's the important thing."

He gazed down at her, blue eyes murky with emotion, and she was nervous suddenly—until he reached out and pulled her into his embrace, and then a soft, sweet warmth eased through her. Peace, she realized. Jack quieted the storm inside her in a way no one else ever had.

"I'm so glad you made it," she murmured, wishing they could just stand like this, arms wrapped around each other, for the rest of the day.

"I can't stay long. I'm afraid I'm only in town for about thirty-six hours before I have to fly back to Singapore."

"Thirty-six hours?" She slid out of his arms to stare up at him. "You flew all the way from Singapore for thirty-six hours?"

He didn't answer, but she saw the truth in his eyes. He didn't even know Layla, yet he had come back—not just for Sage, but for her. He cared about both of them enough to sacrifice his time and his energy—and probably more money than she wanted to think about in last-minute airline fares—in order to be here for them.

She smiled tremulously, wanting to take that knowledge and hold it close to her heart. When he reached for her hand and slipped his fingers through hers, she felt as light as those butterflies, despite the sadness that lingered.

"Did Sage tell you we're having dinner later at, um, Harry's place?"

He made a face. "She told me. You couldn't find a better venue?"

"Too bad for us, Buckingham Palace wasn't available, so we had to take the next best thing."

He nudged her shoulder with his. "Smarty."

She smiled. She couldn't help herself. "Seriously, I had no control over any of this. Everything was quite firmly taken out of my hands—Sage and Harry cooked it up together. The two of them are becoming quite close."

"Doesn't that strike you as a little…ominous?"

She saw Sage now talking with her grandfather and Harry was…gasp…smiling. "You're not going to like hearing this, but Harry has actually been very good to Sage. He's great at distracting her when she starts to become stressed about the baby and Sawyer and everything." She cast a quick look around to make sure no listening ears were nearby before she continued. "I think the two of them are now in cahoots about the whole Angel of Hope thing."

"Why do you say that?"

"A few times, Sage has casually mentioned she has to go run some errands with Harry, and then the next thing I know, I hear rumors about another secret Angel mission, mysteriously coinciding with her errands. I don't know. I can't quite see her doing the sneak-and-run thing while she's almost seven months pregnant, but I was thinking maybe she's the wheelman, driving the getaway car."

He chuckled. "I'm not sure I want to try picturing any of that. I thought he would have stopped after we figured out his game."

"Apparently not. The Angel is still making visits."

She had spent years being angry at Harry, hating him for causing Jack to leave, but she couldn't deny that Harry had helped Sage through this difficult time. If nothing else, he had provided a much-needed buffer against the kinds of whispers or stares that Maura had endured as an unwed mother.

Just like Laura Beaumont, most people in town didn't dare say anything offensive to Harry. Now that Harry's relationship to Sage was beginning to emerge, Maura's daughter had benefited from the trickle-down effect of her grandfather's power and influence.

"I'm sure you're not eager to spend more time at Harry's but…will you come?"

He squeezed her fingers. "Of course. I just endured a twenty-two-hour flight with three connections. I can probably survive a few hours of good food and pleasant company, even if they're in less-than-desirable surroundings."

HE COULD THROW a pretty damn good party when he set his mind to it.

Harry watched the fifty or so people who had come to celebrate Layla's life interspersed among the spring flowers and purple helium balloons Sage had insisted on for decorations. Everybody looked as though they were having a good time.

And why shouldn't they be? The music was nice, the food was delicious and he was serving free booze.

In the spirit of the Angel of Hope, Sage had even come up with the idea of combining the meal with an activity to help somebody else. That's just the kind of girl she was, and he was damn proud of her.

Along one length of the wall, two quilts had been set on frames for people to tie, and a group of women—and a few men—worked on all four sides of each. Sage wanted to donate them to the VA hospital in Denver, which he figured was a fine idea.

He hadn't entertained much since he'd built this house. Truth was, he'd always figured there weren't that many people in town he wanted to spend much time with. Maybe he had been wrong about that, as he had been wrong about so many other things. All his preconceptions seemed arrogant as he listened with an odd sense of satisfaction to the various conversations flow around him.

"Hey, Gramps," Sage said suddenly at his elbow.

"You know I hate it when you call me that," he lied.

She only winked in answer, seeing right through him. God in heaven, he loved this girl. She looked a great deal like his Bethany when she had been young and lovely and free of the demons that would plague her so cruelly later in life.

Fate was a strange and mysterious thing. Who ever would have guessed a year ago—when he had witnessed the accident that had changed so many lives—that one day he would find himself here, hosting a gathering in remembrance of a girl he didn't know, for this unexpected granddaughter he already loved fiercely?

"We need to put up another quilt. One of them is already almost done. Can you believe it? So do you remember where we put that green yarn after we went to the store?"

He frowned. "How should I know? That was a week ago. You'll have to ask Mrs. Kingsley where she put it."

"She said to ask you. According to her, she remembered seeing a bag of yarn in your office and had planned to ask you where you wanted her to keep it, but when she went back later, she couldn't find it anywhere."

He thought for a moment, hating the random absentmindedness that seemed to have come once he'd hit his late sixties. "Oh. Right," he suddenly said. "I put it in one of the desk drawers. I forgot all about it. I'll go find it for you."

"Thanks." Sage kissed him on the cheek before she returned back to acting as the de facto hostess of this gathering.

Harry headed for his office in the opposite end of the house. Now that he thought about it, he wouldn't mind sneaking a cigar while he was gone. All this socializing was exhausting for a guy who still preferred his dogs to large crowds.

His office was quiet and warm, faced to catch the afternoon sunlight. He unlocked a drawer and pulled out his humidor. Quite a thing when a man had to lock up his own smokes so his housekeeper didn't throw them out. After picking a cigar and a clip and cedar matches, he opened the sliding door that led to a private terrace, where he enjoyed sitting and smoking and looking out over his ski resort.

Damn the doctors anyway, he thought as he puffed, leaving the door open. And damn Mrs. Kingsley too. Her nagging caused him to hide out here on the terrace to enjoy this rare pleasure, even on snowy days in January, so the fresh air would hide the revealing scent and smoke.

He took another puff—five or six were all he would allow himself per cigar, a criminal waste, really—and savored the taste just as he caught a flicker of movement inside his office. Maybe Sage had come looking for him and her yarn.

Before he went to the trouble of stubbing out the cigar in the ashtray he kept hidden under a bush, he peered around the curtains to check and realized with considerable shock that his visitor wasn't Sage. Instead, her grandmother stood inside the room, her attention fixed on the Colville hanging in his office. The painting was one of his favorites, of a storm rolling over a meadow in the mountains. The colors were rich and vivid, and he could almost smell the ozone in the air when he looked at the clouds.

Mary Ella McKnight must be enjoying it as well. She didn't appear to notice him—she was too busy gazing at the painting, with her hands folded together at her chest as if she were a nun at prayer.

It seemed too private a moment for him to witness, almost as if he had peeped in a window at her dressing.

This was his house, he reminded himself. Hell, not just his house, his private office.

A shaft of sunlight arrowed in from the window and seemed to encircle her, giving her an ethereal glow. He had often thought her the most beautiful woman in town, even now that she had a few wrinkles around her eyes and bracketing her mouth. The green eyes she had passed to all her children seemed to blaze in her features and her mouth was rounded, as if on an exclamation.

He hardly dared breathe as he watched her, but despite his best efforts to remain still, he must have made some sound. She frowned first, as if sensing someone on the periphery of her awareness. Then she turned fully toward where he sat on the terrace, and a curious mix of guilt and horror crossed her features.

"Oh! I'm sorry. I had no idea anyone was here. What are you doing out there?"

Watching you. Yearning. He held up the cigar. "Hiding from my housekeeper. Want a puff?"

He made the offer as a joke, but Mary Ella was always good at surprising him. After a pause, she strode to the terrace and, with a defiant look, she plucked the cigar from his fingers and held it to her lips like a seasoned aficionado. His insides did a long, slow curl to think of her lips touching the place where his mouth had just been.

She puffed only slightly and held the smoke in her mouth correctly before she blew it out and handed the cigar back to him. "My ex-husband used to enjoy a cigar once in a while. Certainly nothing as fine as that one."

Her husband had been a narcissistic asshole. He had always thought so, and that had only been reinforced when the idiot had walked away from Mary Ella and their six children.

"Go ahead and finish it if you want. I've had my quota for the day."

"I never quite developed a taste for it." She looked embarrassed. "I'm sorry to intrude. I was admiring the Colville in the living room, and Maura told me you had another one in here. I only wanted to see it. I love her work. Even if she wasn't a dear friend, I would love it. I actually own a small landscape she gave me for my birthday a few years ago. It's my most treasured possession."

He couldn't pass up an opportunity to talk to Mary Ella when she wasn't sniping at him. "Would you like a tour of all twelve of mine?"

She gaped at him. "Good heavens. You really have that many?"

"When I find something I like, I don't see any reason to deny myself."

"You could save a few for the rest of the world, couldn't you?"

Her sharpness almost made him smile. If he kissed her, would her mouth taste tart like pie cherries or sweet and lush like bings? He was unbelievably tempted to find out.

"Come on. I'll show you my collection. If you're such close friends with Sarah Colville, maybe you can convince her I'm not such a bad guy and she should consider selling me more."

"Hmmph."

Despite the derogatory sound, she followed him as he walked out of his office and down the hall toward the den.

She had the same reaction to each one as she'd had in his office, rich and wholehearted admiration. He saved his favorite for last, a huge landscape in his bedroom, ten feet wide, a spill of sensual poppies on a field of vibrant green.

"Oh, stunning!" she exclaimed, her face as radiant as the painting.

Seeing her sheer joy at something he also loved seemed to weave a spell of intimacy around them. He wanted to march out and buy a dozen more paintings just for the sheer thrill of showing them to her.

"Thank you for the tour," she said, her voice and her eyes soft, and he wondered if she too sensed the subtle tug between them.

"You're welcome," he said, his voice gruff. He should be the one thanking her. He had never appreciated his own treasures as much as he did seeing them through her eyes.

"And while I'm choking on my gratitude here," she said, "I would be remiss if I didn't thank you for hosting this gathering. Sage told me you insisted, which meant a great deal to her. To all of us, really. It was…oddly kind of you."

"Believe it or not, I do have the occasional moment of odd kindness."

She gave him a half smile. "A few months ago I wouldn't have believed you possessed a shred of goodness, no matter what evidence I heard to the contrary."

They were standing very close together, he realized. What would she do if he reached a hand out and brushed that loose strand of hair away from her face and kissed her, as he had been aching to do since he had seen her gazing up at the painting in his office like a novitiate in front of the Blessed Virgin?

Knowing Mary Ella McKnight, she probably knew karate and would take him down to the floor.

"I just have one question for you," she said, her voice a soft breath on the air.

"What's that?" he asked, just as softly.

"Are you the Angel of Hope?"

He froze, his mind racing with a hundred different ways to answer that—and the hundred different questions he wished she might have asked. *Will you kiss me?* headed that particular list.

"Sage told you. That little snitch. She swore she wouldn't tell a soul. The mystery was all part of the fun, she said. And what does she do? First chance she has, she blabs to her nosy grandmother."

"Sage didn't tell me a thing," she assured him calmly. "It was only a wild guess, but thank you very much for confirming the suspicion I've had for a while now."

He swore, loud and long. That was twice now he had been fooled by McKnight women. How in the hell had he managed to amass such a fortune when he could be such an idiot sometimes?

"How did you guess?"

She shrugged. "Process of elimination, really. It had to be somebody with plenty of financial resources and time on his or her hands. And, to be fair, I happened to be walking past Mike's Bikes one day a few months ago and saw a quite unusual sight through the window that presented a huge clue."

"Oh?" he asked warily, guessing already what she would say.

"I had to ask myself why Harry Lange would be looking at child-size bicycles. And lo and behold, a few days later I heard the Angel had dropped a brand-new bicycle off on the porch of poor little Polly Ellis the very day she learned she had to start a second round of chemotherapy."

"Completely circumstantial."

Her smile spilled over with triumph. "Absolutely. But you just confirmed it."

Early on, he had decided to do most of his Angel shopping online or in Denver, where he had a better chance at anonymity. The Polly Ellis situation had come up quickly and he hadn't wanted to wait until he had a chance to make the arrangements, so he had gone against his better instincts and shopped locally.

And look where it got him. Ratted out by his own stupidity.

On the other hand, maybe it wasn't such a bad thing that she knew. Instead of prickling with animosity—which he knew damn well he fully deserved—Mary Ella gazed at him with a soft light in her eyes.

He caught his breath suddenly when she reached a hand out and rested it gently on his arm. "You've done a good thing for Hope's Crossing, Harry. This town needed something to bring us together. All of us knew deep inside that something good and right was missing in our town, but no one knew how to fix it and bring us together again. As usual, you took the lead."

Goose bumps erupted on his skin where she touched him. He didn't know what to say, so he did the only thing he could think of. He covered her hand resting on his arm with his opposite hand. Her fingers were small, slim. Delicate. A low ache began somewhere inside him, wistful and subdued. He missed the softness of a woman's hand in his. He hadn't realized how very much until right this moment.

He was vaguely aware through his own yearning that her fingers had stiffened when he touched her, but she didn't pull away. If he was going to be an idiot for Mary Ella McKnight, he might as well go all the way. Take a chance. Jump off the cliff. Float the rapids.

Live.

With his heart in his throat, waiting any moment for her to slap him or shove him away or yell, he reached a hand out and acted on his earlier impulse, pushing her hair aside. The strands were silky and he wanted to rub it between his fingers, maybe bury his face in it. Instead he slid a hand over her cheek, still soft despite the few fine wrinkles there, and leaned in to steal the kiss he had been thinking about for longer than he cared to remember.

"Don't you dare," she ordered in that bossy English-teacher tone he had always secretly been crazy about, though he wanted to think her voice sounded husky and strained.

"Go ahead and stop me," he growled.

She didn't.

And when she kissed him back with a fierceness that shocked both of them, it was everything he dreamed and more.

When they emerged from his bedroom sometime later, Mary Ella's cheeks were pink and her hair was a little messier and he was pretty sure he just might have lipstick on his jawline.

"This doesn't change anything," she muttered as they made their way through the house to the living area.

His laugh was rough and amused. "You can tell yourself that, but we both know better, don't we?"

Sage was the first one they bumped into back at the party. She gave them both a curious look, and he wondered if anyone else could sense the tensile connection between him and Mary Ella now. "There you are. What happened to you?"

Love. That's what happened, missy. Not that it's any of your business.

"Did you ever find the yarn?" she pressed when he didn't immediately answer.

Yarn? It took him a moment to remember the errand she had sent him on earlier. First he'd been distracted by the cigar and then by the even more tempting forbidden treat of Mary Ella.

"No. And I've been over the whole house." It wasn't *quite* a lie—he had traipsed through every room, but he had been showing Mary Ella the Colvilles instead of looking for yarn. "Let me go take another look in my office."

"No. Forget it. We'll just use the red that we already have. It will look fine."

"I'll look anyway." He brushed a kiss on his granddaughter's forehead, then squeezed Mary Ella's arm slightly. She trembled just a little, which made him grin broadly, and he walked away whistling—*whistling,* for hell's sake—the tune to "I've Got You Under My Skin" as he headed to his office.

In his office, the woody, cedary smell of cigar smoke was stronger than it should have been. He frowned and looked around. The whistle died on his lips when he spotted Jackson on the terrace, in the same spot where he'd been when Mary Ella had come in a half hour earlier—and enjoying one of the same cigars.

"Make yourself at home," he said, still feeling so great after kissing Mary Ella McKnight that he could almost look at his son without the customary sorrow and guilt.

"Sage sent me in here to look for you. Something about yarn. I didn't find you, but I did happen to spy an open box full of particularly fine Coronas and couldn't resist."

He frowned at the dark circles under Jack's eyes and

the lines of exhaustion bracketing his mouth. "Maybe you would be better off finding a bed and taking a nap instead of stealing my cigars. You look like hell."

Jack shrugged. "Give me a break. I was up two nights straight before I left Singapore trying to wrap things up so I could get away, then spent the next twenty-two hours either flying or waiting around in airports."

He wanted to tell Jack not to let work completely consume him or he might one day find himself alone and unhappy, but he choked back the words. This didn't seem the time for lectures, especially not when he was just so damn happy to be with his son.

"I'm sure it means the world to Sage that you made the effort to be here."

Jack narrowed his gaze as if parsing the words for mockery, then appeared to accept them as genuine. "I had to try, even if it was tough." He paused. "Maura tells me you and Sage are becoming close."

He loved her with the same fierceness he loved her father. "Are you going to try to tell me you don't want me in her life?"

What would he do if that were the case? He had treated Jack so horribly he didn't know how he could ever atone. He had tried in small ways. Oh, his will was written to leave everything to him, even before Jack had come back to town, and over the years he had worked behind the scenes to steer juicy projects his son's way.

He knew it wasn't enough. If Jack wanted him to stay away from Sage, he would have to accept that as penance for his sins, even though it would kill him. Possibly quite literally.

He waited for Jack to say the words that would crush him, but his son only puffed the cigar. "Why would I make you stay out of Sage's life, as long as you continue to treat her well?" he finally asked.

Gratitude and relief almost made Harry weep, much to his dismay. "She's a good girl," he said gruffly. "I…care about her very much."

"I can tell," Jack said. "Word is you don't entertain often. Yet here you are flinging open those big gates for Sage."

It was such a small thing. Why was everybody making such a big deal about it? Had he really become such a recluse that people considered him another Howard Hughes, hoarding his fingernail clippings and his used tissues in his mansion?

He stood for a long moment while Jack smoked. His son didn't seem to mind his presence, and Harry was aware of a fragile happiness bubbling inside him. He was here, with his son, and for once they weren't fighting. He was half tempted to relight the long stub of his own cigar, still in the ashtray on the table, but he didn't dare. Smoking even one was risky with his bad ticker, and for the first time in far too long he had plenty of things to keep him alive.

Including his granddaughter, he suddenly remembered, who would be ready to put him in a nursing home for dementia if he let himself become distracted by one more thing.

"I should probably go," he said with deep regret. "Sage sent me in here to find something for her. She's going to have my hide if I don't get back out there. You're welcome to stay as long as you'd like. Have another cigar. Hell, have two or three."

Jack nodded, and Harry hurried to his desk and opened the drawers until he found the bag of yarn. He gazed at his son out on his terrace in the spring sunshine, with one of his cigars in his hand, and Harry smiled with a deep, contented joy before he hurried back out to find his granddaughter.

CHAPTER EIGHTEEN

JACK SAT FOR a while in the very comfortable chair outside his father's office, watching a few clouds scud across the snow-topped mountain peaks. He wasn't quite sure what had just happened between the two of them, but it seemed somehow significant, as if they had crossed some Continental Divide in their relationship.

He wasn't sure he could forget everything his father had done, but maybe it was time, at last, to find room for a little forgiveness. Harry had certainly made mistakes. Those tramlines and ski lifts etching their way up the greening hillsides were a prime example.

Could Jack find some semblance of peace with his father? He was mellowing, he supposed. Maybe age and experience had leaked away some of the hot anger of youth, or maybe it was due to becoming a father himself. He still didn't know if he could move beyond their past, but for the first time in two decades, he realized he wasn't averse to trying.

He saw a flash for a moment as someone headed out across the sloping lawn, headed toward the horse paddocks just beyond the grass. Maura, he realized. He recognized her slim frame and the lavender dress she wore, which flowed around her legs with every step.

A deep yearning stirred. He had missed her this past month while he had been overseas. In the past, he had always enjoyed the traveling aspect of his job, the hands-on involvement on a project, but all he had wanted these past weeks was to come home to her.

The constant flow of emails and phone calls and Skyping—their modern-day long-distance courtship—had only heightened this ache to be with her. Every time he talked to her only whetted his need to talk to her the next time.

They traded stories about their day, she asked his business advice, they laughed and joked and rediscovered each other. Every time they ended a call, he felt the keen loss of the connection and had to force himself not to pick up the phone and call her right back.

So what the hell was he doing sitting here by himself when she was out there, a strong, beautiful, vibrant woman instead of an image on a monitor or a voice on the phone?

He tossed the cigar in the ashtray on the terrace and vaulted over the three-foot stone fence surrounding the terrace, probably built to keep out the animals and the rabble, and headed toward her.

She didn't seem aware of his approach and appeared lost in thought as she leaned on the top railing of the paddock, watching a few elegant, undoubtedly expensive, horses graze inside.

"Hey," he finally said when he was only a few steps away.

She turned in surprise, and her expression seemed to instantly light up with joy when she saw him. "Jack. Hi!"

He was helpless against the tide of warmth that flowed through him, sweet and cleansing, washing away everything that had come before. He was in love with this woman. Deeply and profoundly.

He had loved the girl she had been, sweet and generous. His first love. But the woman Maura had become—

a woman of courage and strength and grace—she was *everything* to him.

"Where did you go earlier?" she asked. "I looked around some time ago and you had disappeared."

"Sage sent me on an errand and I ended up stealing—and then very much savoring—the guilty pleasure of one of my father's cigars."

She smiled while the breeze played with the ends of her hair.

"Why are you out here by yourself?" he asked.

"Brodie and Evie and Taryn just left. Taryn was tired."

"She looked good."

"Doesn't she? If you had seen her a few months ago, you would be completely stunned at how far she has come. So I was walking them out to their car and the sunshine felt so good, I couldn't resist walking back here to see Harry's view from the back."

He leaned his elbows on the railing next to her, relishing the sunshine on his head and the earthy smell of springtime around them. He wasn't sure he had ever been so exhausted, but just standing here beside Maura filled him with a sweet, seductive peace. "It turned out to be a beautiful day."

"Yes." Out of the corner of his gaze, he saw her draw her bottom lip between her teeth. "Do you think the butterflies will survive?"

"Of course they will." He didn't know a damn thing about butterflies, but he wasn't about to tell her otherwise. "You said Sage researched this out. If the butterfly people said it's warm enough for them, I'm sure they'll be just fine."

She narrowed her gaze. "You would say that even if you thought they were all doomed, wouldn't you?"

"Yeah. Probably."

Her laughter rippled over him, and he finally couldn't resist the overwhelming need to pull her into his arms. With a sigh, she settled against him, wrapping her arms around his waist and lifting her face for his kiss.

He managed to bank his wild desire—for now—and kept the kiss soft and gentle, with all the tenderness inside him.

Finally, when he wasn't sure how much longer he could be noble and considerate and mindful of the solemnity of the day, he slid his mouth away and caressed her cheek with his thumb.

"I think the butterflies will be fine. Despite how lovely and fragile they look, they're survivors, accustomed to weathering storms. A great deal like someone else I know." He paused, gazing intently at her, his heart pounding in his chest like one of those horses on a racetrack. "The woman I happen to be in love with, actually."

She stared at him, her eyes huge in that soft, lovely face, and he thought he saw a quick blaze of joy there before her lashes came down. "Jack…"

"I really didn't intend to say that. Either the cigar or my fatigue must have loosened my tongue. This isn't the time or the place, today of all days. I just wanted you to know where my head and heart are."

He wrapped his hand around her fingers and brought their clasped hands to his chest. "Right here. With you."

She still didn't say anything, only continued to gaze at him out of those eyes as green as the new growth around them. Had he ruined everything between them? Moved too fast? Spoken when he should have shut the hell up?

"You don't have to say anything," he said. "I know you're not ready for this. Not with everything going on in your life. We can talk again when I come back for good in a few weeks."

"Not for good," she whispered. "Only until you move back to San Francisco."

"What if I didn't have to go back to San Francisco?" He couldn't quite believe the words were coming out of his mouth, but even as he spoke them, he realized he meant them completely.

She stared at him, her eyes huge. "What?"

"I have a partner who handles the administrative side of things at the main office very well. I don't see why I couldn't keep the office here in Hope's Crossing and use that as my central base."

Her laugh had a disbelieving edge. "You *really* must be exhausted. You do realize what you're saying, right?"

Over the past few months, he had witnessed genuine concern and caring in Hope's Crossing and had come to see that perhaps he had viewed the town through the sometimes skewed perception of youth. No doubt he could still find pockets of intolerance and small-mindedness in Hope's Crossing, but the majority of the people he had come to know were warmly generous. Why wouldn't he want to live here?

"I would still have to travel sometimes. That's the nature of my job. But I would always come back to you."

Her fingers still nestled in his and he could feel them tremble in his grasp. He lifted them to his mouth and kissed the soft skin at the back of her hand. "I love you, Maura. I want to be with you. Whether that's here or in San Francisco or in Singapore. It doesn't matter to me."

MAURA COULDN'T SEEM to catch hold of any of her scattered thoughts. She could only stare at him, trying to gauge whether he spoke truth. She was inordinately aware of their surroundings—the fading afternoon sunlight, the soft breath of a spring breeze, the horses now cantering through the pasture behind Jack.

Joy seemed to burst inside her, bright and lovely and *right*. Her love for him was a sweet ache in her chest, a quiver in her stomach, but she couldn't find the words to tell him. Instead, she did the next best thing. She reached on tiptoes and kissed him, their still-clasped hands caught between them.

He hitched in a breath and returned the kiss, his mouth warm with the taste of cinnamon. He kissed her with such soft tenderness she could feel the ache of tears behind her eyes. The past weeks ran through her mind, the late-night phone calls where neither of them wanted to be the first to hang up, the sharing and the teasing and her inexorable journey toward falling in love with him all over again.

"I love you, Jack," she murmured. "Some part of me never stopped, all these years. I had the reminder of you every day when I would look at our daughter, so curious and determined, just like her father."

"She's become a beautiful, strong woman. Like her mother."

Could they really have a second chance together? It seemed a miracle, somehow. A rare and precious gift, after the hellish year she had endured. She smiled against his mouth, aware of a subtle shifting and settling inside her, a quiet peace she had never expected to find with Jackson Lange, of all people.

Over his shoulder, she caught a bright flash of yellow-and-orange out of the corner of her gaze and she shifted in his arms for a better view.

"Jack! Look!" she exclaimed.

He followed the direction where she pointed, to where a monarch butterfly dipped and danced among the early-spring flowers of Harry's landscaping.

"Do you think that's one of the butterflies from the ceremony?" she asked. "Surely it wouldn't have made it all the way up the canyon. That's three miles at least."

"Stranger things have happened. Maybe he hitchhiked in somebody's car."

"It is. I'm sure it is." She watched the butterfly alight on a huge, plump peony, its wings bright and cheery, and felt the last icy fingers around her heart crack and break away. It was almost as if Layla had sent her a sign, promising her all would be well.

She lifted her face to the sunshine and to Jack, suddenly sure of it.

EPILOGUE

"SOMETHING'S NOT WORKING. I think we might have cut the angle wrong." Maura held up a board that was supposed to fit against another one, but quite obviously didn't.

Jack, looking extremely sexy in jeans, a tight T-shirt and a low-slung leather carpenter belt, raised an eyebrow. "Excuse me. Who's the professional, again?"

Laughter bubbled up inside her. "You're an architect, not a carpenter."

"And you run a bookstore and coffeehouse."

She gestured at the pile of lumber scattered around them on the path beside Sweet Laurel Falls, where they were supposed to be helping build the small, delicate gazebo Jack had designed.

"So we're both completely out of our league here."

He gave her a wry look and hooked his hammer back on the loop of his belt. "Yeah. Basically."

She laughed and couldn't resist kissing away the disgruntled look on his gorgeous features, wondering how it was possible for her to love him more every moment of every day.

As usual, he was easily distracted when she kissed him, and he wrapped his arms around her, pulling her close. "How about we forget this whole thing and go back to your place and make out for a few hours?" he murmured. "We can let Riley finish up here. He's dying to take over."

She had to laugh. Her younger brother had gone back to the community center for more lumber, but for the entire morning he'd been trying to boss around all ten of the volunteers working on the gazebo for the Hope's Crossing second annual Giving Hope Day.

"That's a very appealing idea," she answered Jack. "But since you designed this, don't you want to see the project through to the end?"

"I have no problem letting everyone else do the work and just enjoying the finished product."

She didn't believe that for a moment. The gazebo had been a labor of love for Jack, his gift to her and to the town. Even after Harry stepped in to donate all the materials, Jack had been excited about the design. When it was finished, this would be a lovely place for people who wanted a shady spot to enjoy the falls. She could even picture her and Jack—and Puck, of course—sitting here, sheltered from the elements, in the middle of a summer-evening rainstorm.

While she was undeniably tempted by the idea of sneaking away to her house for some rare alone time, she knew they couldn't. "Claire would kill me if she found out we bailed. You know Riley would rat us out to her in a minute."

He gave her a smile full of enticing promise. "Later, then."

"Deal," she said, her voice slightly husky. The past six weeks had been wonderful between them, filled with more joy than she could have imagined.

A week ago, in this very spot, he had asked her to marry her. She gazed at the falls—their spot—wishing with all her heart she had been able to give him a wholehearted yes. Oh, how she wanted to, but she had asked him to be patient a little while longer. With Sage's baby due in less than a month, the timing didn't feel right. For now, she felt that they needed to concentrate on their daughter and the difficult choices she faced.

Jack had argued a wedding might be exactly the distraction Sage needed. Maura saw his point, but she still couldn't feel right planning the rest of their lives together while everything in Sage's world was still unsettled—even her choice of an adoptive couple with which to place her baby.

In the end, he had held her close. "I've waited twenty years. I can wait a few more months," he had promised.

As she watched him measure the board again and recalculate the angle, she loved him even more for his patience and his steady strength.

"You're right. The angle is wrong and now this one is going to be too short. Can you go grab me another board and I'll recut?" he asked.

"Of course." She hurried to the stacked lumber and picked one of the correct size. Around her, the other volunteers were hard at work on the base of the gazebo. As she watched them, Maura remembered the previous year's service day, just six weeks after the accident, on what would have been Layla's birthday.

Her emotions had been scraped raw. She had only been able to attend a few hours before she had had to escape the crush of sympathy.

Everything was different this year. The loss would always be part of her, an empty spot that nothing else would fill, but she had made the choice to move forward, to live instead of hiding away in her grief.

Layla would have wanted exactly that.

She was carrying the board back to Jack's work area when her cell phone suddenly rang with Sage's distinctive ringtone. She set the board down on the grass with the others before she answered.

"Hey, Mom," Sage said. She sounded breathless.

"Hi. How are things going down at the library?"

Sage was under strict orders to sit quietly and help repair dilapidated books at the library. "Um, I guess fine. I have a…little problem. Well, not really a problem but…"

"What's wrong?"

"I think my water just broke."

For the first time, she recognized that what she had taken for breathlessness in Sage's voice was actually fear.

"Are you sure? You're not due for three more weeks!"

"Yeah. Pretty sure. It's hard to mistake that when the ground at your feet is suddenly soaked. Fortunately, I was already in the bathroom, so it was easy to clean up with some paper towels."

Maura fought down panic. Not yet. Not today. "Okay, just sit tight. I'll grab your father and we'll be right there."

"Mom, wait. Harry's with me. He's already planning to drive me to the hospital. I was thinking you could meet us there. That will be quicker than you coming down here first. Can you just stop at the house and grab the bag we packed?"

"Yes. Yes, of course. Give me ten minutes."

"Thanks, Mom. I love you."

"I love you. Honey, hang in there. It will be okay." Though she tried to sound confident and breezy, she didn't know how anything possibly would be okay.

"What's wrong?" Jack asked, instantly alert the moment he saw her face.

"Sage. Her water broke and she's heading to the hospital now. Harry's taking her."

He swore, some of the color leaching from his face. "Okay. Looks like Riley gets to be in charge, after all."

They raced to her house, stopping only long enough to

make sure Puck had food and water and to pick up Sage's bag, then Jack sped to the Hope's Crossing hospital.

By the time they pulled into the parking lot, her hands were shaking on the bag she clutched on her lap.

"Where do we go?" Jack asked. She quickly gave him directions to the new women's center and its state-of-the-art birthing rooms that she had toured with Sage during their birthing class.

At the nurses' station, a too-chipper RN told them a room was being prepared and that in the meantime they could find Sage and Harry in a small family waiting room down the hall.

When Maura pushed open the door the nurse had indicated, she found Sage looking tense and upset. Her daughter jumped up from the sofa and sagged into her arms. "I'm not ready, Mom," she wailed. "I thought I had a few more weeks!"

"I know, honey."

"I can't have this baby yet. I haven't even picked an adoptive couple. I've been trying and trying to pick the best one and…they're all good. None is any better than another. What am I going to do? This is my baby. I can't just flip a coin!"

She started to cry, and Maura held her closely, her heart aching. Everything was in place legally for the adoption. Sawyer had readily signed away any parental rights, and Sage had been working with a wonderful adoption agency. But despite all the weeks of counseling and discussion, Sage obviously wasn't prepared for this emotional tumult. Giving a baby up for adoption was a courageous decision but certainly not an easy one.

She was trying to find impossible words of comfort when Harry spoke from his spot on the sofa.

"Am I the only one with a brain in this family?" he growled.

This was *so* not the time for one of his cantankerous fits. Maura needed her mother here to mellow him out. Their budding relationship had caused a shockwave of epic proportion to roll over Hope's Crossing, but even *she* couldn't deny that Mary Ella was good for Harry. And, amazingly, he had been good for her too.

She was about to snap at him—the best she could manage under the circumstances—when Harry rose, still a commanding figure. "I can't believe none of you have figured this out yet. For hell's sake, the answer is obvious, isn't it?"

"What haven't we figured out, Gramps?" Sage asked, her voice small and forlorn. Harry shook his head, his eyes softening as he looked at her.

"You two—" he gestured to Jack and Maura "—should just get married already, and then you can raise the baby. You're both still young. Hell, you're young enough to pop another one out yourselves, aren't you?"

Maura gaped at him, aware of Jack's features going taut beside her. Sage stopped sniffling and pulled out of her arms to stare at her grandfather.

Suddenly Maura's whole life seemed to rearrange itself in her head. Everything she thought was right for her and for Jack seemed to shift and settle into a new picture.

A son.

She and Jack could be parents again. At last he would have the chance she had taken from him—to be a father, from the beginning. For sticky toddler kisses and coaching soccer games and helping with math homework, all the things he'd never had the chance to do with Sage.

Her mind started racing with possibilities, but just as

suddenly she forced them to a screeching halt. As much as that picture suddenly seemed perfect to her, it wouldn't be fair to Jack. Surely he wouldn't want to start the rest of their lives together changing diapers and fixing bottles and rocking a colicky baby....

"I couldn't ask that of you," Sage finally said into the gaping maw of silence that stretched out between the four of them.

"Why not?" Jack asked, his voice a little ragged.

Maura stared at him. "Do you... Are you saying you would...actually consider it?"

"I want to marry you, Maura. You know that. I want to have forever with you. I hadn't expected an instant family to be part of that picture, but that's what we would have had twenty years ago if things had worked out differently. We're older now. More mature. Certainly we're both better equipped to deal with a child."

He smiled broadly. "Besides. This wouldn't be the first time I suddenly and unexpectedly became a father."

She gave a rough laugh at that, thinking of the strange and twisting journey their lives together had taken so far. This was a crazy idea, adopting a child before they were even officially married, but somehow it seemed exactly right.

Sage sank back down onto one of the sofas, gazing at them both with a raw, almost painful hope. "I don't want you to feel pressured or anything, but this would be beyond perfect. Maybe that's the reason I couldn't make a decision. Maybe in my heart, something like this is what I wanted all along but was afraid to ask—or even let myself think about."

Maura gripped Jack's fingers. He squeezed tightly, out of nerves or anticipation or simply love, she couldn't tell.

"You have to be sure, darling," she said. "And you'll have to be very clear in your own head that if we do this, we wouldn't just be babysitting for you until you're in a better place to be a parent. This would be our child. We would be the mother and father."

"I can't imagine two better parents for my baby, Mom." Sage gave a watery smile and Harry wrapped an arm around her. "I was a really good big sister to Layla. I think I can be a great big sister to your son too. It would be super cool to have a little brother."

Without releasing her hand, Jack reached for a tissue from a box on the table and passed it to her. That was the first moment she realized she was crying, tears of joy and anticipation and no small amount of fear.

A baby.

Dear heavens. They were going to have a baby.

She didn't have time to fully adjust to that before the chipper nurse from out front bustled into the room.

"Okay. We've finally got your birthing room ready. If you'll come with me, Sage, we'll get you settled first, and then your family can come in."

"Okay." Sage gave a nervous smile and followed the nurse. She seemed lighter somehow, freed of the fear and uncertainty she had been carrying along with her baby.

After she left, Harry stood up, a look of sublime self-satisfaction on his weathered features. "I parked in one of the emergency-room spots. I should probably go move my car, even though they wouldn't dare ticket me."

He headed out, leaving the two of them in the waiting room alone.

Maura was nervous suddenly, still unable to believe the enormity of the decision they had just made. "Are you sure about this, Jack? It's not too late to change your mind. We can figure something else out. I don't want you to feel obligated to something you didn't want."

He wrapped his arms around her, and she felt some of the tension seep away. "Do you want to know a secret? The idea of adding to our family isn't completely foreign to me. I'm embarrassed to admit that adopting Sage's baby never even occurred to me, but lately I've caught myself wondering what it would be like to have another child with you. Harry's right. We're both young. Young enough, anyway. Plenty of couples don't even get started until their late-thirties. I guess I was waiting to see if you might be thinking along the same lines, or if you figured you had done your time raising young children."

"I love being a mother. If things had gone differently in my life, I would have wanted at least one or two more."

After her divorce, she had just accepted that part of her life was gone. The idea of shopping now for a crib and buying baby clothes and having to rearrange her work demands to accommodate a new life was both overwhelming and intoxicating.

"I never would have pressured you," Jack assured her. "But I can think of nothing more beautiful and *right* than raising a son together."

She caught her breath, dizzy at how quickly the pathway of her life had suddenly veered off in a completely different direction than she'd started on that very morning. Outside the window, the rest of the world was carrying on as usual, the citizens of Hope's Crossing busy helping each other, while in here a new life was about to enter the world and a family was shifting and changing to welcome it.

She looked out the window at a beautiful June afternoon, rich with promise. A lush, wild rosebush bloomed there, its flowers a vivid pink in the sunlight. Somehow she wasn't at all surprised to see a flicker of orange amid the pink as a monarch butterfly flitted from flower to flower.

Another message from Layla? Maybe. She had seen butterflies everywhere these past few months, but perhaps that was only because she was finally ready to notice them again.

She reached for Jack's hand, this wonderful man she had once loved and lost, then found again.

She smiled at him, her heart nearly bursting with happiness. "Let's go have a baby."

* * * * *